WESTON'S TREASURE

GEMINI GROUP

RILEY EDWARDS

Weston's Treasure
Gemini Group Book 3
Riley Edwards

Cover design: Lori Jackson Designs

Written by: Riley Edwards

Published by: Riley Edwards/Rebels Romance

Edited by: Rebecca Hodgkins

Proofreader: Julie Deaton, Rebecca Kendall

Weston's Treasure

Print ISBN: 978-1-951567-03-3

Ebook ISBN: 978-1-951567-00-2

First edition: December 24, 2019

To my family - my team – my tribe.
This is for you.

CONTENTS

PROLOGUE

Silver

Weston Beil was infuriating.

And what made everything worse was he'd been semi-right. Not that I lacked experience, because I didn't. I had more time on the water than every man on the team Weston had put together, including the members of the Coast Guard.

I'd grown up on the water. Literally. I'd lived on a boat since the day I was born. My dad was an adventure diver and instructor and part-time treasure hunter. Whatever money-making scheme he'd had always revolved around the water. Since birth, my father had been grooming me to take over his business.

Not that I had taken over my dad's diving company or decided to be a treasure hunter—instead I'd opted for a career as a professional mariner. A career path that at the moment was debatably the wrong choice.

I was sure my father was probably out cruising the beautiful cerulean waters of the Caribbean enjoying the view from his wheelhouse while I was currently handcuffed to a water pipe in the hull of a motor yacht.

Good times.

That was the part Weston had been correct about.

He'd warned me—the operation to stop the drug trafficking was dangerous. He'd repeated *ad nauseam* that criminals, and most certainly drug dealers, did not take kindly to someone stopping their racket.

So, Mr. Know-It-All Weston Beil had been right. And the taste of crow made my stomach roil. Which sucked, because if I got out of this alive, I'd be eating a huge plateful.

The yacht rocked back and forth, a motion I'd always been accustomed to but that now was making me queasy, as I tried to figure out a way out of this mess.

I had no idea what the captain and the first mate had planned for me, but considering I was surrounded by bricks of cocaine; I didn't figure it'd be pleasant.

No one was coming to my rescue. If I wanted to live, it would be up to me.

Damn, I wished Weston were there, and that

thought churned my belly for a variety of reasons. I was not and had never been a helpless female and I wouldn't turn into one now. But I couldn't deny the big man was strong and the air of danger that surrounded him was intoxicating. Had he not been such a dick, I would've said he was probably the hottest man I'd ever laid eyes on. And there was the fact that despite him being a huge asshole I was half in love with him.

Weston would know what to do. The captain wouldn't have been able to overpower him and handcuff him to a fucking pipe.

Shouting upstairs had me shrinking back against the steel.

I needed to hurry up and figure something out before I turned into fish food.

1

Silver Coyle could write a book on how to annoy the fuck out of men. And if Weston got her out of her current situation, he was suggesting it.

Actually, it wasn't a matter of *if* they could do it, it was simply a *when*. The alternative would mean they failed their mission and Weston never failed—neither did his teammates. So it was a matter of time until the infuriating woman in question would be rescued. And she'd hate that. Hate that it was Gemini Group coming to her aid, most especially Weston himself. He'd warned her, yet she refused to listen. He'd told her she was skirting the line. But Silver, being as stubborn as she was brave, hadn't listened.

The game she was playing was dangerous, and just as he'd predicted she'd been burned. Now she was being held hostage by a group of drug traffickers and as much as Weston wanted to say I told you so, he wouldn't. At least not until Silver was safely back at his house, under his watch and protection. Something else she was going to pitch a fit about and Weston couldn't wait for the battle that would ensue.

He'd never met a woman as feisty as Silver, not even his teammates' women could hold a candle to her and that was saying something. Nixon and Jameson had chosen well, both of their women fit them seamlessly. Not that Weston was looking for a woman, but Silver had disaster written all over her, and if he didn't lock her down, she'd fuck the whole mission. It was *not* because she was the only woman who he'd ever met who sparked something deep inside him. And it certainly was *not* because he couldn't stop thinking about her. So much so, the woman had invaded his dreams. Nope, it was all about this mission.

One that he and his team had been planning for the last month. It was a multiagency takedown and neither Homeland nor the Coast Guard needed her interfering.

But she had interfered and now she was in the hull of a ninety-foot Feadship named the *Dora B* and Weston would bet she was not happy. He'd watched as she boarded the mega motor yacht to pilot it down the C & D Canal.

Then he watched as she was pulled from the wheelhouse through the companionway and marched to the aft deck before she disappeared back inside. That had been an hour ago. Now that the team was certain they were clear of commercial traffic it was time to make the rescue. Something else Alec Hall, their contact at DHS, would be pissed about—dead drug dealers floating down the Chesapeake and Delaware canal. Thankfully it wasn't his job to clean up the mess they were about to make.

"Ready?" Nixon asked.

"Oh, yeah," Weston answered.

"I think you're enjoying this a little too much." Jameson chuckled and clapped him on the shoulder.

"You've met her. Two birds, one stone."

"How do you figure that?" Jameson pressed.

"We get to take out the trash and piss her off at the same time," Weston answered.

Nix shook his head and smiled. "I think the pretty Silver has wormed her way under our boy's skin."

"If you mean, she's annoying as fuck—affirmative. If you're implying I have a hard-on for her, that's a no. I'll give you this, she is fine as hell, but she can't follow directions—hence her current incarceration—and she has a gigantic chip on her shoulder. Couple that with the blinding, 'I hate men' neon sign she flashes and that's a hard no for me."

"She's just strong-willed," Chasin joined in.

"You think maybe we can get her ass off the boat and away from the bad guys instead of waxing on about the woman's disposition? Which to add is irritating."

"Sure," Nix responded, sounding amused at Weston's frustration. "Holden," Nixon radioed the last man on the team and the only one not currently on the small fishing boat tailing the *Dora B*. "We're ready when you are."

"You have fifteen minutes, maybe seventeen until you have company," Holden told them.

"Five more than we need," Nixon replied, then turned to his team. "Let's roll."

A few minutes later Weston was climbing aboard the *Dora B* courtesy of a dive ladder that had been left in the water. His head peeked over the aft deck's railing. Not seeing anyone, he hefted his weight onto the teak surface and motioned for the team to follow.

Four men silently split up, each having a job to do to clear the boat. Weston made his way through the salon and easily found the crew stairs leading down to the cabins and storage below. With no guards patrolling the lower level, Weston made quick work clearing the galley and crew cabins. He reached for the last closed hatch and a volley of gunfire rang out above him.

His heart rate ticked up and he prayed the team's assumption was correct and Silver was being held below deck. Part of what had taken them so long to board was surveying the vessel. They couldn't see much through the portholes but there had been no sight of Silver on the upper decks. The hull was the smartest choice for the drug runners, but then again, smugglers weren't always the brightest and Silver could be anywhere.

Weston may've thought Silver was too hard-headed for her own good but he didn't want to see her hurt and he certainly didn't want her dead. On that thought, and an overwhelming urge to protect the brown haired beauty, he went through the open door and looked around.

Goddamn it, no Silver. Bricks of cocaine were stacked on pallets, and the stench of pot filled the room. Weston stepped farther into the small room, his rifle pulled up to his shoulder as he scanned. He moved toward the pallet of coke when he caught something in his peripheral flying toward his head. He quickly ducked, but a second object flew through the air, then another one, hitting the flash compensator on the end of his barrel. White powder exploded and dusted the room.

Another brick of coke hit him in the head and he barely recovered as Silver darted out from behind the stack of drugs, arms flailing, lashing out blindly. A tiny fist made contact with his bulletproof vest. He knew it had to have hurt, but to her credit she never stopped fighting. Weston let go of his rifle—the sling attached swung it to his side—and he wrapped her up in a tight bear hug, trapping her arms.

"What the fuck?" he growled.

Her foot made contact with his shin and Weston winced as pain shot up his leg.

"Goddamn it, Silver, stop."

Some of her fight started to wane, either from exhaustion or recognition, but Weston held tight.

"Let me go," she demanded.

"Not until you calm down," he returned.

"I am calm," Silver seethed.

"You don't sound calm."

"Seriously, Weston, you wanna do this now?"

Silver was right, he didn't have time to debate her bristly tone, and he really didn't have the time to process why relief had washed over him when he'd pulled her into his arms.

"Are you hurt?"

"Just my pride. And my wrists are sore from the cuffs."

"The cuffs?" he questioned. He glanced around the room and spotted a pair of open handcuffs and a chain lying on the powder-coated floor.

"Just get me out of here and I'll explain later."

Damn if she wasn't demanding. And the fuck of it was, instead of being irritated he liked it. Something else Weston didn't have time to think about.

"When we go up, you stick to my back, and this time when I tell you something you listen without question."

Silver's nose scrunched and her brows pulled together in irritation but she didn't argue which was a damn miracle. The girl could bicker about anything.

Weston pulled his rifle back to the ready and gestured for her to follow. They hit the stairs leading back to the upper deck when gunshots rang out. Silver moved so fast plastering herself against his back, Weston nearly stumbled forward. He needed to tell her she couldn't keep her arms around his stomach in case he had to move quickly and fire his weapon, but he didn't. He liked the feel of her clinging to him. Seeking his body for protection.

They took the steps together, her behind him, still

holding on, though loosely due to the incline. He stopped them at the top and maneuvered Silver so her back was to the wall as they sidestepped down the hall toward the aft deck.

Jameson came around the corner, meeting them in the salon, and gave him a nod. "We're clear."

Even though his friend had assured Weston there were no more drug smugglers still breathing, he didn't move away from Silver—very aware of her body still pressed against his.

"We're out," Nix declared as he joined them in the salon. "Holden's ready."

The group made their way to the aft deck. Chasin went over the railing and down the ladder. With one foot on the gunwale and the other still on the ladder, Chasin waited to help Silver.

"You're next," Weston said.

She didn't hesitate to climb over the side. Weston immediately felt it, the loss of her body next to his, her looking to him to keep her safe. The moment they'd shared was gone and back was the capable and stubborn Silver.

And now was not the time to ponder why that left him feeling uneasy.

2

The time had come.

The bird was cooked, it was plated, and now I was going to have to eat it.

Weston hadn't said a word during the quick boat ride back to the dock. He'd been quiet in the car as Nixon drove us to Kent County. The others had formally introduced themselves though I'd briefly met Nixon and Jameson the day I stormed into Gemini Group's office and pitched my fit. But other than assessing I was not injured—though my ego and pride had taken one hell of a hit—I was surprisingly fine.

The topic of why I was on board the *Dora B* was remarkably avoided. That was, until we reached an old farmhouse tucked away down a long dirt lane and surrounded by wilting corn. Though I didn't grow up in the country, I'd lived in the area long enough to know the corn would soon be harvested. I vaguely wondered what the bare landscape would look like with clear views of the woods in the distance.

Weston slid out of the SUV, reached in for my hand, and helped me out. But the minute my feet hit the dirt his face turned to granite.

"Are you out of your goddamned mind?" he roared.

I jerked in surprise before I squared my shoulders and prepared to go head-to-head with the jerk.

"I had every right to board that ship. Delaware rules state anything over ninety-feet flying a foreign flag requires a pilot until they reach the Maryland line. So not only did I have the right, it's my job."

"You knew the *Dora B* was on radar. You were under orders not to approach and certainly not to be the pilot to guide it down the canal. You were told to stand down."

"I don't take orders from anyone, Weston. I had a job to do and I did it."

"And that's the fucking problem. The sole reason I recommended you being pulled from this operation. You don't listen. You don't know when to stand the fuck down and watch. You're all gung-ho to rush in and

I told you that was dangerous. I told you that was going to get someone hurt. I told you to stay the fuck away from the *Dora B* and let us do our fucking job. Now it's fucked and you did that."

There it was—the 'I told you so'. The crow I'd have to eat because he was right. He did tell me, and I did fuck everything up. But he was also wrong.

"You're right," I spat the words out even though they tasted like shit and there'd be more where those came from. But first I was setting the record straight. "You did tell me all of that. But I didn't rush anything. I boarded because it is my job. I was told to pilot the ship and I couldn't say no. When I went aboard I didn't ask questions, I didn't look around, I didn't check their charts, I did nothing but steer the ship."

"You couldn't say no?" Weston asked incredulously.

"No."

"Never crossed your mind to find an excuse?"

"Excuse? Like what?"

"I don't know, maybe you had diarrhea. Maybe you started that time of the month and needed the bathroom. Maybe lying and saying you ate something bad and needed to throw up."

I couldn't believe he said that. Who says that?

Started 'that time of the month'? What, was he ten and couldn't say menstrual cycle or period? Not that that would've been any better and really, it was a hell of a lot better than discussing diarrhea.

"Oh, for fuck's sake, are you crazy?"

"No, I'm not. But you sure as fuck are."

"You think maybe we can take this into the house before the neighbors hear the two of you shouting?" Nixon asked.

I looked around, saw two pickups, an old Jeep Wrangler with the top off—vaguely thought that it was cool as hell—then to a sexy black Charger. What I couldn't see because of the corn was if there were neighbors who could hear. I also thought about how I didn't want to go into the house. No way, no how. Weston would continue to berate me and I'd had enough of him.

Hell, I'd had enough of him months ago when I'd met him in DC and his smug ass had recommended me being taken off the team to take down the drug traffickers. Further, I'd had enough of my body's reaction to him. He was a dick, but somehow my girly parts hadn't gotten the memo we hated him and they tingled with awareness every time he was around.

I'd convinced myself I'd been imagining the twinges in the time I hadn't seen him. But when we'd been on the yacht and I heard gunshots, in a serious moment of weakness and fear I'd hidden behind his huge frame. My front was plastered to his muscled back and for some unknown reason, which I was going to blame on distress, my pussy clenched. It was insane but I'd heard in extreme situations your body went haywire and I was going with that theory.

So, no, I wasn't going into the house. I wasn't spending more time with Weston Beil and his pheromones that oozed like a signal pulling me in, yet warning me he was all man and I couldn't handle his vitality. Hell to the no, I was going home.

I just didn't know how I was getting there considering my car was back at the dock in the employee lot and I didn't think Uber was available all the way out here in the middle of nowhere.

Yet I still announced, "I'm going home."

"No, you're not."

I ignored Weston and turned to the men huddled close to tell them thank you for rescuing me, but stopped dead. Four overly large men stood with identical looks of amusement.

"What's funny?" I snapped.

"Nothing." Holden chuckled.

"Then why are you smiling?"

"No reason."

"No reason? So you all normally just stand around looking badass with smiles on your faces?"

"We look like badasses, huh?" Chasin quipped, adding a wink for good measure.

Whatever, I didn't have time to stand around embarrassed by my blunder. They all knew they were hot, and standing with their feet shoulder-width apart, their arms crossed over their chests displaying their biceps, made them hotter. All except Weston. His arms weren't over his chest, they were on his hips, which not only made his biceps bulge but also drew my attention to his waist, which then drew my eyes to his stomach where I was sure a six-pack hid under his shirt.

It was a vicious cycle, my gaze not knowing where to land. There was no part of Weston that was safe to look at. His male beauty was overwhelming no matter where I looked.

Damn him for being so hot. Dickheads should not be allowed to be good-looking. This was why women were always getting themselves into trouble, picking the wrong men, overlooking an asshole's attitude because he was big and had muscles. Weston was a prime example of sexy as all hell but off-limits.

"Before I go—" I started but Weston cut me off.

"You're not goin' anywhere."

"I wanted to thank you all for saving me," I told the group and ignored Weston.

"Once again, you're not fucking listening."

"I'm ignoring you, Weston, there's a difference."

"Christ," he growled. "Get your sweet little ass in the house before I toss you over my shoulder and carry you in there."

"You touch me, asshole, and we'll have problems."

"Problems? Sweetheart, you've already got problems." His hands went from his hips and crossed over his chest and I was wrong—Weston, like the rest of the guys, could get hotter. Stupid, *stupid*, stupid girly parts not understanding the difference between hot and plain old jerk. "And how exactly are you gonna stop me, Silver? Throw some more bricks of coke at me?"

Asshole.

"The only problem I have is you. One I'll forget all about as soon as I leave here."

"If you think that, then you're naïve and haven't been paying attention."

Gah. He was annoying.

"Then tell me, Mr. Know-It-All, what am I missing?"

"You sure you didn't ask any questions today?"

"Positive."

"You didn't snoop around? Spook the men moving

the drugs? Didn't look at them funny? Didn't act weird?"

"No to all of that."

I seriously wished he'd move this along so I could go home.

"Then you've been compromised."

Say what? Compromised?

"I don't know what that means."

"You've been burned, sweetheart. The traffickers were tipped off, that *you* tipped off the authorities. Which means you got problems."

It took my brain a moment to fully comprehend what Weston was saying. It was impossible. No one knew I'd been talking to the Coast Guard or Homeland Security. I hadn't taken any time off of work to go to DC, I only went when I was off rotation. I hadn't kept any documentation of what I'd found and hadn't written anything down. There was no way anyone knew.

"You're wrong," I told Weston. "And stop calling me sweetheart, it's condescending."

"Serious as fuck, that's what you're gonna bitch about? Someone tried to kill you today and you're worried about me being condescending?"

Well, when he put it like that, it seemed I did indeed have bigger fish to fry. However, me being me, meaning I was stubborn as all-hell, I was latching on to the part about him being a jerk rather than freak out that someone had tried to off me.

"Yes, that's what I'm bitchin' about, *sweetheart*. And if you don't like it there's a way to put an end—"

I didn't have a chance to finish my hissy fit because Weston moved, and he did it so fast I didn't have time to prepare before his shoulder hit my stomach and I was airborne. Surprisingly he hadn't hurt me in his endeavor but it did piss me right the fuck off.

"Put me down."

He didn't. He kept walking toward the house and when I lifted my head I saw Holden behind me with a broad smile.

"This isn't funny, Holden."

"It sure as fuck is." He shook his head, still smiling.

"If you think so, then you're just as much of a jerk as Weston."

"Right."

The brick walkway gave way to wooden steps, then a porch, and finally Weston stepped over the threshold but didn't put me down. He continued into the living room and set me on my feet.

"I don't even know what to say to you," I told him once I was steady and staring at his angry face.

"You can start by saying thank you for saving your

ass today. Then you can promise me you'll stop being stupid. After that, you can give me your word you're not gonna run and get yourself into more trouble."

"Don't hold your breath."

"Fucking stubborn," he snarled.

Damn right, I was.

It was also my biggest problem. I blamed it on my mother. It was because of her incessant belittling I was hell-bent on proving my worth. Her constant nagging had made me hard-headed, always out to do the opposite of what she'd told me. She hated my dad, hated that I loved him, hated that I wanted to be like him, hated that I loved the water. Basically, she hated everything about me and told me so.

But more than all of that, it was because of her, my self-esteem was shit and I over-compensated by setting out to do things that would show her I was more than who she'd said I'd turn out to be.

Only right now, the one thing I was trying to do was protect myself against a man who had saved my life, was continuing to try to protect me, even if he was doing it the only way a jerk knew how and that was to be a bossy, condescending prick.

So I was grateful I was so obstinate. A weaker woman would've caved under the intensity of his stare, she would've allowed her gratitude to outweigh her sensibility. But lucky for me, my hard head was screwed on tight and I wouldn't budge no matter how tingly I got.

And damn if every nerve ending in my body was rapid firing just from the look in his eyes.

Down, girl. Stay strong.

3

Weston had been wrong. Silver couldn't write a book—she could fill a motherfucking library to the brim.

Never in his life had he met a woman who had no idea when it was time to stop with the pig-headed bullshit and admit she was in trouble. And what the hell was it about her eyes that shone the truth, yet her mouth ran away like a train headed straight for Bullshitville, but she couldn't stop the derailment.

Weston knew she understood she was in trouble, he saw it the moment it happened, when his words had finally penetrated her thick skull and it had settled over her that she'd been targeted—that the drug dealers knew she was the one to give up the *Dora B.*

Yet Silver continued to be combative.

He was seriously considering handcuffing her in

his bedroom so she couldn't go out and find more trouble when he remembered she'd been cuffed earlier.

"How'd you get out of the cuffs?" he inquired.

"Picked the lock," she said proudly.

Weston was almost impressed until her smile turned smug and he was reminded she was exasperating.

"Picked it, with what?"

"With a bobby pin."

It wasn't difficult to pick handcuffs—one of the reasons the team preferred zip ties with securing a prisoner. But it wasn't necessarily easy either. It would be something she would've known how to do or she wouldn't have figured it out so quickly, and she'd had herself uncuffed and hiding before Weston had entered the room.

"You got random cuffs laying around at home to practice with?"

Weston's back shot straight at Chasin's bad attempt at flirting with Silver.

"Bet you'd like to know," she sassed.

"Damn right, I would," Chasin continued, and ire turned into jealousy, which only further pissed Weston off.

He didn't get jealous, never had looked at anyone— male or female—with envy of any sort. Yet there he was, standing in front of Silver jealous as fuck that his friend was playing with a woman who he had no interest in. Yet he was resentful of the easy banter.

It was time to move on before Weston did something regretful, like tell his friend to back the hell up and stop talking to Silver like she was some chick he was trying to pick up. And if that's what Chasin was trying to do, Weston would shut that shit down.

He didn't want her, but he didn't want any of his friends hooking up with her either. He told himself it was because he didn't like her, therefore he didn't want her around, but Weston knew that was a lie.

"Before you boarded the *Dora B* was anyone acting funny?" Weston asked, in an effort to move the conversation away from Chasin.

Without missing a beat, Chasin chuckled, catching on immediately that Weston didn't like the banter.

"What do you mean?" Silver asked.

Gone was the playful tone she'd used with his teammate and back was the bitchy snarl. And Weston couldn't help thinking there was something seriously wrong with his head and his dick. The more spiteful Silver was the more turned-on he became. He wanted to blame it on his recent dry spell, but he knew that was bullshit. He'd gone longer without sex and had still had full control over his dick. But not now. Not when Silver had a scowl on her face and fire in her belly.

She was downright hostile and all Weston could think about was if they ever found themselves naked in his bed, it would be explosive. No, it would be uncontrollable. Volatile. A chain reaction of obscene passion that would have catastrophic consequences. Weston knew without a doubt one time with her wouldn't be enough.

She'd ruin him.

Hell, she already had.

His dick now thought bitchy was the new sexy.

"Any of your coworkers? Your boss? Was someone watching you when you parked? Anything," Weston prompted.

"No. I was on day two of my rotation and everything was normal. Matt and Rodger were on with me and they both were acting normal." Silver stopped speaking but jerked her body to attention. "Oh my God."

"What?" Nix snapped.

"Work... Matt and Rodger... the ship. That's beyond dangerous, that ship cannot just be left there, a cargo—"

"Relax, Silver—"

"Relax? Have you lost your mind? The cargo traffic

through the canal is heavy. A yacht cannot be left unattended to drift down—"

"If you would stop interrupting me, I could explain. Alec Hall has already taken possession of the ship," Weston explained.

"But my job—"

"As of today, you're taking a leave of absence."

Silver's gaze cut to Weston and she tried her best to intimidate him. *Silly woman.* It would take more than her pretty hazel eyes and dirty look to make him back down. But it was a cute try.

"I'm not taking a leave of absence. And Matt and Rodger have to be wondering where I'm at."

"Alec took care of that, too," Nixon cut in. "As far as your coworkers are concerned, you got sick and were rushed to the hospital. And Weston's right, as of now you're on sabbatical. We'll figure out what excuse you're gonna give, but I think you should go with illness, since they already think you're in the hospital."

"That's crazy," she protested.

"No. What's crazy is you not taking the threat seriously," Weston told her.

"But we don't know..." Silver stopped speaking and frowned.

As shocking as it was, and it was astonishing, she looked like she was at a loss for words.

"You're right," she relented, and it looked painful for her to admit.

So, the woman did have it in her to be reasonable, she just chose to be a pain in the ass.

Good to know.

Weston wasn't sure what to do with this piece of information and as much as he wanted to celebrate that he'd won, he knew better. Silver was like a opossum—playing dead, but really she was lying in wait so she could claw you and scratch your eyeballs out when your defenses were down.

For now, he'd keep his mouth shut and eyes open.

"What now?" she asked.

"Now we wait for Alec," Nixon interjected. "The only good part about today is someone's gonna be pissed their coke wasn't delivered. Hopefully, they're pissed enough to slip up."

"What does slip up mean?" Silver continued.

"It means, so far whoever's on the receiving end of the shipments has been careful and we can't get a lock on the leader. A lieutenant picks it up from the dock, distributes it to the captains, from there it gets cut, packaged, then given to the street soldiers for distribution," Weston explained. "We've identified everyone but the head of the organization and until we do we can't move in."

"And you think someone knows I figured out what they're doing?"

This time when Silver asked there was a hint of trepidation in her voice. Weston hated the sound but was relieved she was finally understanding she'd placed herself in the middle of a serious shitstorm.

"Wouldn't take much," Holden told her. "The men we're dealing with are not stupid, they pay attention. And if they have someone on the inside, helping them move the drugs down the canal and into the harbor, it would be even easier."

"You think someone I work with is in on it?"

"Absolutely. You don't move millions of dollars of coke unless you know you have safe passage," Chasin weighed in.

Weston hadn't taken his eyes off Silver. She was clever—hell, she'd been the one who'd put the pieces together and brought it to the Coast Guard and the DHS. He was waiting for her to come to her own conclusions about the situation and when her brows pinched together, Weston knew she was closing in on the reality of the state of play.

"If it's an employee they'll have my address," she blurted out.

There it was, she was figuring it out.

"And if it's someone in the Coast Guard..." Silver

didn't finish her sentence and she didn't need to, the men in the room all understood what that meant.

Silver hadn't gone in quietly, she hadn't anonymously reported the issues. She'd marched her happy ass straight into the Coast Guard station in Baltimore, uncaring the station was actually a repair yard, and she'd demanded to speak to the Captain. It wasn't her best play but luckily Captain Stewart had taken her concerns to heart and used his contacts at Homeland to help her.

"Captain Stewart is on the up-and-up and no one on Alec Hall's team would turn on you," Nixon commented. "It's someone you work with."

"I can—"

"You're staying here," Weston told her before his brain had fully engaged, allowing his mouth to speak without thinking of the ramifications.

Weston felt his teammates staring. They hadn't talked about what to do with Silver or where they were going to stash her until the operation was over, but the more Weston thought about it the more he realized staying at the farmhouse with the team was her best option.

Though he wasn't sure he'd make it through the first twenty-four hours of her being in his space.

A gag or hearing protection might be a worthy

investment if he had to be around her for any lengthy period of time.

"I am not staying here," Silver protested. "I can find a hotel."

"Actually, Weston's right," Chasin agreed. "You staying here means we don't have to rotate security detail."

"Security detail?" She gaped. "I don't need a detail."

Christ, just when Weston thought Silver was finally taking the situation seriously she sank back into her stubborn ways. Only this wasn't her being pig-headed, it was her being careless and stupid. And since Weston knew she wasn't stupid he was back to thinking she was obstinate and careless.

"Are you purposely trying to get yourself dead? Or are you just so goddamned determined to be a pain in the ass, you're gonna fight against us even when we're trying to save your ass?" Weston growled. "Serious as shit, woman, I cannot for the life of me figure you out."

Silver's eyes flashed hurt and Weston felt like a dick, but as quickly as she'd allowed some vulnerability to creep in, she masked it and spewed her vitriol.

"I don't need anyone to save my ass and I certainly have no desire to get dead. I can take care of myself. I don't need you—"

"You don't? Funny, I think it was my team that got you off that yacht. And before you say it, yes you'd got yourself out of the cuffs, which I admit was impressive. What wasn't, was you thinking you were gonna somehow escape by throwing bricks of cocaine at your captors. What the fuck did you think you were gonna accomplish by that? Have them OD as powder floated through the air? It was stupid and potentially deadly. If that coke had fentanyl in it, we'd both be dead right now. So, I'm sorry to burst your stubborn-ass bubble, sweetheart, but this isn't something you're just gonna get out of. And the only way you're gonna be safe is by me and my team making you that way. Unless you got some mad tracking and sniper skills we don't know about. By all means, now's the time for you to share you're really an undercover assassin. But I have to say, knowing what I know about you, I know you're fucking not. So we're your best option. Like it or not."

"I don't like it," she snapped. "Not one fucking bit."

"You don't have to. But what you have to do, is accept it."

"I don't have to—"

"Goddamn, woman. Listen to yourself. We're offering to protect you. To keep you safe. The alternative is you're picked up again, only next time when I find you, it won't be amusing. Mainly because you won't be tossing drugs at my head, then you won't be walking off the yacht with your arms around me. It will be me carrying you in a fucking body bag because you'll be fucking dead."

Weston watched as Silver paled. She didn't frown, she didn't spew shit, she simply shrank into herself as her shoulders hunched forward, and damn if Weston didn't hate it. Hated that she looked sullen and beat down—and what was worse was that Weston had been the one to put the look on her face and he knew it. Felt down to his soul that he'd been a prick and gone too far.

But he didn't know any other way to make her see she needed them. Needed him. And he wasn't lying—it would be him carrying her lifeless body, because for some asinine reason he felt responsible for her. Through all of her prickly, brash bullshit, Weston still couldn't stop thinking about her. Hadn't stopped since the day he'd met her. Could not get her fire out of his belly, and her go-get-it attitude out of his head.

He'd never simultaneously disliked and wanted a woman so badly.

4

Before I'd left for college my dad had sat me down and told me, I had to let my mother go. He'd warned me there would come a time when my ambition would be tainted with her bitterness if I didn't put her behind me. He'd explained that my determination and drive to excel had to be my own and not because my mother had told me I was worthless.

I thought about that conversation a lot through the years. What was my true motivation and purpose to push myself to succeed? Why did I always have the need to prove I was better than what she thought I was?

My dad was a good man if not a little selfish in some ways. He was also reflective and caring. He didn't want me to carry the burdens my mother had piled on my shoulders.

His warnings had come to fruition. The day had come where I was holding onto the bad stuff, the bitter, the burden, the need to prove something that was not mine to prove. And it was going to get me killed. I was being stupid and I knew it. I needed Weston's help. I needed them all but I didn't know how to accept it graciously, so instead, I behaved like a bitch to show them all I was strong and capable.

But I was not capable of getting myself out of this mess. And as much as Weston had been a first-class dick, he'd been correct, I didn't have mad gun skills. I couldn't track down who had caught on to what I was doing and stop them. I couldn't protect myself against a gang of drug dealers.

"Listen, Silver—"

I put my hand up to stop Weston. I hated that he no longer sounded angry. His tone had changed to gentle and compassionate. Two things I didn't want from him.

"You're right. Is that what you want to hear? I can't do it on my own. But I don't want to burden the rest of you with babysitting me."

Damn, and I was back to eating crow and it tasted

shittier this time around. I was tired of having to admit I was wrong.

A logical person would simply modify their behavior so they didn't have to utter the admission. But unfortunately for me, I had a hard time with logic and an even harder time holding my tongue. Especially around Weston. He seemed to have the uncanny ability to reach inside of me and pull out the bitchiness.

"No, I want you to tell me you understand you're in danger and you'll stay here so I can protect you," Weston said.

And that was when it happened. When I stopped being an irrational bitch and looked at Weston. Really saw him for the first time through clear eyes.

Instead of seeing him as an opponent, I considered the possibility that maybe he'd been trying to look out for me all along. Not that I liked the way he'd gone about it, but he'd done it all the same. Hadn't he been the one to warn me in the first place? The rest of the men I'd met with were all too happy to let me be the one to board the ships and snoop around. After all, it was within my right to check the navigation charts.

But not Weston. From the very beginning, he'd expressed his concern for my safety.

"I understand. But..." I saw Weston's eyes glitter with annoyance and rushed to finish, "I'd like to help."

"How can you say you understand and still make that offer?" he inquired.

"I don't mean, be on the front lines. But I have something to offer. I know those waterways. I know the routes they'd take and what time of day they'd take them. I'm aware I'm in danger. This isn't me being stubborn, it's me offering to help so we can wrap this up. The faster that happens, the faster I'm out of your hair and we can all get on with our lives."

As true as that statement was, it was a depressing thought. My normal life consisted of working, going home alone, having an occasional beer with one of the guys I worked with, maybe talking to my dad on the phone if he had service, but mostly it consisted of me being by myself.

Pretty damn sad for a woman my age.

"I'll take you back to your apartment so you can pick up what you need," Weston offered.

"Do we have a deal?" I pressed.

"Yeah, your help will be needed." Weston hadn't stopped staring at me and something had changed—his light brown eyes were no longer spitting daggers at me, instead, they looked kind. Understanding. Gentle, even.

All the more reason for me to invest all of my time and energy into taking out the drug dealers. It was hard enough keeping my body's reaction to Weston in check when he was being an asshole, I had a feeling it would be damn near impossible if he was being nice. And neither one of us needed me to throw myself at him, even if I really wanted to know what his hard muscles felt like under my hands. It would have to remain one of the many wonders of the world, never to be explored.

FIFTEEN MINUTES later I was in Weston's Jeep Wrangler. But the surprising part was, I was wearing his sweatshirt. Before we'd left he disappeared upstairs, then minutes later reappeared with a hoodie and thrust it at me, explaining he still had the top and doors off his Jeep and he didn't want me getting chilly.

It was thoughtful.

It was out of character.

It also made my belly whoosh.

I didn't like this side of Weston, or more to the point, I really liked it—therefore he needed to go back to being a jerk so I could continue to dislike him.

"Why a professional mariner?" he asked, pulling my attention from inspecting the interior of the Jeep. Which, just to add, was sparse. No radio, no bells and whistles of a new car, nothing. It was bare bones and weirdly it fit Weston.

I wasn't sure how I felt about his personal question but I answered anyway.

"My dad—"

"You're gonna have to speak up, babe."

I started again, this time loud enough he could hear me over the street noise. "My dad is a boat captain. Has been most of his life. When I was growing up he wanted me to take over his dive business but the thought of taking inexperienced divers out day in and day out had no appeal. He's also a part-time treasure hunter—always chasing the next big find. So even though I knew I didn't want to follow in my dad's footsteps I loved the water. And up until that point I'd lived on boats my whole life—"

"Lived on boats?" Weston cut me off.

"Yep. From the day I was brought home from the hospital to the day I left for maritime college. The first week I lived on dry land was a little strange."

I left out the part about how I couldn't sleep because the bed was too soft and too still. And the sounds freaked me out. I was used to being lulled to sleep by the rocking of the sea and the constant thrum of the engine noise that drown out all other sounds.

"And your mom?"

After all these years my reaction was involuntary and immediate. It happened every time someone asked about her and I was grateful Weston's eyes were on the road and he couldn't see how my body stiffened at the mention of her. "Is she a waterman, too?"

"I'm not sure what she is," I told him, trying to keep my voice neutral.

"Come again?"

"She left when I was ten to go live in Florida. She'd come back and visit every few months and stay on the boat until she couldn't take it anymore and leave again. When I was about fifteen she stopped coming around altogether. Two years later my dad was served with divorce papers and that was the last he heard from her."

"Last he heard from her? What about you?"

"She ceased to exist for me when I was fifteen."

"Damn, Silver, I'm sorry."

I wasn't, I was happy she left when she did and wanted nothing to do with me. Her last visit had been horrific. She and my dad had argued the whole time, and before she left, she told me I was nothing more than a water rat and would end up exactly like my dad —a loser with nothing to show for my life.

"Nothing to be sorry about. It was a long time ago,

and trust me, my dad and I were better off with her gone."

If it was so long ago, why do you still dwell on it?

I mentally chastised myself for going there and struggled to find something to steer the conversation away from my bitch of a mother.

"What about you?" I asked. "The Navy, huh? Did you always want to go into the military?"

"Yep. Though I thought I was gonna join the Air Force. I grew up in Montgomery, Alabama, next to Maxwell Air Force base. My mom's a teacher and used to volunteer on the base as a STEM advisor, and my dad coached a youth baseball team on the base as well. Since my dad was the coach I got to play on the team. It was love at first sight. I knew then being on that base, seeing the comradery, feeling the sense of purpose and community, that the military was for me. I started learning everything I could about the military entrance exam, I studied day and night so I'd be ready to take the ASVAB. Mom wanted me to go to college first and enlist as an officer. Dad recognized I had no interest in going to college first and made me a deal. He'd support me, even sign the papers to allow me to enlist at seventeen if I promised to get a degree as soon as my GI bill came available."

I was so enthralled with Weston's story I barely

noticed we were already in Chesapeake City going over the high-rise bridge.

"You can't leave me hanging," I complained. "What happened next?"

Weston chuckled and much to my surprise I found I really liked the sound. It was deep and rich and wholly manly.

Damn him.

Maybe I didn't want to hear the rest of his story. Maybe I was better off thinking he was an animatronic robot who didn't have what sounded like a good family, a past, a real life. It was easier to think of him as an unfeeling jerk who thought I was incompetent and unworthy of being a part of his operation.

"I took the ASVAB my senior year, scored exceptionally well, thanks in part to all my studying. The other part is credited to my school teacher mom who thought anything less than a four-point-oh GPA was unacceptable. My recruiter took one look at my ASVAB and PT scores and told me I'd be perfect for Special Reconnaissance. Once he'd mentioned special forces, I began to research more and found the Navy was where I wanted to be. The Air Force recruiter was not happy when I showed up with my parents a week later and signed a Navy contract."

"I bet the recruiter was unhappy, but it sounds like you made the right choice."

"Yeah, I did. Couldn't imagine my life any other way."

My eyes drifted closed and I wondered what that would be like, to be so happy with your life, with the decisions you've made, with the family you were born into, you couldn't imagine any other life. I'd spent my life wishing my father hadn't reproduced with the Spawn of Satan. How different would my life have been if my dad had picked someone else to be my mother?

The Jeep slowed and my eyes opened to find Weston pulling into my driveway. And suddenly I wondered what he'd think of my apartment. I loved it though I hadn't done much to the interior, but the view of the canal and the twenty-minute drive to work was what had sold me on the location.

I wasn't sure why I cared so much about what Weston thought of me or how I lived. It wasn't like we were friends. Hell, in a few days when this was over, he'd forget all about me. But I guess old habits die hard.

5

Weston followed a very quiet Silver to the front of an old three-story brick building. She opened the front door and Weston quickly grabbed the door to allow her to precede him.

"I'm on the third floor." Silver told him something he already knew.

Not that Weston would tell her, but he knew a lot about her. Not the personal stuff about her parents that she'd revealed during the drive, something that Weston couldn't stop dwelling on. He'd wanted to ask more questions, find out why she thought she was better off without her mother in her life. He couldn't imagine what it would be like not to have a mom who loved and supported him. Sure, his own mother had been strict when it came to his education, but Margie Beil was always around to help.

As they climbed the stairs, Weston thought about the things he did know about Silver—she was born in Florida, was homeschooled, went to the Maritime College in Delaware, graduated second in her class. She furthered her training and became a maritime pilot, and she belonged to the Delaware Pilots Association. She also had an ungodly amount of hours on the water.

Silver Coyle was smart, an exemplary captain, and when she forgot she had a chip on her shoulder the size of the Grand Canyon, she was easy to talk to and genuinely nice.

Too bad she remembered more than she forgot.

Silver stopped at a wall-mounted box that housed a fire extinguisher and opened the glass door. Before Weston could ask what she was doing she reached around behind the canister and retrieved a key.

"My purse with my keys are still at the boatyard," she explained, and Weston wanted to kick himself in the ass for not remembering that important detail. "My spare."

She held the key up for him to see and he stopped himself—though just barely—for berating her on her choice of hiding places.

"I'll send someone to gather your stuff from the yard," Weston told her as they walked down the hall to her door.

He knew her apartment occupied the entire third floor, therefore no one would use that hallway except for her, but he still didn't like that there were only two overhead lights to illuminate the space. During the day, it wouldn't be an issue with all of the large windows on the outside wall but at night it would be dim.

The tiniest prickle started at the base of his spine and he reached out and grabbed Silver's hand, slowing her down.

"Does anyone else have a key to your apartment?" he asked softly.

"No. Just me."

Weston's gaze went to her door. His eyes zeroed in on the frame, and his free hand went to the holster on his hip.

"How sure are you that you closed your door all the way when you left for work?"

"What?" Her brows furrowed and he was fast learning she looked damn cute with her forehead wrinkled.

"The door, Silver. Did you close it all the way and lock it?"

"Of course I did. I use the deadbolt every time I leave."

Shit, goddamn. He was worried she'd say that. The sidearm his hand had been hovering over cleared the holster and Silver's gaze flitted to the gun before coming back to his face. Concern washed over her pretty features, and as much as he wished he could reassure her, he couldn't. Not right then, while the fine hair on the back of his neck stood up and his instincts were screaming at him.

With a tug, Silver stumbled back and Weston quickly tucked her behind him.

"Just like before, stay at my back. If I tell you to run, you run."

"Kay."

Weston blew out a relieved breath when Silver didn't hesitate or argue.

"Reach in my front right pocket and grab my keys."

Silver's hand dove into his pocket and fished around, bumping his dick in the process. The more her fingertips grazed the head of his cock, the harder it was to fight his body's natural reaction to a beautiful woman touching him, even if she was innocently trying to find his keys. And it was most certainly the wrong time to get a hard-on.

"Other pocket," he grunted.

Wordlessly, her hand went to his other pocket and Weston was damn grateful his dick was out of her reach. Silver pulled his keys free and he felt her hand brush his ass as she shoved them in her jeans, then quickly plastered herself against his back.

He started to walk toward the door but stopped briefly to pat her clasped hands around his waist. "Can't have you holding onto me in case I need to move. Just stay close."

She nodded her answer against his back and took a half-step away from him. And just like before, Weston immediately felt the loss of her touch.

He toed the already-cracked front door open. With his gun pulled up and at the ready, he scanned the front room and was damn happy Silver was shorter than him and her view would be obscured.

The place was completely ransacked, all of her shit torn to pieces. How no one below her apartment heard the bookcases being knocked over, Weston did not know. He also didn't know how the hell he was going to maneuver around the room without stepping on books, broken glass, ripped-open couch cushions, and tipped-over chairs.

But he needed to hurry the hell up and figure it out

so he could clear the house. Making a decision he didn't want to make but knew he had to, Weston reached behind him and took Silver's hand and skirted the wall until he found a place to stash her.

"Stay right here, with your back to the wall," he whispered.

He didn't have to be looking at her to know the moment she saw the devastation. The quick inhalation of air and whimper was enough. As much as he wanted to pull her into his arms and comfort her, he couldn't—there were three more rooms to clear.

Weston tried to pull his hand out of hers but she held tight. He glanced over his shoulder, finding a wide-eyed and pale Silver.

"Please don't leave me," she whispered.

"Not gonna leave you, I just have to clear—"

"Don't leave me, Weston, please."

Those five words hit Weston's soul like an atomic bomb and stopped him dead. Sheer panic and desperation shone in her eyes and she was looking at him like he was the only thing standing in between her and her worst fear.

Damn, why did that feel so fucking good?

"Okay, sweetheart, stay right behind me."

It was not the best plan, having her following him, but neither was leaving her unprotected. Clearing the rooms went a lot slower than Weston would've liked, but fortunately, there was no one in the apartment. Unfortunately, the bedroom, bathroom, and office were worse than the living room.

Total loss. Silver's home was destroyed.

After Weston had closed and dead-bolted the door, Silver finally moved from his side and walked to what was left of her kitchen.

Dishes, pots and pans, countertop appliances were all on the tiled floor shattered to pieces.

"There's nothing left," she whispered with tears brimming in her eyes. "Everything's gone."

The first tear broke free and rolled down her cheek and that was all it took for Weston to pull her into his arms and hug her close. Something he shouldn't have done but only realized his mistake when her face hit his chest, the top of her head coming just below his chin—she was a perfect fit. And when the side of her cheek nuzzled, sending waves of rightness over Weston's body, he knew he was in trouble.

They stood in silence, Weston at a loss for words and Silver trying to process her home being decimated.

He didn't want to rush her but they couldn't stay there, so he gently brushed her hair away from her face, another mistake—a huge one. He'd liked the feel of her pressed close but liked the way her soft strands glided through his fingers just as much.

"Silver, sweetheart, we have to go."

She nodded her head and looked up at him with red-rimmed eyes and Weston wanted to beat the people responsible bloody.

"I still need to get some—"

"No, honey, leave it. We'll stop at the store and pick up what you need."

He knew he needed to stop with the silly pet names, but each time one slipped past his lips it felt right. Which was a shocking revelation considering he'd always hated endearments of the sort in the past and had never used them with any other woman before. He also found he hadn't hated when Silver had called him 'sweetheart', even if she'd meant to be sarcastic and snarky.

Wasn't that some crazy shit?

"Okay," she readily agreed and for once he didn't like her easy acceptance.

Especially knowing it was because she was traumatized. He hadn't thought it possible but he actually missed her stubborn, know-it-all attitude. He would take her sass any day of the week and twice on Sunday over the wobble in her voice.

Weston started to move away but stopped when Silver whispered, "I'm scared."

And it was then in that moment, with Silver pinning him in place—all pretense gone, all the walls down—he knew he would meet death before she met harm.

"I promise you, Silver, swear it, I'll keep you safe."

6

I'd known pain, the emotional kind that eats at you from the inside. The kind that nags and belittles you until you believed the lies others told you, the untruths your mind replayed. I knew what that felt like, I'd lived it, was *still* living it.

But this was worse than that kind of pain. The truth had smacked into me with a force I couldn't deny.

I was in danger.

More danger than I'd thought I was already in.

I couldn't pretend my way out of it. I couldn't lie to everyone around me and front like I was someone who was invincible.

So while I'd known pain I'd never known this kind of fear and it scared the hell out of me. It terrified me even more to admit it. But standing in my apartment with everything I owned in shambles, with nothing left, I no longer had the luxury of hiding.

I needed help. I needed someone to protect me. Two things I didn't want to need but did all the same.

"Let's get you out of here," Weston mumbled. But before he pulled away he bent forward and kissed my forehead.

I knew he did it to be nice—the peck was meant to be reassuring and comforting but it wasn't. It sent my heart rate skyrocketing and reminded me of things I'd never have. Sure, Weston was being nice to me now, it seemed like deep-down he was a good person, being that he'd offered me gentleness after everything I'd lost. But I knew it wasn't real, not like a man would brush his lips against the forehead of woman he cared for.

I wasn't that to him and never would be. So his kiss was torture.

Weston led me out of my apartment, even unnecessarily locked the deadbolt after us and continued down to his Jeep. He didn't let go of my hand until he asked me for his keys, and it was only then because I needed my hand to reach into my pocket. After that, he helped me in, buckled the seat belt for me, and jogged around the front and climbed in.

It wasn't until we were well over the Chesapeake City Bridge and I noticed he was going the wrong way did I finally speak.

"Where are you going?"

"Middletown."

"Delaware?"

"Unless you know another Middletown, then yes."

He was being a smartass and I wasn't sure how I felt about him being friendly. Actually, that was a lie, I did know—it freaked me out.

"Why are we going there?"

"You need clothes and there's nowhere to shop in Kent County and I'm starved. As much as I love pizza and Procolino's has the best I've ever had, I can't eat another slice. So we'll find a place to eat, too."

I didn't live in Kent County and even I knew, no one turned down Proc's, which meant he had to be over pizza, as in *over* it, if he was swearing off the eatery.

I didn't know what to say to him about his thoughtfulness so I went back to silence. The problem with that was, silence meant there was nothing else to do but think. And thinking was not what I needed to be doing right then. It had been a long time since I'd needed my dad, but right then, all I wanted was my dad to wrap me up in one of his bear hugs and tell me everything was going to be all right. That I'd get through this. That I could rebuild my life. That all the shit in my house that had been broken could be replaced.

"What are you thinking about?"

"That I miss my dad."

Weston nodded like he understood and said, "You know all of that can be replaced. The important thing's that you're safe. I know it sucks, the prospect of starting over, but shit is just that, Silver—shit."

Okay, so, I may've been gaping at him. It was like he'd read my mind and then somehow channeled my dad and told me exactly what he'd say.

"When I was about eleven, the boat we lived on caught on fire. My dad grabbed me, two life preservers, and jumped overboard. When we were floating in the water waiting I asked him why he didn't try to put out the fire. He told me that a boat can be replaced, but he could never replace me. He said, shit is shit and that's what insurance is for. I didn't get it then, I was kinda upset that everything we had was on fire and I was floatin' in the water in the middle of the night. But he was right. So, I know you're right, too. But I feel like I'm back in the cold water floating all alone with nothing again."

Weston took his hand off the gear shift and reached over and laced our fingers together.

"You're not alone."

Shit. Shit. Damn.

Why on earth was he being so nice? This side of Weston was more than I could bear. I should've pulled my hand away and told him not to touch me, but I didn't. I should've told him he didn't need to be nice to me, I may've had a moment of weakness but I wasn't going to break.

Yet I did neither of those things. Instead, I sat in Weston's Jeep as he kindly drove us to buy me clothes, wearing his sweatshirt—that indecently smelled divine, and I did it all holding his hand.

"I like your Jeep," I blurted.

"Yeah?"

"Yeah, it's cool driving around with no top or doors. It feels like you're free."

I was sure my hair was already a rat's nest from the first leg of our trip and it would look even worse when we stopped in Middletown, but I didn't care. I lifted my chin, closed my eyes, and let the fresh air whip through my hair.

"It does. But if you really wanna feel free I'll take you for a ride on my bike."

"You have a motorcycle?" My eyes popped open and I looked over at Weston.

"Yep. You ever been on one?" he asked and glanced over at me.

Our eyes locked. It was quick—just for a second—before he had to look back at the road, but I could swear something passed between us.

"No."

"You'll love it."

I was sure I would, though I didn't think it would be a good idea. I'd learned a few things over the course of the day. When Weston wasn't being a jerk, he was irresistible. I'd also come to the conclusion my girly parts really liked when I was close to him. Riding on the back of his motorcycle would mean my crotch would be pressed against his ass—and just to note it was a spectacular sight. I wasn't sure what exercise he did to make it as tight and firm as he did, but whatever he was doing, he shouldn't stop.

"Here," Weston said, and reached behind him. His hand came back with a baseball cap.

"That bad, huh?" I laughed.

"No, you look great. But your hair is whipping you in the face. I should've offered it earlier."

"It's like you can read my mind," I mumbled.

"What was that?" He leaned closer.

"I said you can read my mind. I was just thinking about how messy my hair was gonna be."

Weston pulled to a stop at a red light and looked over at me.

"It's a little knotted. But it's...." He shook his head and didn't continue.

"It's what?"

"Nothing. It's fine." Weston shifted in his seat, then leaned back and pulled his phone out of his pocket and handed it to me. "My texts are blowing up, can you check them for me?"

"Your texts?"

"Yeah. Can't while I'm driving."

I looked at his phone then back to him. "But what if they're private? Like from your girlfriend or something."

Okay, so I was fishing and it wasn't my finest moment, and my question wasn't as smooth as I thought it sounded in my head. But now that I'd asked, the inquiry hung between us.

"Babe." He laughed but said no more.

Sweetheart, honey, babe. I wasn't sure which one I liked more. What I did know was I shouldn't like any of them.

"Is that your answer?"

When the light turned green, Weston shifted into first, then into second, and I couldn't take my eyes off his hand on the gear shift. Actually, I couldn't peel my eyes from the muscles in his forearms. Who knew watching a man drive was so sexy? My gaze moved to his thick thighs, before they went to his stomach—which I knew was rock-hard since my arms had been wrapped around him twice—then up to his chest, which was just as solid, and I knew that, too, because my face had rested against it—then to his throat.

Since I was staring so intently I not only heard but saw as he cleared his throat, pulling my attention to his face. Gone were all traces of annoyance that were normally present when he looked at me. His features weren't set in stone, but they were intense, and he was also looking right at me.

"Two things," he started and I lost his eyes as they went back to the road. "I'm a grown man, I don't do girlfriends. And second, if I had a woman, my lips would never have gotten anywhere near you."

I shivered at his response and it had nothing to do with the chill in the air. I was more than comfortable with his hoodie on and he had the heat blasting at my feet. No, it was the steel in his voice. The vehemence in his tone. Weston was making it clear, he wasn't the kind of man who would kiss another woman—even a friendly kiss—if he was already involved with someone.

Why does that make me so happy?

"Silver? The texts," he prompted.

"Right." I went back to the phone and pressed the home button. "It's locked."

Weston rattled off his security code and my mouth fell open. "You just gave me your code."

"And?"

"And...I don't know. You don't know me. Your phone's private, now I know your code."

"You gonna jack my phone from my room and send out spam emails to all my contacts?"

"No. That's crazy. But I could take it and nose through all your pictures."

"Knock yourself out, honey, but I think you'll be disappointed."

"Not a picture-taking type of guy, huh?" I laughed.

"No, there are thousands of pictures on there, but nothing exciting."

I was teasing Weston, but now I wanted to look to see what pictures he had and what he considered not exciting. Who was the real Weston Beil and what did he think was photograph-worthy?

I unlocked his phone and found he had four text

messages. I tapped the icon and pulled up his text strings.

"You have three from Nixon and one from McKenna."

Seeing a woman's name made my stomach bottom out. Just because he didn't have a girlfriend—or a woman as he called it—who he was serious about didn't mean he wasn't seeing one. And a man as good-looking as Weston could be seeing a lot of women, there was no doubt his options would be varied and his field wide.

Damn.

I couldn't compete with the type of women who would flock to Weston.

Wait. Full stop. Back up. I didn't even want to compete for Weston's attention.

"Start with Nix."

I clicked on the string and backed up three messages and read them out loud.

"Chasin is driving up now to go over to the apartment. Holden is going by her work to pick up her stuff." I reread the text to myself then asked, "What are they doing?"

"Chasin will go to your apartment and check it out, see if he can figure out who broke in and why. Holden's going to the yard and he'll pick up your stuff. While he's there he can get a read on Matt and Rodger."

"Get a read?"

"Yeah. Right now, everyone you work with is potentially the one that sold you out. Holden wants a face-to-face with everyone. Your stuff still being at work gives him the perfect excuse."

"But Matt and Rodger won't give it to him."

"They will, he can be convincing. What's the next message say?"

I looked back down and read the next three.

"Alec reported in, 1.5 mil in coke. He's not happy there are three dead men, but happy with the bust." Three dead men. Holy shit. Then the next. "McKenna is working on pulling traffic cams and any private CCV in the area." *McKenna?* And the last. "I'm headed back to my place. McKenna put fresh sheets on your bed for Silver. Check in later. Meeting at the office 8 AM."

So maybe McKenna wasn't his woman—either that or she was crazy and didn't care another woman was going to sleep in her man's bed even if he wouldn't be in it with me. I still didn't know a woman alive who would be okay with that.

"What'd Micky say?" he asked.

"Who's Micky?"

"McKenna."

Gah. He even had a cool nickname for her. My

belly swooshed and I was reminded again what an idiot I was. Weston was off-limits and I had to remember that. No matter how hot, how sweet he could be, how badly I wanted to ride on the back of his bike, how insanely good it felt to be in his arms, how desperately I wanted to know what his skin felt like under my palms.

I couldn't ever do any of that.

7

Silver had gone quiet after she'd read the message and Weston knew it was a lot to process so he didn't rush her. A man she barely knew was going to enter her home, albeit it was trashed, and among the rubble would be personal items. A second man she didn't know was going to invade her space even more and go to her place of work and get her overnight bag and purse—if it was still intact.

So Weston gave her time. But when he stopped at another light he glanced over at her and gently asked, "You okay?"

"Yeah. No. I don't know. Depends on what you're asking about."

Weston was surprised by her honesty and also thrilled she wasn't hiding from him.

"Let's start with Chasin going into your apartment."

"I don't care about that. Everything's ruined. What's he gonna see? My tampons all over the bathroom? Mildly embarrassing but whatever. My underwear thrown all over my room? I could be wrong, but I'm pretty sure he's seen women's underwear."

Jealousy and irrational bitterness bubbled in his gut, thinking about his friend seeing Silver's panties. Weston had caught a glimpse of pink scraps of lace on Silver's bedroom floor and he sure as fuck didn't want his friend seeing them, let alone touching them.

"Maybe I should call Chasin and tell him I'll go back tomorrow," he grumbled.

"It's whatever, seriously. Weston, I don't care about anything in that apartment. Everything's gonna be thrown away."

Fuck, he hated that for her, hated the melancholy in her voice.

"So if you don't care about that, then why do you look upset?"

She was quiet for a moment and he wished she'd hurry up before the light turned green and he couldn't look at her when she answered.

"Will McKenna be upset I'm staying at your place?"

What the fuck? Why was she worried about McKenna?

"Why would McKenna care?"

Silver pulled her bottom lip into her mouth, a gesture that was so sexy when her teeth sank in and started to worry the corner of her mouth, all of Weston's good intentions flew out the window. Not that there were windows in his Jeep—but the sentiment was the same.

Without thinking, he reached over and used his thumb on her chin to pull the abused lip free, then turned her face toward him. Wrong thing to do. When her hazel eyes met his, the electricity between them couldn't be denied. Even looking wounded and forlorn, Silver was the sexiest woman Weston had ever seen.

"I'm gonna be sleeping in your bed."

Weston still didn't understand her concern but his cock jerked in his pants at the reminder. And if he had his way, he'd be in that bed with her sooner rather than later.

"I can promise you, Nix's woman could care less who I take to my bed."

"Nix's woman?" Something flashed in Silver's eyes, something that looked a hell of a lot like relief, and his cock took notice of that, too.

"Yeah, babe. McKenna is Nixon's woman. They're engaged. Micky also works for Gemini Group. She does all of our computer work."

"Oh."

Realization dawned. *Fuck yeah.* Silver had been worried McKenna was his. And by the look on her pretty face, she didn't like that thought.

There was a lot Weston wanted to say, but none of it could be said while he was driving. It was a conversation that needed to be had when he had her undivided attention, and that wasn't happening right now. But the conversation would be had.

"What'd Micky say?" Weston prompted when the light turned green.

Unfortunately with his concentration back on the road, he lost sight of Silver. But not before he saw her look back down at his phone.

"Working on traffic cams. But I want eyes and ears in the boatyard. We'll work on that tomorrow. Please tell Silver if she needs anything me and Kennedy have her back."

Weston thought about letting Silver sweat it out a bit wondering who Kennedy was, but that would be a dickhead move that's only purpose would be to feed his ego, knowing Silver would be jealous.

"Kennedy is Jameson's woman," he told her. "He used to live at the farmhouse with us but moved in with Kennedy. So now it's just me and Chasin in the house and Holden lives in his Airstream."

Weston found the shopping center he was looking for and pulled in. There weren't many options in Middletown, but in a pinch Silver could find the necessities.

"Holden lives in a trailer? Is there not enough room in the house?"

Weston found a spot, pulled in, engaged the emergency brake, and cut the engine.

"Don't let Holden hear you call his baby a trailer." Weston chuckled. "He's crazy about that damn thing. When he bought it, it was junk. He spent two years between deployments and missions fixing it up."

"Two years?"

"Yep. And by the time he was done, he'd spent enough money on the damn thing he could've put a down payment on a house."

"Why did it take him so long?"

Her innocent question was not something he wanted to answer while sitting in his Jeep in front of a TJ Maxx. At least not fully.

"We were gone a lot," he answered, and Silver seemed to understand his need for privacy.

"Right."

Shit, maybe she didn't understand.

"Not a conversation I want to have sitting in my Jeep."

"I get it."

"No, babe, you don't. I'm not saying I won't tell you. All I'm saying is it's not something I want to talk about while we're both hungry, and especially after the day you've had. We'll table the conversation for another day when you're not stressed out, worried, haven't been held against your will, and my team's not rummaging through your stuff."

Silver's face paled and Weston wanted to kick his own ass for being such an inconsiderate asshole. Not that he'd meant to be, but he certainly shouldn't have brought up the day's events.

"Silver, I—"

"You don't need to say anything. I know what you were trying to say. It just feels weird."

"What does?"

"Everything that happened. I'm kinda on autopilot. Like it doesn't seem real. Or like, all of that didn't just happen today. I don't know. It's hard to believe this morning I was handcuffed in the hull of a ship and now I'm sitting here with you. I don't know if I thanked you for saving me."

"You did."

"Right. In the middle of my temper tantrum. It probably didn't sound sincere or heartfelt, but I really do appreciate it. I knew I wasn't getting off that ship."

Weston really wanted to let her get it all out, tell him everything she was bottling up, but now was not the time. He wanted to be able to pull her into his arms and hold her when she finally processed her kidnapping.

"Hey," he called and her gaze came to his. "Let's get you some clothes, eat dinner, and get you back to my place. After that, we'll debrief. I want to hear everything. But I want you to feel safe when you unload it. I want to be able to touch you. And I can't do that here."

"Why?" she blurted out then blushed. "Forget my question."

"Not a chance." Weston smiled. "I want you to have clothes so you're comfortable—you'll be staying awhile. I want to feed you because I know you're hungry. I want you to feel safe when we're talking because I swore to you I'd protect you. And I want to be able to touch you because...*fuck*...because it feels right. Because I think we both feel it. Because I keep trying to ignore my reaction to you but I'm failing miserably."

The pretty pink in her cheeks deepened, and damn

but Weston wanted to know if it had traveled under his sweatshirt down to her chest.

"Am I wrong, Silver?"

"You're not wrong," she whispered and some of his worry waned. "But it's crazy, right?"

Instead of answering, Weston climbed out of his Jeep, made his way to Silver's side, and helped her out of the vehicle. His sweatshirt hung on her, the curves he knew she had hidden from his sight, and his baseball hat concealed her face. Needing to watch her as he spoke, he tipped her chin up so they were looking at each other, then moved his hand to the nape of her neck, wishing her soft hair was down so his fingers could tangle in the strands.

"Wanna know what I thought when I first saw you?" he asked.

Silver's eyes widened but she nodded. *Brave girl.*

"You took my breath. You strutted yourself into that meeting room and the first thing I noticed was your confidence and it was sexy as fuck. Then I took in your shiny brown hair and I wondered if it was as soft as it looked. Then I looked at the rest of you— from your gorgeous eyes to your fantastic figure—and I was fighting to remain seated. And as the day went on, the more you laid out what was going on the tighter my gut got. I didn't want you anywhere near these assholes. The next time I saw you, we'd had time to go over your intel and I knew it was more dangerous than we'd originally thought. And I really didn't want you putting yourself out there. The thought of something happening to you was abhorrent. I knew you'd be pissed, but I'd rather take your anger than have you caught up in the middle of a dangerous operation."

"Why didn't you say that instead of recommending I be pulled because I lacked experience?" Her tone held no ire, just curiosity.

"Because I couldn't very well tell Alec Hall and the Lieutenant Commander I was having strong feelings for a beautiful maritime pilot, who by the way was nothing more than a stranger to me, yet I wanted to protect her at all costs. Both men would've looked at me like I'd lost my mind, and for the record I had. And the truth is—and I know you hate it but I hope you can understand it now—you do lack tactical training. And that doesn't say anything bad about you or make you less competent on the water. How could you understand our battlefield tactics when you never learned them?"

Silver's body went solid and Weston prepared for her response. He knew it had been only a matter of time before her stubborn side made its comeback.

"You made me look stupid in front of them," she argued and tried to pull away.

"No, I didn't," Weston told her and tightened his hold. "Neither man questioned your ability or the information you brought to the table. We all trusted your instincts and the intel you'd gathered. We were impressed by the manner you collected it and precautions you'd taken. You're smart, Silver, and your intellect was never in question. What was, was your safety. And at the risk of pissing you off further, there will never be a time that I agree to anything that will put you in harm's way."

"But you didn't—"

"Babe, seriously. I did know and I was right. You're back to fighting a losing corner and trying to protect yourself from someone you don't need to hide from or guard yourself against. I won't hurt you. I won't belittle you or question your competence. I know you're strong and capable. I know you're a good captain. I know you're skilled in navigation. I know you can handle any watercraft you board. But, honey, you cannot tactically outmaneuver my team. And we cannot keep you safe while you're swinging your ass out there. There are too many variables."

Some of the stiffness started to fade but she was still holding herself back.

Baby steps, patience, and a healthy dose of self-control. Two of which Weston knew he sucked at. He was all about action. Once he'd zeroed in on his target there was no stopping him from accomplishing his mission. The self-control—Weston had that in spades, but the sexy woman in front of him pushed him to the brink of breaking and tested him like no other.

"I already told you, you were right about that," she snapped, and Weston wished to God Almighty he could kiss the sass right out of her.

It wouldn't take much to lower his mouth and take hers. And once he did, he knew she'd forget all about her snit. But Weston was smart enough to know that kissing her in the shopping center was not his best play. Not that she'd fight him, but they were at least twenty minutes from home and if he started something now, that drive would be knocked down to fifteen and they would skip shopping and dinner altogether.

"Come on, let's get you some clothes."

He stepped away but grabbed her hand, and much to his surprise she didn't fight it. Not when he walked her across the parking lot and into the store. Not when she was picking out clothes, and the only time she dropped his hand was to pull something off the rack and toss it in the cart. Then her hand went back to his and Weston pushed the load one-handed and didn't mind one fucking bit it was difficult to navigate the thing without the use of both his hands.

For the first time in a long time, he was content.

And he was also pleased as fuck, Silver was the one reaching for him.

8

If Weston was bored when we'd been shopping he'd done a good job hiding it. The only snag was when we'd gotten in line and I remembered I had no purse, therefore no way to pay. An argument ensued, right in the checkout line of TJ Maxx. Then when I relented because I had no choice but to get a few things because I had nothing, and tried to put back most of it, Weston looked like he was going to lose his mind.

His grip on my hand tightened, something else that had been frightening and exciting at the same time. We'd held hands like teenagers the whole time we were walking around the store. At first, I wanted the connection—it had only been that morning I'd been taken prisoner and thought I was going to die, but shortly after we got into the store I continued to seek out his touch simply because I liked it.

I knew I was borrowing trouble, but couldn't for the life of me stop myself. It was stupid and I was going to get burned, but at that juncture, I didn't care, and a part of me knew the pain of his departure from my life would be worth it.

Dinner was great, except when I tried to order a cup of soup, since again I had no way to pay. Weston got pissed and ordered me crab cakes, a salad, and a bowl of lobster bisque. When I protested the amount of food he'd ordered he simply growled "babe", something I'd learned was his go-to word. He could use it as an answer, a statement, or as a question. It was mildly annoying but when the food came I'd forgotten all about my irritation.

Another thing I learned that didn't annoy me was Weston was funny. He didn't crack jokes or have an arsenal of one-liners—it was the way he told mundane stories. He was animated when he talked, and his delivery was hilarious. It was also very apparent he was close to his team, respected them as partners in the business they owned together, but it went beyond that, they were like brothers. And he genuinely liked his friends' women—McKenna and Kennedy.

He told me a little bit about what they'd gone

through and encouraged me to take McKenna up on her offer to talk. I was still on the fence about that. Growing up I didn't go to a regular school, so I'd never had friends my own age. That made making them in college difficult. There was also the fact that most of my classmates were men, so I'd never really had women friends. I knew my classmates' girlfriends but none of them were ever particularly nice to me. And part of me understood those women probably didn't like that I was hanging out with their boyfriends even if it was strictly platonic.

I was afraid McKenna and Kennedy would treat me the same way and not want Nixon and Jameson to help me. And truthfully I needed the help more than I needed friends so I thought it was best to stay to myself. Besides, after this was over it wasn't like I'd be around them.

So, shopping was good, dinner was better, the drive home was relaxed, but now that we were back at Weston's house alone in the kitchen I was no longer feeling the calm the evening had afforded me. I was on-edge and didn't know what to do with my hands. I was fidgeting and it pissed me off I was acting like a dumb schoolgirl with a boy she had a crush on.

Which may've been the case—not the schoolgirl part—but the dumb crush was a definite possibility.

Weston finished pulling two bottles of water out of the fridge, set them on the counter, then twisted so he was leaning against it with both his hands at his sides holding onto the edge. The new position did nothing to settle my nerves. Now I had the perfect view of his front. Top to toe, the man was gorgeous and by the smirk on his face, he knew it.

"Come here, Silver."

"No way." I shook my head for emphasis.

I didn't mind the few feet of space between us.

"Do you think I'd hurt you?"

"What? No. Of course not."

"Do you think I'd do something that would make you uncomfortable?"

Oh my God. I didn't like where this was going, mainly because I sucked at lying and there'd never been a time when I successfully pulled off a fib. Not even a small, white one. Everyone could tell when I was being dishonest so I just bluntly told the truth. But right then, I wanted to lie. I wanted to hide from Weston because the truth would be embarrassing.

"No."

"Then why aren't you movin'?"

"Because I'm afraid if I do, I'll do something that will make *you* uncomfortable."

His smirk turned into an out-and-out mega-watt

smile and sweet Jesus my panties dampened and it was a good thing he hadn't let me put any clothes back or I'd have to do laundry every time he smiled like that.

He didn't look sexy, it went so far beyond that it wasn't funny. This man could and would devastate me. No man should be as beautiful as Weston. It should be outlawed. A crime against the sisterhood.

"Babe, come here."

I shook my head and my feet stayed cemented to the floor. At least there was that, I was paralyzed by his good looks. Never had I ever been so mesmerized by a smile. But in my defense it was wicked and the promise behind it was something, in my current state of arousal, I couldn't understand.

"Then I'm comin' to you," he announced and even though I wanted to run as I'd mentioned, I was freaking paralyzed. I couldn't get my legs to move but had no problem with running my mouth.

"Oh, no. You need to stay right where you are."

"Why's that, Silver?" he asked, pushing off the counter without waiting for my answer.

"Because you're dangerous," I blurted out.

My outburst did nothing to stop his approach and if it were possible his smile grew as he stalked toward me. My feet came unglued and I stumbled back, hitting the counter behind me, trapping myself between the Formica top and an unforgiving wall of muscle.

Weston's hand went to the hat I was wearing. He pulled it off my head and tossed it behind me. Perfect. Great. Splendid. Now I was standing in front of the sexiest man alive with wild Jeep hair combined with hat head. What else could go wrong? I probably had bad crab breath and lettuce stuck in my teeth. I wanted to slink away, run and hide. But I'd missed my chance. Weston was so close I could feel his body heat rolling off of him even through the thick material of the hoodie I was wearing. Which got me thinking about the sweat I could feel running between my boobs. Another mortifying thought.

"Glad you understand that." Weston's gravelly voice pinned me in place.

"Understand what?"

"That I'm dangerous. That I will step between you and anyone who means you harm. I will protect you with my life. But the one thing you never have to worry about is me hurting you. Not mentally, not physically, not emotionally. I wouldn't be standing here with you if I wasn't sure this was where I wanted to be. Don't have a magic eight-ball so I can't predict the future. I can't promise you a white dress and picket fence. But I can promise you I'm not looking for a quick fuck. I don't have time for games and you don't deserve them, so straight out, while we're figuring out what's going on with the case, I wanna explore what this is between us. And I mean both emotionally and physically."

Maybe I was dead. Was it possible to be killed, then go into a dreamlike state and spend the day with a man you didn't much like at first, but it turns out he's a really great guy who's simply reacting to your bitchy attitude? Then after said day, go home with him, whereupon he sets out to rock your world, say a bunch of really nice things, then tell you he wants to explore you physically?

No? That was an impossibility? Then that meant I was alive but I had to be imagining what Weston had said. No way would a man like him be interested in a plain-Jane woman like me.

Not a chance in hell. I was a nobody, a loser like my father, unsocialized, a freak, I had nothing to offer and the one thing my mother had pounded into my head was, if you had nothing to offer you were worthless. Therefore, I was as worthless as she always said I'd be.

"Silver?"

My gaze moved from the spot on his t-shirt up to his face and it hurt so damn bad to look at him.

"That's not possible," I told him.

"Which part, babe?"

"Everything. All of it. I'm not worth your time."

"What the fuck?" His growl was low and menacing.

"What I mean is, I have nothing to offer a man like you."

Weston's face turned to granite. Hard and unrelenting. Maybe he was realizing he'd been wrong about me. There was nothing to explore.

"Again. What. The. Fuck. What does that mean, nothing to offer a man like me? What kind of man do you think I am?"

"A good one," I blurted out. "You deserve better than me. I have nothing. I don't even know how to act around people because I grew up alone on a boat. Growing up, my friends were older treasure hunters and drifters. I don't know anything about family or true friendship. I'm a loner, it's who I am and I know it. I'm toxic and I don't want that to leak onto you. I've always known I'd be worthless—"

"Shut up," he growled and my spine shot straight.

"Don't tell me to shut up."

"Fuckin' hell, woman, I've heard some fucked-up shit in my life, seen even more. But never have I heard a good woman beat up on herself the way you just did.

I'm guessing by our earlier conversation, it was your mother who put that venom in your head."

"It's not—"

"Sweetheart, what you just spewed was rancid. Pure poison. And the fuck of it is, I know you believe it. And that shit is so jacked it ain't funny. So, new plan, while we're exploring what's between us, I'm gonna unravel that for you. I'm gonna make you see it for the lie it is. And just to warn you, it's gonna be painful. Once you see what I see, you're gonna know you've been living a lie."

Oh, no. No, no, no. I didn't want that. I didn't want Weston getting that close. I didn't want to face the truth of who I was.

"That sounds painful. I don't think I want that."

"It will be. And I bet you don't. But it's happening all the same. I will not have a relationship where you hide behind a mask of stubbornness and pretend to be a character in someone else's fucked-up story. You are not what your mother said you were, and you certainly didn't become what she told you you would."

"I have nothing to give—"

"Kiss me," he ordered and I jerked back.

"What?"

"You heard me. Kiss me, Silver."

Hell no. That would hurt worse than talking about

my mother. Getting a taste of something only to have it ripped from my reach. No way.

"Why?"

"Because I want you to. Unless of course I misread how you were looking at me earlier."

Jesus, was there anything I could hide? Seriously, this was getting worse by the second.

"I wasn't—"

"Babe, you were looking at me like you wanted to fuck me right here in the kitchen. And if you deny it, you're lying. There was no missing the hunger in your eyes, which if you were paying attention, mirror my own. So please, for Christ sakes, fuckin' kiss me already."

One second I was trying to come up with a rebuttal and the next I was attacking him.

There was no other way to describe it. I'd literally launched myself into his arms, slammed my mouth on his, and didn't wait for an invitation before I pushed my tongue between his lips. And then there he was, one hand dove into my hair, the other clamped onto my ass and he hauled me closer. All the while our tongues clashed and dueled. It was not a soft and sweet kiss, it wasn't a first kiss, it was a battle of wills. Me proving to him I wasn't what he wanted and him proving I was.

There was no stopping the mew of protest when he

pulled his mouth from mine. Then without warning my sweatshirt was up over my head and my t-shirt got tangled in the mess of material, so that went, too. Both his hands went under my pits and he lifted me to the counter. I was in a haze of disbelief and amazement.

On instinct—because there were no coherent thoughts, not when Weston was touching me. Not when he looked at me. And certainly not when I kissed him—my legs went around his waist and I locked my ankles, bringing his hips closer, his dick closer, and his mouth closer.

"Mouth," he demanded, and I instantly complied.

This time when I kissed Weston, my hands weren't lamely at my sides, they roamed. I touched and clawed everywhere I could reach. I couldn't get enough of his taste, the faint smell of soap, the way his hard body fitted against mine. And in a moment of clarity I wondered what the hell I was doing—why hadn't I removed his shirt so I could feel his bare skin?

I was still contemplating my dilemma when Weston pressed his hips tighter to my core and excitement shot through me. There were layers of clothes separating us, but his hard-on couldn't be missed. It was there, right there, rubbing against my clit and the feel of it was so good I couldn't stop myself from taking more. I moved my hips, needing more friction, needing him closer, needing the orgasm that was building.

"Christ," Weston growled, and shoved his face into my neck. Not giving me a chance to mourn the loss of his tongue tangling with mine, he started licking and nibbling on my neck and that felt really good, too.

Weston's hands went to my ass and pulled me closer to the edge of the counter, my legs spreading wider, and I rubbed myself harder. That felt even better.

"I cannot wait to get you in my bed. Naked. Laid out before me so I can see every part of you," he said against my skin. His hand traveled up my back. He unhooked my bra and used his chin to push the loose material of one of the cups away. "Cannot wait to taste you."

His mouth latched on to my nipple, and like everything else Weston did it wasn't gentle, it was rough and demanding and oh-so-good. My hips bucked and a moan tore from my throat.

So close.

"Don't stop," I begged.

"Not stopping, babe."

He moved to the other side but this time before he sucked my sensitive nipple into his mouth he bit down. The pain felt erotic, illicit, and shot straight to my pussy. I'd never felt anything like it, and as my insides clenched and my clit hummed I wanted him to fill me up so bad I was ready to beg. Ready to rip my pants off and take him right there in the kitchen.

More. I needed more.

9

"More," Silver demanded.

Good Christ, the kiss had not gone to plan. Weston had meant to prove a point, however, the second Silver's lips had touched his, he couldn't for the life of him remember what that point was. Then she went wild and let loose and he lost all control. Everything about Silver felt right. Her tongue in his mouth, her body pressed against him, her legs wrapped around his hips, and most especially her pussy grinding on his cock in her quest to get off.

Jesus fuck, but she felt good. Never had a woman ignited for him so quickly. Never had a kiss turned him on so much. He hadn't meant to allow it to go this far, but now that Weston had tasted her pretty pink nipples, had seen the way they pebbled before his mouth had even touched them, he was all in and nothing would stop him until she was moaning her orgasm.

The hell of it was, he might be joining her. The hell part was because he was going to shoot off in his pants like an untried virgin. Just knowing her pussy was wet and she was close to coming was enough to make his balls tingle and his cock throb.

Silver's back arched and her heels dug into Weston's lower back. Both actions made him grind into her harder. He fisted her hair, forcing her head back so he could have a go at her neck.

"Babe," he mumbled against the base of Silver's throat, and loved the way she shook in his arms. "Get yourself there."

"Can't," she panted.

The thick layers of material between them made it impossible for Weston to touch her the way he wanted.

"What do you need, honey?" he asked as he nibbled his way down her chest. Goddamn, she had great tits. Not too big, not too small, perfect handfuls. Firm, perky, and the best fucking nipples he'd ever seen.

"I don't know," she complained. Frustration and need laced her tone.

Weston knew exactly what she needed, he was just

afraid he'd lose the last thread of his control if he gave it to her. He bypassed her gorgeous tits—going lower he licked a path down to her belly button and Silver's legs unlocked and fell open, giving him much-needed room.

He didn't ask when he unbuttoned her jeans, but his head did come up and when their eyes locked he was pleased to find she was on board with his new plan. Silver's hand left his hair so she could lift her ass off the counter as Weston tugged her jeans over her hips and down her legs.

So much hunger and need shone from her hazel eyes it nearly took Weston to his knees. But in the end, it was the plea that did it.

"Please," she begged, and his gaze left her face, traveled down the length of her body, his cock now in a constant state of pulsing, something he'd never in his life felt. He zeroed in on her pussy.

Fuck, she's hot.

"Open your legs for me." Silver didn't delay complying with his demand and Weston wasted no time stepping between them.

His hand went between her legs, and he was wrong —she wasn't hot, she was scorching. And so fucking wet with arousal she was dripping.

"Kiss me." The words no sooner left his mouth then Silver's was straining to follow his order. Their mouths crashed together and their tongues met, and he remembered something he'd forgotten. It was surprising he hadn't remembered, then again with his head full of the sight of her wetness, maybe not. But right then, with Silver's tongue gliding against his, he remembered—the woman could kiss. Weston had no idea how one moment she'd follow his lead, and then flawlessly she'd take over and take him where she wanted. She took everything she wanted and the results were spectacular. Without delay he teased her pussy, working two fingers inside of her.

He kept a perfect rhythm. Every time her tongue spiked out to brush his, he pushed in farther until she was bucking and groaning and her pussy was pulsing around his fingers.

"More?" he asked, breaking the kiss.

"God, yes," she panted.

Weston added his thumb to her clit and gave her more.

"Wes—" she started to moan but the rest of his name died on her lips as she shuddered and her pussy clamped down.

Silver's orgasm tore through her and Weston felt it, heard it, and couldn't tear his eyes off her. Not for anything. Nothing could've made him stop watching. If it was possible, Silver looked even more beautiful, her eyes were glassy and unfocused, her face slack, her lips parted as she whimpered. Brilliant—all of it. He waited for her pussy to relax before he pulled his fingers free and finally tasted them.

"Taste good?" she whispered.

Her dirty question shot straight to his cock, it had been by sheer force of will he didn't come. No, it had been a miracle and he knew it wouldn't take but a touch for him to go off.

"Fuck yeah," he answered, and lowered his mouth to hers, licking her bottom lip so she could share in the goodness.

"I think I should be embarrassed," she said against his lips and Weston stiffened. "But I'm not."

Thank fuck, because she had not one thing to be embarrassed about. The woman was crazy-sexy. Wild, unafraid, she lost all inhibitions and damn if that wasn't hot.

Weston pulled her closer, his hands going to her ass, and he lifted her off the counter. Silver's legs went around his waist and her arms around his shoulders.

"What are you doing?" she squeaked as he started to move through the kitchen.

"Taking you upstairs."

"I can walk."

"No doubt."

He continued through the living room and made it to the stairs before she spoke again.

"Then why aren't you letting me?"

"Don't want to."

He had no idea why he was carrying her other than he wanted her in his arms. Something he'd never felt with any other woman he'd been with. Never had he desired to carry a woman anywhere. And the hell of it was, he wasn't even carrying her to his bed to fuck her. He just wanted to feel her wrapped around him. He wanted to take care of her after the shit day she'd had.

Maybe he'd taken it too far in the kitchen, but Weston couldn't summon up remorse. There was no guilt that he'd allowed things to go as far as they had. The only thing he felt was satisfaction.

"Um. We need to bleach the countertop." It took a moment for her statement to register and when it did Weston's body shook with humor. "I mean, that's kinda gross."

Weston lost the battle and silent hilarity turned into an audible chuckle.

"Nothing gross about you coming around my fingers, babe."

"It is when you gave me that orgasm on the kitchen counter where people cook. Not sure there's enough bleach in the world to disinfect the area. We may need to use Lysol, too."

It was a good thing Weston had made it into his room and to the side of his bed before he busted a gut and dropped her from laughing so hard.

Silver bounced as she hit the bed and suddenly Weston didn't find a damn thing funny. The only clothing Silver had left was her bra loosely hanging from her forearms. The scrap of lace resting across her stomach made all kinds of illicit memories flit through his mind.

"Weston?" she called out.

"Yeah?" His eyes didn't move from the perfectly trimmed triangle of hair between her legs. Even though he'd felt it, knew her pussy lips were devoid of any hair, seeing the pink, glistening flesh had him enthralled. It was as gorgeous as the rest of her.

"You're making me nervous staring at me like that."

"Like what? Like I want to lick you clean, taste your excitement as it leaks from your pussy instead of off my fingers?"

"Yeah, like that," she confirmed.

Weston's gaze went to hers and he didn't see nervousness or even embarrassment. He saw hunger that matched his own. "Goddamn, you're sexy. Every part of you."

Pink hit her cheeks and he really wished he could join her in bed, but she was right, he needed to get back downstairs and clean up the kitchen. The last thing he wanted was his teammates to come home and find her clothes on the floor. Not that he gave two shits what Holden or Chasin would think, but Silver would. And he'd never allow her to be embarrassed. His teammates wouldn't judge, they'd never even bring it up to her if they found her discarded clothes, but she didn't know that.

"Bathroom's through there." Weston pointed. "Make yourself at home. I'll be right back." Silver's brow raised in question and he continued. "Gonna grab your clothes, sweetheart."

She smiled and nodded and Weston's chest started to feel funny when she made no move to cover herself, no sign of trepidation, no shyness or regret. Silver simply laid in his bed smiling up at him, like she trusted him. Like she didn't have a shit day, like she hadn't been taken and chained up, like they hadn't been at each other's throats since the day they'd met.

He didn't understand it but wasn't going to question it. Without leaning over her to kiss her the way he wanted to, knowing if he started something he'd never make it back downstairs, he turned to leave and was at the top of the stairs when Silver yelled.

"Don't forget the bleach!"

With a smile, Weston descended the steps. He was still smiling when he bleached the counter, and wiped the cabinet door below where she was sitting—just in case—the smile didn't leave his face until he collected her clothes off the floor and heard the front door open.

Fuck.

Holden and Chasin rounded the corner and came to a stop when they took him in. There was no hiding the crumpled clothes, no getting rid of the smell of bleach that permeated the room. Neither man missed it.

Holden smiled outright and Chasin looked like he was fighting one.

"Not a fucking word," Weston warned, keeping his voice low so Silver wouldn't hear.

"Don't know what you're talking about," Holden quipped.

Chasin made a production out of lifting his chin and sniffing loudly. "Late night kitchen cleaning?"

"I've smelled less bleach trying to clean up blood after a takedown," Holden added.

Dicks. Weston stood silently in front of his friends and waited for more.

"Never been happier to live in my Airstream,"

Holden started. "At least I know which surfaces to avoid."

He was full of shit. Holden had never had a woman in his Airstream. Hell, when Holden lived in an apartment when he was restoring the old junker he'd purchased, he'd never had a woman there either. And it wasn't because the man was celibate, Weston had seen him go home with plenty of women over the years. But always back to their place, and he never spent the night. Something the team had given him shit about. Holden Stanford took booty call to a whole new level of impersonal.

"Either of you got anything else?" Weston asked.

"Just point to the place I should avoid," Chasin continued.

Weston didn't rise to the bait and confirm what his teammates knew.

"No? So I'll be on a treasure hunt for the—"

"I wouldn't go there," Weston growled and Chasin chuckled.

"Right. I'll just eat out... I mean, get takeout for the next few weeks and use the table. That is, if it's safe."

Fucker.

Done with the conversation, Weston moved it along to something important.

"Did you get Silver's shit from the boatyard?" Weston asked Holden.

"Her car was broken into. Thankfully it doesn't look like her apartment, but someone was on a mission to find something. I have her bag and unless she just throws wrinkled clothes in there, someone's been through that, too. Her wallet and other girly shit is still in her purse, but she'll have to go through it to see if anything is missing."

"Shit."

What the hell were they looking for and who in the fuck were they? During one of the meetings with Homeland, Silver was very clear she hadn't written anything down or taken any pictures. But the drug smugglers wouldn't know that—neither would the inside man working with them.

"Did Matt or Rodger give you anything?"

"I told them I was Silver's man and there to pick up her stuff," Holden explained, and for some ridiculous and unexplainable reason, Weston hated that Holden had lied and said *he* was her man. She didn't belong to his teammate and hearing it filled him with resentment. "They seemed more shocked she had someone in her life than they did hearing she was in the hospital with some unknown ailment. If either of them is worried she has something, neither showed it. They'd called in a man named Gary to take over Silver's rotation and he seemed concerned about her illness, but his concern was if it was contagious because he has a newborn at home. Just so Silver knows, she has a kidney infection. A bad one, don't know how long a hospital stay is for one of those or what the recovery time is, but the dude was relentless, wanted to call the hospital, scared to shit his kid would catch something."

"Don't know either, but Silver's kidney infection just became a seriously bad one that will require a long recuperation time. And her apartment?" Weston glanced over to Chasin.

"Total loss."

"Saw that, brother. Find anything?"

"Spent hours sifting through the rubble. The only thing I got from my efforts is to tell you, your woman has a seriously sexy underwear collection."

A growl slipped out, giving away more than Weston had intended, and both men smiled at his outburst.

"Chill the hell out, it's not like I pocketed a pair to—"

"Swear to Christ, I'm gonna beat the hell out of you if you finish that."

"Too fuckin' easy." Chasin chuckled. "Nothing there,

no prints on the doors, the cabinet doors, bathroom, nowhere. The place was clean other than all the broken shit. One thing I found interesting is, whoever was in there was thorough. Every cushion was cut open, mattress, cereal boxes emptied, even dumped the tampons."

"Saw that," Weston confirmed. "They knew what they were doing, and they knew they had the time to do it, which meant they knew Silver was on the *Dora B* so they put that time to good use."

"We need to ask her if there's something else someone could be looking for," Holden said.

"Like what?"

"Anything. Maybe she stumbled onto something else. I know dealers will go to great lengths to protect their shipments, 'specially ones as large as what they're hauling through the canal, but it won't hurt to ask if she's noticed anything else going down."

Weston was doubtful, but it never hurt to investigate all avenues. And on that note, Weston remembered he had a beautiful woman in his bed he'd like to get back to exploring—every sound, every curve, every taste. Weston wanted to learn everything he could and standing around talking, albeit about important shit, wasn't cutting it.

"We'll brief in the morning," Weston offered.

"Right." Holden laughed, but wisely kept the rest of his comments to himself.

"Weston," Chasin called.

He stopped and turned to look at his friend.

"You sure you know what you're doing?"

"Nope."

"Shit's complicated, brother, you really wanna go down that road?"

Weston thought about Chasin's question mainly because he was trying to get his temper in check. He didn't question where his teammate stuck his dick and didn't appreciate him not returning the favor. But more importantly, Weston didn't like the insinuation that Silver wasn't worth the complication. Though Chasin did have reason to be concerned—after all it was just that morning Weston was bitching about the woman being annoying and stubborn.

What a difference a few hours and a smile make.

"Everything worth your time is always complicated."

And with that, Weston headed for the stairs hoping like hell he wasn't making a mistake. He'd like to believe he'd stopped thinking with his dick sometime in his twenties—at least hoping he thought with the right head most of the time—but the naked woman in his bed told a different story.

Even if Weston was feeling something out of the ordinary for Silver, the fact he'd finger-fucked her on the counter in the kitchen he shared with Chasin told him his dick had been in charge.

All he'd wanted to do was kiss her. Show her there was something between them. But all Weston had done was prove there was a crazy physical attraction between them. That, and she was the sexiest fucking thing he'd ever touched. So really, he'd demonstrated his dick was a hundred percent in command.

10

After Weston left the room, mortification set in.

I was a little in shock, I'd actually allowed that to get out of hand. Even more appalling, I'd fully participated and even begged for it.

On the counter. In the kitchen where anyone could've walked in and caught us and with a man I despised. Or at least I'd hated him right up until the point he pulled me into his arms and let me cry on his chest when I saw the wreckage that was my apartment.

Actually, if I was being truthful with myself, I stopped hating him when he gave me his sweatshirt to wear so I wouldn't be cold while we drove in his Jeep. That small act of kindness was all it had taken. Which was totally sad, that I was that easily impressed by a man.

Now there I was, lying in Weston's bed with one of his t-shirts on. Oh, I'd also rummaged through his dresser when he left the room and my nudity hit me with a double smack in the face, further reminding me I'd behaved like a bitch in heat with a hound dog. Or maybe I was the hound dog mounting the bitch. Either way, I was the one who'd attacked Weston's mouth like I hadn't had a kiss in the last ten years. Which wasn't the case, it'd been three years since I'd kissed a man. Three very long, very lonely, very dry, three years. Longer than that since I'd had an orgasm. Way longer.

Good God, I was pathetic.

So, I was in Weston's bed, listening to hushed voices drift up the stairs but I couldn't make out what they were saying. Then I could hear someone tromping up them. I pulled the sheet up to my neck and prayed to all things mighty and holy I wouldn't burst into flames when Weston returned.

He stepped into the room, came to a stop, dropped my clothes on the floor, and chuckled.

Thankfully my prayer worked, I didn't catch on fire. Which would've been a shame because Weston's bed was totally soft and his sheets softer, but my face heated for a variety of reasons. One being, I didn't have on panties and I was very aware of the fact when wetness started to gather.

Damn, *damn*, damn. I was a total slut.

There was no disputing Weston was good-looking. Tall, broad shoulders, lean but muscular body he obviously worked for and the results were out of this world. His unruly brown hair reminded me of why it was messy and that my fingers had been in it and I could now testify to the fact it was soft. I could also swear to the fact he was the best kiss I'd ever had. And he was also the only man who'd ever been able to get me to orgasm with very little effort.

But even with all of that, and considering he had indeed given me said orgasm with frightening speed, I shouldn't have been getting wet at the sight of him. Yet there I was, drenched and most likely leaving a wet spot on his sheets.

I was also blushing because he was smiling at me. And it was not a friendly 'hi, nice to see you again' smile. It was a pleased smile from a man who knew I was easy.

"Babe," he said with humor in his tone, and I wanted to yank the sheet over my head and pretend he wasn't standing there laughing at me.

But I didn't get the chance. He shut the door, turned the lock, and stalked to the bed.

Oh no!

"We need to talk," I blurted out.

"We do," he confirmed, and pulled his shirt over his head, dropping it on the floor, before he turned his back to me and sat on the edge of the bed.

Someone upstairs hated me. I couldn't say it was God because I had a lot to be thankful for. Well, not a lot, but I had my health, and I'd heard that was something one should be tremendously grateful for, so I was —grateful that is. But whoever God's right-hand man was, he certainly hated me. My mouth was nearly watering at the sight of Weston bare-chested, and once I'd gotten a look at his back, my mouth was no longer 'nearly' anything, it was simply watering.

Good Lord, I'd never seen a back look so strong. His shoulders might possibly be the sexiest part of a man's body I'd ever seen. I wanted to reach out and touch him, run my hands over the muscle and sink my teeth into his flesh.

Where the hell did that come from? What was I, a vampire?

Weston stood, dropped his pants, exposing his boxer-brief-covered ass and I nearly choked. This had to stop.

"We...um...should talk now," I suggested.

"Scoot over," he returned.

"What? Why?"

"So I can get in. I sleep on the side closest to the door."

"Why?" I semi-repeated, mostly to buy time, not because I actually cared what side of the bed the man slept in. I only cared he seemed to think he was sleeping in it with me.

"Because I'm the one with the gun, and if someone gets into the room they have to get through me before they get to you."

There was so much to process for that one simple statement that wasn't actually simple—it was huge. But I didn't have time to think about why my belly got warm and my heart started to swell, that he wanted himself between me and an imaginary threat.

I didn't want to think about why that felt so good, and how no one had ever considered my safety—save my dad. But no friend, male or female, had ever cared to protect me.

"You're sleeping in here?"

"Yep. Scoot over, babe, I'm wiped."

"You're wiped?"

Could I sound anymore like an idiot?

"Babe. Seriously, move over."

"You can't sleep here."

"Why's that?" Weston's lips twitched.

"Because I'm not that kind of girl."

Okay, so I could sound more idiotic. Seriously? That was my reason? I wasn't that kind of girl. Of course I was, and I showed him how big of a slut I was not even thirty minutes ago.

Weston was no longer smiling when he yanked the sheet down, scooped me up, put a knee to the bed, and moved me over a few feet.

His gaze left mine, went to the bottom sheet. Mine followed and there it was—soggy proof. My humiliation knew no bounds. Weston's eyes came back to mine, and when they did, they weren't full of mirth like I thought they'd be. Instead, they were gentle and soft.

Why me? That was all I could think about when he ignored the wet spot and climbed into bed. All thoughts about talking—gone. All the reasons why he couldn't sleep in the same bed as me—gone. As a matter of fact, I never wanted to speak to or see Weston again.

And yes, I knew I was behaving like an immature idiot. I knew, and I was so embarrassed, I didn't give a damn I was acting like I was two and not thirty-two.

"Not liking the deer-in-the-headlights look, sweetheart."

"Stop calling me that," I snapped, and Weston jerked in surprise.

"And we're back there again," he mumbled.

"We never left *there*," I stupidly said.

Stupid because in the blink of an eye Weston's big body was looming over me. One elbow planted near my head, the other on the bed by my hip. He wasn't touching me but he didn't have to be to scare the bejeezus out of me.

"Sure we did, and that wet spot under my ass is proof."

"I knew you couldn't wait to rub that in my face and embarrass me."

If it was possible for every muscle in Weston's body to simultaneously bunch, they did.

"Come again?"

"You heard me."

"You're right, I did. I was just hoping I heard you wrong. You serious with this shit?"

"Well, it didn't take you long to bring it up."

"I didn't bring it up to embarrass you, I brought it up to remind you, we had most certainly checked your snarky attitude. The proof of that is when I put you in this bed you were dripping wet for me. So much so, your pussy leaked onto my sheets."

"I can't believe you said that."

"You can't?" He gave me a taste of his own snarky attitude. "Well, let me finish with this, since you're already in a state of disbelief. Seeing that spot, knowing

I was the reason your pussy was dripping, remembering that I was the one who made you so wild you fucked my fingers until you exploded, my name on your tongue, my fingers inside you, my mouth on your tits, made me so fucking hard I was getting lightheaded. I liked seeing that wet spot. Any man would, knowing he was the reason it was there. So do you remember now?"

I said nothing because I was speechless. No one had ever spoken to me the way Weston had. Not that I'd been in bed with that many men. Two to be exact. And three more fooling around on the couch, but none of them had been so crass. None had uttered the word pussy in my presence, let alone talked about what their fingers had done to it.

"You ready to check that attitude again?" he asked.

"No."

"At least she's honest," he muttered. "What did you mean, when you told me you weren't that type of girl?"

"I'm not easy," I told him.

"You sure as fuck aren't."

"That's not how I meant it and you know it. I've never done that before."

"Done—"

"Seriously, you're gonna make me spell it out?"

Not even Weston when he was acting like a jerk would be so obtuse.

"Which part have you never done?" he asked.

And the only reason I answered was because he'd lost the attitude and sounded concerned.

"None of it. In the past, I've chosen the men I've been with carefully. I've dated them before I allowed them to kiss me. I've never attacked a man like that. I've never spread my legs on command. I've never done any of that on a kitchen counter. So I'm not a slut."

Oh no! Back was the stone-faced, pissed-off Weston.

"Babe, even if you had done all of that and did it regularly with a variety of men, it still wouldn't make you a slut. You're a beautiful, adult woman, with a healthy sex drive—"

"I don't have a healthy sex drive. I haven't even had sex in..."

And it happened again, I was running off at the mouth, sounding like a fool.

"All right, let me break this down for you. And I know you wanna have this conversation about as much as you want your fingernails ripped out, but it has to be had." Well, thank God he understood my plight, though it didn't sound like he was going to let me off the hook. "First, I had my fingers inside of you

—I know it's been a very long time since you've had sex."

"Kill me now," I grumbled. "I don't even wanna know how you could know that."

"Babe, you are tight as hell. Virgin-tight and there's no way you're getting sex on the regular when all it took was a few strokes of my thumb on your clit and you went off the way you did. And before you twist that up in your head, I loved it, all of it. Every sound you made, how you held nothing back. You feel good, you taste good, and, sweetheart, you looked gorgeous coming around my fingers. With that said, I wasn't getting in bed with you to fuck you. I certainly didn't think you were some foregone conclusion and I could come in here and expect you to spread for me. What happened downstairs got out of hand and that's what I wanted to talk to you about."

I wasn't sure what was worse, Weston using the word pussy fifty-two times or the sound of regret in his tone.

At this juncture, I *really* didn't want to talk. I wasn't sure what I would do if he told me what happened was a mistake—even if he was right and we shouldn't have gone there—it would kill to hear him say it.

I didn't want to hear it, therefore I got smart and

brought my hands up to his chest and started to shove him off of me.

"Move," I demanded.

"Not until we talk."

"I get it."

"No, Silver, I'm learning you don't get shit and I'm gonna have to spell it out for you."

"I think I've had enough of you spelling things out for me."

Weston's face broke out into a wide smile—another one of his half-smirk, half-I-have-a-really-great-secret—kinds, and I wished he'd stop doing that. It was hard enough to breathe with him braced over me, muscles on display—not all of them of course, but I had the perfect view of his chest, shoulders, and biceps.

"You're wearing my tee," he noted.

It's worth mentioning he didn't look put-out by this. If anything his face had gentled and he was looking at me funny.

I had five-hundred and fifty-two sarcastic and bitchy comebacks on the tip of my tongue but wisely I kept them to myself.

"Yep," was what I settled on.

"Back to what happened," he started.

"You don't—"

I got nothing else out. Weston rolled to his side,

bringing me with him, tagged my thigh, brought it over his, and held me captive.

'Captive' being a relative term since it felt good, and therefore I didn't struggle all that much. Though I knew I should've. Our new position was dangerous. If Weston moved or pulled my leg higher, my bare pussy would be pressed against his thigh.

"So, straight up, I only meant to kiss you. After hearing you spout off the garbage in your head, I had a point to make. But honest to God, the second you came at me and your lips were on mine, I couldn't for the life of me remember what my point was. From there, everything that happened was without thought. I allowed need to take over when I should've stayed in control. So now we gotta talk about it and I think I know where you're at with all of it, but I have to make sure."

"Where I'm at?"

"Sweetheart, I didn't exactly ask if I could undress you and take you on the counter."

That was sweet he was asking me now, and Weston being sweet was a different kind of dangerous. When his voice gentled and he was showing concern for my well-being it was hard to remain bitchy. It was like he doused my bad attitude and I was powerless to keep it, even if it was the smart thing to do.

"*I* kissed *you*," I reminded him.

"You did. But that didn't give me the green light to take your shirt off."

He was right, it didn't. But I hadn't told him no. I'd lifted my arms and aided him in his endeavor. I'd even begged him to give me more and definitely helped him take my pants off.

"If I didn't want it to happen I would've told you no."

"Good. That's what I needed to hear. The second part of that is, in the future if I'm doing something you don't like or going too fast I need you to understand if you tell me to stop I always will. No matter what we're doin', how far we've gone. I will always listen to you."

In the future? My belly started to flutter and not in a bad way, in a really, really good way that scared me even more. 'In the future' meant he was planning on doing that again, and I liked what we did the first time so much, I knew I'd like it even more the second time. Which meant when all of this was over and we went our separate ways, it was going to *not* feel so great. In other words—I'd be heartbroken.

I didn't have the experience to handle a casual affair. I didn't understand what casual even meant. So I figured in an effort to quell future heartbreak it was better to experience the embarrassment of telling

Weston that now. Better a moment of mortification than months of nursing my shattered heart.

"Weston?" I sighed.

"Right here, babe."

"I don't regret what we did. I liked it—all of it."

"That's good, because I fuckin' loved it."

Oh, hell, he wasn't making this any easier saying stuff like that. And it was hard enough with my cheek to his chest and his hand resting on my thigh.

"But I don't think it should happen again."

"Right." His mocking tone couldn't be missed.

"I'm actually being serious. This is me being straight with you. I've never done this."

"Told me that already."

I had, but he must not have understood—I hadn't done any of it. I was so lost I wasn't even sure how I was going to explain all the reasons why we wouldn't be fooling around again.

"Silver," Weston prompted.

"We can't do it again because I don't understand what *it* is. I don't understand why I behaved the way I did with you when the last man who kissed me had taken me out on four dates before he kissed me at the door. The kiss was so bad, I turned down date five."

"Yeah?" I could feel Weston's body shaking with

silent laughter and I would've gotten pissed if it wasn't kind of funny in a sad way.

"And before him, I dated that man for three months before I let him get his hands down my pants. *That* was so uneventful, I allowed him one more try and after an hour of him fumbling around, I *think* I had a mini-orgasm, but I still broke it off with him because, well, I don't need to explain why. It's been over five years since I've had sex. And that man had waited me out, done and said all the right things, but after we finally made it to bed, *he* broke up with *me*. I think you're smart enough to put two and two together and figure out I'm completely inexperienced. I'm out of my element. I don't do casual. And if I couldn't even please a bumbling idiot who had no clue what he was doing, I could never please a man like you."

"A man like me? We're back to that shit? I thought I explained that your line of thinking is completely jacked."

"I mean, a man who is obviously extremely experienced."

"Extremely?"

"Don't be an ass. You said it yourself. You barely had to touch me and I turned into some crazy lust-drunk idiot. Clearly, you know what you're doing, and you do because you have experience—something I don't have. And I doubt you were in a relationship with all those women who gave you that expertise. So you know how to do casual. I do not. Which means I will be the one who's left heartbroken—not you. And that's why nothing can happen between us again."

There, I'd said it, and surprised I wasn't as embarrassed as I thought I'd be. Now that he knew the truth we could put what happened behind us. I'd store the memory for a different day and sift through the encounter when I was alone in my apartment and I could reminiscence about how good he'd made me feel. How wanted. How sexy. How cared for.

I would never forget Weston Beil—not as long as I lived.

11

Weston was trying his best not to bust out laughing. He didn't like hearing Silver talking about the men she'd been with in the past—he downright hated it. However, he didn't mind knowing none of those men had given her what he had. And he fucking loved that she hadn't lit up like fireworks on the Fourth of July when any of them had touched her. Because she damn well had for him.

It also wasn't funny that she'd had a shit sex life in the past. But again, he liked knowing in the future she'd have a great one, and he'd be the one to give it to her.

The thing he didn't find amusing at all was that Silver was trying to pull away. That and she thought he wanted something casual. Nothing he was feeling toward her was casual. But she was mostly right about his past and the women he'd been with. There'd been a few who had been around longer than the rest. Some who he'd dated. Some he'd been monogamous with. But none had been serious. Not in the sense he could see them going the distance. All of them had been missing something.

Try as he might, Weston couldn't find what was missing with Silver. So there it was—she was right, he'd had plenty of women, enough to know when he found something he liked, and smart enough to know not to let it go.

"You say that like it's a bad thing," Weston started.

"Which part?"

"All of it. Lust-drunk idiot? Babe, I call that a sexy-as-fuck siren who made me lose my mind and nearly come in my pants. Wanna talk about things that I've never done? I've never—not since I stopped being a boy —almost come in my pants. Not one time. Yet with you, I was sweating bullets thinking I'd shoot off and you'd think I was some idiot. I've never lost my control with a woman the way I did with you. Never taken a woman on the counter because I couldn't wait another second to touch her. I've done casual plenty of times and I'm only telling you that so you'll get this next part. Never have I had anyone turn me on the way you do. Let loose, get wild, and take what she wanted in a way I seriously got off on. You don't need experience, babe, you're a goddamn natural. And just so you're crystal clear, I do not want casual with you. If you're with me, you're only with me, which means I am only with you. No one else enters our relationship while we're exploring what's between us."

The only indication Silver gave she heard what he'd said was the twitch of her hand. And Weston only felt that because her palm was resting on his chest.

"But you don't even like me. You said it yourself, I'm stubborn."

"I'm finding I like your stubborn."

"That's crazy. No one likes stubborn. It's annoying."

"Then I must be crazy."

"Weston, seriously, when this is over and I go home, back to work, back to my life, it won't work out."

"Why?"

"Because I work two-week rotations. Meaning I live at the yard for two weeks. It will get old."

Now she was grasping at straws, the tiny red ones a bartender puts in frilly pussy drinks. They were so thin but she was fighting to get a handful.

He couldn't deny that her being unavailable two weeks out of the month would suck, but it wasn't a deal-breaker. Weston's work schedule was unpredictable and that sucked, too. But it was certainly doable.

"We'll cross that bridge when we come to it."

"And what I'm trying to tell you is when it comes and you find you don't want to cross it, I'll be the one heartbroken."

Fuck, her honesty was killing him. He'd said he didn't want to start a relationship where she masked her feelings and goddamn if she hadn't torn that bitch off and was laying herself out there. Something that Weston respected a whole hell of a lot. He actually envied her courage.

Weston's hand left her thigh and went to her jaw. He gently lifted her chin and captured her eyes. So damn pretty. Even with the hurt he was learning she'd lived through, they were still bright and pure. Honest when she wasn't spitting fire.

"I promise, I won't hurt you."

"You say that, but you won't be able to stop it. I won't be able to stop it."

"Do you think I'm stupid?"

"What?" she startled. His question obviously took her by surprise. "Of course not."

"Then you'll have to trust me that I'm smart enough to know what I got with you is worth moving forward. Trust me to know that if I wasn't sure, I'd cut you loose."

"What do you think you have?"

"Treasure."

Silver's eyes drifted closed and Weston silently waited her out, letting his words settle, and hopefully penetrate.

"See. That right there," she said when she opened her eyes, "is how I know I'll be shattered when you figure out I'm not enough for you."

He wanted to argue—rail against the stupid doubts her mother had planted—and he would've if he thought his words would help. But Weston was also smart enough to know words meant shit. She'd heard enough of them in her life, unfortunately, the wrong kind, so she wouldn't believe anything he said.

The thing that would make Silver believe was action. And it was a good thing Weston was an action man. He wasn't good with flowery sentiments, didn't have the time or inclination, not that he wouldn't give what he could to Silver with his words, but he'd show her. And that was what would make the difference.

"Take a chance," Weston pleaded.

"But—"

"I'm not asking for a commitment in blood. Just the chance to see where this goes. Enough trust that I wouldn't be asking if I wasn't sure this is what I want."

"You'll trample my heart."

"I'll have a care, Silver. I will not hurt you. Take a chance."

"I'll think about it," she relented.

Weston debated the wisdom of graciously accepting her answer and letting the topic drop. But quickly came to the decision he would not hold back, he wouldn't be someone he wasn't when he'd asked her for openness. She deserved to know where he stood and who he was. Nothing good would come from hiding it when she'd find out anyway.

"You should know that while you're thinking about it I won't be sitting around twiddling my thumbs."

"What? Does that mean you'll be..." she trailed off, too flustered to ask what she wanted to, but the hurt in her eyes was enough for Weston to puzzle out what she was trying to ask.

"Told you once and I meant it. No one enters our relationship, so you shouldn't have to ask that question. But I'll clarify, I won't be seeing other women. But neither will I let you lock yourself in your head trying to come up with excuses why this won't work. You go ahead and take your sweet time, because while you are,

I'll be proving to you I'm worth the chance you're gonna have to take. So in the end, you're gonna take it, and you'll know I'd never hurt you."

Goddamn, Silver was beautiful when she was off-kilter. Her eyes went unfocused, probably trying to form a rebuttal, one that Weston had no interest in hearing. Not because he didn't care about what she was thinking, because he did—he cared about everything that had to do with Silver. But because of the way she was looking, how she felt pressed against him, he found there were other ways he wanted to spend their time together in his bed.

And luckily for him, Silver getting used to his touch, his kiss, and the feel of him wrapped around her, was step one in his plan to make her believe.

Weston lifted his head the scant distance needed and brushed his lips against hers. The sexy mew she made sealed the deal. He licked her full bottom lip and returned the favor. Fuck yeah. She may not have been experienced but he'd been right—she was a natural. Her tongue plunged in his mouth and Weston fought to control the kiss, keeping it slow but less powerful. She tasted like heaven. Their tongues continued to tangle together and Weston thought he'd been wrong. It wasn't heaven he was tasting—it was treasure.

His treasure.

He'd waited a long fucking time to find it. Never would settle for anything less. Knew it was out there somewhere. And he'd been right. Being that Weston was as smart as he was—he was holding on.

Silver Coyle would not be the one who got away.

12

Instead of waking up refreshed, I'd woken up with dread in my stomach. Surprisingly it had nothing to do with my current dilemma involving Weston. That dilemma being, I'd cuddled close to him all night. This of course was after he'd given me a fantastic orgasm, told me he wanted to explore things with me, called me treasure—and come on, what woman wouldn't want to explore things with a man who said that?

Then he'd kissed me a second time. That kiss was much different than the others. It was hot, full of passion, but he was trying to tell me something and maybe if I'd had more familiarity with the opposite sex I would've been able to read it. So all I knew was how it made me feel—and I felt great. Too great.

It was already happening, I could feel it creeping

in even as I was trying to push it away. Sleeping curled up next to Weston after the day I'd had where I wasn't sure if I'd still be breathing at the end of it, only to be safely tucked to his side, was too much.

So this morning I'd taken some time to try to figure out how it was possible I could feel any sort of feelings for him this soon, when a thought hit me. It was unpleasant and it worried me. Was I the type of woman who would cling to a man because he'd been nice? Was I that desperate for someone to be kind to me? I thought the questions but couldn't find the answers. At least not the ones I wanted because all evidence was pointing to the affirmative. I was that kind of woman and I was desperate. Both disturbing and disappointing answers.

But none of that was why I was dreading the day. After Weston's delicious goodnight kiss, he informed me the team would be over in the morning to 'brief' and Alec Hall would more than likely show up at some point, too.

I was not looking forward to briefing in any way that word could mean. I didn't want to talk about my stupidity or how I'd been chained up in the bottom of the *Dora B*. I'd eaten enough crow and was afraid anymore would make me gag. I didn't know Alec all that well but he was intense, same as Weston and his team, so I suspected Alec was going to be pissed.

Weston said there had been drugs and dead bodies to clean up, and though I'd never done either it didn't sound like a good time. Not to mention, I was a tad bit worried that Weston and the guys would get in trouble —*for the dead bodies*. I would never be able to live with myself if something happened to them because I'd gotten myself into a bind.

"Babe?" Weston called from the other side of the closed door.

I was in the bathroom getting ready. Thankfully I was not the type of woman who wore makeup because yesterday during our shopping extravaganza we'd only picked up clothes. Ditto on hair products. It was a good thing I didn't gunk up my hair or do anything special because I had none of those either.

But I'd at least showered and had on clean clothes.

"Yeah," I answered.

"The guys are here. Are you ready?"

No.

"Sure," I said and opened the door.

Weston was close—he'd been standing right outside the door—but when I'd opened it he got closer. I took two steps back and he continued forward. His bathroom was small so all it took was one more shuffle in retreat and my back was against the wall and suddenly Weston was *right* there. One hand was on the tile next to my head, the other coming to my chin, lifting it.

Why did I have to like that so much?

His lips came to mine and I liked that more. But when he pushed his tongue in my mouth only to tease me with a quick swipe against mine, I figured I liked that the best. It was different in a playful sort of way. He wasn't trying to start something but still wanted a taste. I liked that he wanted that. That he didn't hold back and he showed me.

I also figured that was the real reason I was starting to have feelings for him. It honestly made me feel safe. Something I hadn't had a whole lot of in my life. Even when I'd thought he was being a jerk, he was being honest, I just didn't like what he was being honest about.

Weston Beil was real. He was straight. He hid nothing.

And with all of that, I knew where I stood with him. And currently I was standing with his lips pressed against mine wishing no one was downstairs so maybe I could get more of what he gave me yesterday. That being the orgasm, not the sweet stuff he'd told me while we were in bed.

Yep, I was easy. And I didn't care what Weston had said, I was acting like a slut. I just didn't care because he felt that good.

"How is it possible that every time I see you I'm shocked at how beautiful you are?"

Weston said that. Straight out. Just came right out and told me I was beautiful.

I was screwed. Heartbreak was in my future. It wasn't a maybe, it was a definite. And I had a feeling the hole he'd leave would be huge and ugly and probably never heal. I should start my internet searches on cat rescues now, because no one would ever fill the hole he was going to leave. So cats were in my future, too. Lots of them.

"You have to know when you say stuff to me like that it scares me."

"Why's that, Silver?" he whispered.

"Because it feels so good, and when you take it away, it's gonna hurt."

I watched as Weston's jaw ticked and with his face this close I couldn't miss the irritation that flashed in his eyes.

"We'll see," he weirdly said.

"See what?"

"When you're ready to take a chance and believe, I'll tell you."

"But—"

"You ready to take that chance?"

"I'm still thinking."

"You let me know when you're ready and I'll explain. If you're not ready to make that decision in the next thirty seconds, we've got people downstairs waiting to talk to us."

No, I wasn't ready to make that decision in the next thirty seconds, and maybe not even in the next thirty years. And as much as I didn't want to talk to Alec and the guys, it was better than standing in Weston's bathroom, with Weston's hand still on my face, his thumb gently stroking my cheek, the touch muddling my head. Making me believe we could explore what he was offering. And I wasn't ready to admit that, so I ignored it. Completely pretended I didn't already trust him, I just didn't trust myself.

"Let's go talk to Alec."

Instead of being annoyed I was jerking him around, Weston's lips tipped up. Through a chuckle he mumbled something that sounded like 'we'll see' and dropped his hands and stepped away. I lost his body but he didn't give me time to ponder all the reasons I wanted it back because he was dragging me out of the room.

He didn't drop my hand until we made it to the

stairs. Part of me wondered if he was embarrassed to touch me in front of the guys but the bigger part of me was grateful.

When we hit the living room all conversation came to a screeching halt and five men swung their eyes in our direction. I felt like a zoo animal under their scrutiny. No one hid it, they were all openly staring at me. Chasin and Holden were smiling. Jameson and Nixon's expressions were blank, but Alec Hall had a deep frown and he wasn't hiding that, either. The man was pissed.

Awesome.

"You want coffee?" Weston leaned forward and whispered in my ear. And since he was standing behind me I had the pleasure of feeling his chest against my back. I do not understand why he did this. He wasn't asking me something private. He also didn't have to get close.

"Please," I answered.

Then I understood, because with his lips so close to my ear, all he had to do was turn his face a skosh and he'd be able to kiss my cheek. Which he did. Right in front of everyone and no one missed it.

Alec's face was the only one that registered the kiss. His scowl remained but he added narrowed eyes.

"Sit and I'll grab you a cup."

Weston's hand went to the small of my back, a light, gentle, yet protective touch I liked a whole bunch. I liked what it said more than the feel of it. He had my back, he wasn't going to let anything happen to me.

The gesture gave me enough courage to face off against Alec and the rest of the team—reminding me I was Silver Coyle—stubborn, independent, chock-full of attitude.

"Hi, Alec," I greeted. "Nice to see you."

The big man's body jerked and his frown deepened.

"She's serious with that shit? Hi, Alec. Nice to see you," Alec scoffed.

I wasn't sure who he was talking to or if it was anyone specific, but his response pissed me off.

"What is that supposed to mean?"

"Do you live in an alternate universe or is Weston giving—"

"Don't go there, brother," Weston growled.

"Now what does that mean?" I angrily asked.

"It means you bounce into the room, smile on your face, acting like you weren't locked in the bowels of a yacht packed full of cocaine just *yesterday*."

"I didn't bounce," I told him.

"Now she's splitting hairs."

"Well, I didn't. And I don't think I was smiling either. I know where I was yesterday because I was *there*. I also know that my apartment was trashed and everything I own will be in a dumpster as soon as I can arrange it. What were you expecting? Me to be a slobbering, sobbing, broken mess? That's not me. Weston and his team got me out, I'm fine, they're all fine, and my shit can be replaced. But now that you're being a jerk I'll recant the 'nice to see you' part of my greeting."

"Glad to see a few hours of captivity did nothing to quell the attitude."

I gave Alec a dirty look. One I'd hoped would make him cower under the weight of it, but all it did was make him grin and shake his head.

"Handful," he muttered, then his gaze came to mine and held my eyes. "Glad you're safe and everything worked out."

"Me, too. Sorry you had to clean up dead bodies. Weston told me you weren't happy about that."

"Dead bodies mean paperwork," Alec responded.

It struck me then as odd we were talking about human lives that had been lost like one would talk about taking out the trash, and that made me feel funny inside. Heartless. Cruel.

"Hey," Holden called and I looked over to him. "Don't do that. Don't take that on."

"Take what on?"

"I see it, the guilt starting. Nothing that happened was your fault. The men who lost their lives made their choices. The wrong ones. They were criminals. They were running drugs. And believe me when I tell you, they weren't feeling bad they had you locked up and they weren't thinking twice about ending your life. So let that shit go. All of it."

Holden was right of course, they didn't feel bad about chaining me up. They didn't feel bad when they were dragging me out of the wheelhouse either. And one of them did tell me, he was going to kill me and toss me overboard. But I still couldn't stop thinking about all the ways I'd gotten into that mess in the first place.

Weston came back to my side with a cup of coffee and gestured to the seat. "Sit."

He set the mug down in front of me and I stared down at the blonde liquid remembering I didn't tell him how I liked my coffee, yet the light color of it told me he'd gotten it right.

"How did you know how I like my coffee?"

"Watched you make it more than once while we were in DC."

He had? I was a coffee junkie, therefore he'd have had plenty of opportunities to see me make it. But the fact he'd paid attention enough to remember made my tummy feel funny and butterflies start to flutter.

Butterflies? What was I, ten?

"Thanks," I mumbled because that was all I could say while Alec and his team were sitting around the big country-style dining room table.

I couldn't tell Weston that his thoughtfulness filled me with something that was more than joy, more than happiness, so much more I couldn't find the word. No one had ever paid attention enough to know anything about me. Still to this day, my dad would ask if I wanted Coke or Pepsi when I visited him on his boat and he was stocking up on provisions in preparation for my arrival. The answer to that was neither. I drank Diet Coke in a pinch but preferred iced tea. Always had, even as a kid I'd hated Pepsi.

To sum that up, not even my father paid attention. My mother never cared enough to remember jack shit about me. My coworkers who I spent two weeks at a time with, after years of working with them, still couldn't remember that I hated Hot Pockets, yet every shift Matt brought them in and offered me one. Every. Damn. Time. And I told him each time I thought they were gross.

So I didn't know what to say or how to feel that Weston knew how I liked my coffee. Not because he'd asked and I'd told him but because he'd paid attention. But I did know how to feel when Weston's eyes gentled and he gave me half-a-grin—scared.

He knew what it meant to me and when he reached out and traced the side of my face from my ear to my chin with a single finger before he dropped his hand and walked away, the rest of the room knew, it too. There was no missing it.

"We identified the couriers on the boat. All three men have ties to Jason Scott," Alec stated.

"And you've identified Jason Scott as a captain, correct?" Nixon asked.

"That's our assumption, he definitely runs a crew. But we're not ruling him out as being higher on the food chain. Lieutenant's a possibility but there's no way he's the leader."

"Why's that?" I blurted out, and when everyone's eyes came to mine I wished I'd kept my mouth shut.

"Because Jason Scott is careless. He runs his crew sloppy. He makes calls on his cell to his soldiers. He travels to his drops using the same route every time. A man running a multi-million dollar drug ring isn't stupid and he sure as fuck isn't careless," Alec told me. "We've tagged every man in his crew. Something new we found was one of the men was talking to Avon

Chapman. Avon's been on our radar because of his connection to Jason."

I knew that name, Avon Chapman, I just couldn't remember where I'd heard it.

"Why do I know that name?" I asked.

"Because he's on the news regularly. He's part of a community revitalization project for the Inner Harbor."

Holy shit, Alec was right. That's where I'd seen the man. I didn't watch TV regularly and avoided the news when I was home, but it was on nonstop when I was on shift. It drove me crazy, but since everyone else liked to watch it I kept quiet.

"So this is..."

"Bigger than we thought?" Alec interrupted me. "Yeah, it is. We got community leaders wrapped up with known drug dealers. Which means shit has gotten complicated. DHS is trying to keep this under wraps. The second the Baltimore mayor gets word, we're all fucked. The DEA will be brought in and the mayor will want city police and the drug task force brought in, too. There will be so many hands in my operation it will be fucked. So that brings us to you."

"To me?"

"Someone was looking for something when they trashed your apartment and car—"

"My car?"

"Fuck," Weston clipped and my gaze went to him.

This just kept getting better and better. A bad stench that lingered in the air, and no matter how many windows you opened it just wouldn't go away. If my car looked like my apartment I was officially shit out of luck. I had decent savings, money I'd stashed away for a rainy day, some retirement accounts I could draw from, though I'd take a huge hit withdrawing money early. I could slowly replace my furniture and not have to touch my retirement. But I couldn't do that and buy a new car.

I wondered if my insurance would cover an act of vandalism due to drug dealers ransacking my vehicle looking for something that wasn't there.

Fuck me sideways.

"Babe." Weston's single word filled my ears and I closed my eyes.

It wasn't what he'd said, it was the tone in which he'd said it. Caring, gentle, tender. I couldn't deal with him being sweet.

Not now. And probably not tomorrow either.

California sounded good—maybe I'd pack up and move and get away from all of this.

13

Weston watched Silver's face crumble and he wanted to kick Alec's ass for blurting out that her car was fucked, then his own for not warning her.

He had no excuse, there'd been time after he kissed her but before they'd gone to sleep. He'd had time after Nix had texted to tell her that the meeting had been changed to the house instead of the office.

Instead, he'd found the time to ask her more about growing up on a boat and answer her questions about his Navy basic training. There had been plenty of opportunities, none of which he'd taken because he'd wanted her relaxed.

It was a little bit selfish but in the end, he'd made the decision not to tell her. He told himself he was trying to protect her, and he was, but more than that he liked the way she was cuddled to his side. Stress-free and compliant.

He was an ass and now Silver had been blindsided.

"Your car isn't bad," Weston told her.

Hurt flashed before she asked, "You knew?"

"I did," he confirmed. "Holden told me last night."

She nodded. Then as if remembering last night's activities in the kitchen and the fact he'd come back upstairs with her clothes in hand, her eyes widened and her cheeks pinked. She knew Chasin and Holden had seen the clothes.

"Your purse and duffle are on the couch," Holden informed Silver. "You'll need to go through them and see if anything's missing. And the car's fine, other than your stuff being dumped out of the glove compartment and center console. I drove it to a friend of ours, Thompson. He's gonna dust it and check it for hair and fibers. He should be done by tomorrow and I'll go pick it up for you."

Last night Holden hadn't explained that he'd already taken it to Thompson's place. He was a friend of Nixon's we'd used in the past. They'd gone to school together and now the man worked as an independent forensic expert.

"Thanks," Silver mumbled.

"Not sure there's much to save but when this is

done, if you wanna go through your apartment we'll all be there with you," Chasin added. "If you don't wanna go back in, we'll handle the dumpster so you don't have to."

"You don't—"

"Silver, between the five of us it will take an hour, tops. And even if it took three weeks we'd still do it."

Weston had always known he had great friends— the best. Men that he'd always thought of more like brothers. He'd never doubted Chasin, Holden, Nixon, and Jameson's loyalty, never doubted they'd risk their lives for him, but hearing Chasin extend that to Silver made him all that more grateful to have them at his back—and now at hers.

He was also thankful Holden and Chasin had immediately engaged, taking her mind away from any embarrassment. Yes, they'd seen the clothes, yes they were both smart men, yes they'd known something had gone down between Weston and Silver. But they were not the type of men to be dicks to a woman with the sole purpose of being a dick.

"How well do you know the men you work with?" Alec asked, bringing the conversation back to why he'd traveled all the way from DC for a sit-down.

"Not well," Silver admitted and looked self-conscious. "I mean, I know surface stuff. We talk.

Sometimes after our rotations are over we'll all go grab a beer together, but I wouldn't really call them friends."

Weston tried to tamp down the jealous knot that tightened in his gut. It was irrational and unnecessary. Silver had let all that shit hang out last night, admitting she hadn't had very many lovers. Not that Weston needed to be told, but she'd confirmed all the same. The moment she was in his arms, he'd known. Her touch had been tentative at first, clumsy, not knowing where to put her hands. Her inexperience had been a turn-on, but if that hadn't been enough, when he'd slid his fingers into her tight sheath, his cock damn near exploded at the snug fit.

It had even crossed his mind, there was a possibility she was a virgin. Not that he concentrated on that thought too long, when his fingers were working her pussy and she was grinding down trying to take more.

"What can you tell us?" Alec's question pulled Weston from his dirty memories and he watched Silver as she squirmed in her seat.

"What do you want to know?" she returned, obviously uncomfortable with everyone's attention on her.

"You're an observant woman, Silver." Alec pointed out. "Does anything stand out? Something one of them has said, done, any changes in circumstances, cagy behavior, withdrawn. Anything."

"Well, Gary's wife just had a baby—their first. He seems excited but stressed about being a new dad. Jumpy every time his phone rings. He takes way more calls than the rest of us because his wife is seriously nervous about being a mom. Therefore she calls him like three hundred times a day. Matt's single, lives on his boat, keeps to himself mostly. Rodger's married, a chill kind of guy, always upbeat. Leonard's divorced, his oldest daughter's sick. He doesn't talk about it much but I know the medical bills are killing him. He sold his boat and his motorcycle to pay for her treatment. His ex is kinda bitchy, she comes around sometimes. He meets her in the parking lot and is in a seriously bad mood when he comes back into the boathouse. My boss Travis is a nice guy. Smart, jovial, understanding but still demanding. He expects everyone to be the best they can be." Silver stopped and shrugged her shoulders. "Those are the guys I work with the most. There's another crew and I've filled in with them when someone's been sick or needed time off, but I don't know them really."

"We'll start with Gary and Leonard," Nixon announced. "Do you want McKenna to run the searches or is there someone at DHS you have in mind to do it?"

That question was for Alec and the longer the man took to answer, the more Weston studied his friend. There was certainly something working behind his eyes, but it was in the way Alec held himself stiff that worried Weston.

"McKenna," Alec finally replied.

"There something going on we should be made aware of?" Weston asked.

"Possibly."

"You care to share?" Weston pressed.

"Not yet."

Weston thought about Alec's answer and found it was unacceptable. If there was something going on at DHS he wanted to know. Not for himself, not even for his team, but Silver's well-being was wrapped up in this case and if something was going on that was going to put her at risk he needed to know.

"Normally I'd appreciate your discretion and wait until you were ready to discuss whatever's obviously eating at you. But Silver's ass is out there, she's swinging. Something I was clear from the beginning I didn't want. Things have changed and now not only do I not want her in anymore danger, I *really* don't want it. So if something's going on that's gonna put her out there more than she already is, I need to know. And I need that information now."

"You don't say." Alec's snide comment was out of character and unappreciated. But before Weston could tell him he needed to check his attitude, Alec went on. "I'm not thrilled about some of the pushback I'm getting. I'm not sure if it's simply political red tape or if there's a different reason I'm catching so much shit for pushing this operation."

"You're catching shit?" Jameson inquired.

"I wasn't a few months ago. But the more intel we get and the closer we are to nailing whoever's in charge, the more shit I'm catching. My boss is getting squirrelly—community leaders are involved and I don't like it when people around me start shifting their loyalties."

Weston could understand that. All of it actually— one of the many reasons he himself had turned down offers from DHS and the CIA. Weston had learned a lot during his time in the Navy. More, once he became a member of the Special Forces community. One of those things was, he despised people sitting behind a desk with no real-life or real-time data-making deci- sions that his ass was going to pay for.

Politics and red tape had no place on the battle- field. Or in this situation, encroaching while they were in the middle of an operation to take down a drug lord.

"You think DHS is gonna pull the plug?" Nixon asked.

Alec didn't look pleased when he answered. "Possible."

Weston's gaze swung to Silver—posture ramrod straight, face pale, eyes round. He understood her fear, she was relying on them to keep her safe. But what she didn't understand was she had their protection, and the government contract had fuck-all to do with it.

"Doesn't change a damn thing, Silver," he told her.

"But if Homeland decided they don't want to pursue the case, then everything changes."

"Not a damn thing changes," he repeated.

"But—"

"Babe, do you think for one second we'd let you swing? Do you think *I* would? The answer is, fuck no. Contract or no contract, doesn't matter. DHS pulls out, we go it alone. Either way, you're protected. Alec knows how to cover his own ass and knows how to play the ridiculous games the government likes to play. That doesn't touch you."

"But—"

"Trust *me*."

Weston held her eyes, hoping like hell this was not one of the times she decided to throw her attitude and get stubborn. He was quickly learning how to talk her around, but didn't want to have to do it. He wanted her to trust him instinctively—trust that he would keep her safe.

"Okay."

Thank fuck.

One step closer.

"A word in private," Alec said, and Weston turned to see the man was speaking to him.

With a nod, he stood and headed to the sliding glass door. They'd have privacy but he could still keep his eyes on Silver. She may've acquiesced but he wasn't stupid enough to think she wasn't still scared.

Alec joined Weston on the back deck and turned his back to the window. Whether it was because the other man had sensed Weston's need to keep an eye on Silver, or if he didn't want the others to read his lips, he didn't know and didn't care.

"What's on your mind?" Weston prompted when Alec didn't immediately speak.

"You sure about this?"

Weston's body jerked as his muscles coiled at Alec's question. His eyes also narrowed, not liking where the conversation was headed.

"Not sure that's your business."

"You'd be wrong, it is. Silver Coyle is caught up in

some serious shit. She's in danger and it's my job to make sure she's safe."

"Wrong. That's my job. Your job is to clear the way so I can make that happen."

"This isn't the sandbox, friend. You're on US soil."

Weston didn't appreciate the reference. He was very aware they weren't on the battlefield on a sanctioned mission overseas.

"Your point?"

"My point is, the rules of engagement are different. The unfriendlies you take out are American citizens. So, it is my business when I'm the one cleaning up the mess."

"What the fuck, Alec? You talking about the three dead drug dealers? Three men who kidnapped a woman, planned on killing her, dumping her, then putting one-point-five million dollars' worth of product on the street to kill hundreds more people? You talking about that fuckin' mess? Cause I gotta tell you, it was *us* cleaning up a mess taking out three enemy soldiers who were a direct threat to American lives."

"Hell no, I'm not talking about Silver's rescue. I'm talking about you going rogue and making a mess I cannot clean up. I see you're all fired up to go all-out to protect her. So what I'm asking is, are you sure you wanna put your ass out there for a woman who, last I knew, you could barely tolerate?"

"Told you, shit's changed."

"Yeah, saw that in there."

Now Weston was getting even more pissed. There was something else in Alec's tone, something he didn't like.

"Why are you asking me this shit? What's the real issue here? You gotta thing for Silver I should know about?"

Alec shook his head and frowned. "Clocked her ass the second she hit the conference room. Hard not to notice a woman that hot when she's all attitude and brave enough to throw it in a room full of men. Thought about it for about five seconds, wondering what—"

"Don't wanna hear that shit, Alec."

"Bottom line is, I thought about it. Then I thought twice because that woman uses attitude to cover a soft spot. One I had no intention of looking after. So the thought died. She's hot as hell, no doubt just as wild. What she isn't, is a woman who's practiced enough to know the score. Therefore not my type. So with all that said, I get it why you'd want in there. But you haven't answered my question. You sure about this? Getting involved with her, knowing you get in deep and go all-out it will be not only your ass, your team's ass, but mine at your back, cleaning your shit up."

Weston didn't have to think about his answer, therefore he didn't. He gave it to Alec straight.

"You're correct. The stubborn attitude is bullshit. She hides behind it, but once you crack through just a tiny bit you get to something that's unbelievably soft. My guess is once I get there and she trusts me, it will be better. It'll be treasure. So the answer is—yes. I'm sure. I'm also not dumb. So you can stop worrying about imaginary messes and figure out why you're catching shit at DHS. And while you're at it, you should consider a career change so you're not having to deal with government bullshit."

Alec's lips tipped up and he chuckled. "That a job offer?"

"It is if you want it to be," Weston told him honestly.

"'Preciate it. But I don't think Gemini Group could match my salary. Then there's the cushy office in DC and the company car."

Alec was so full of shit. He didn't have a cushy office, he had a fucking cubicle. One in an office in the middle of DC where the traffic was a nightmare, the cost of living was bullshit, and there was nowhere you could go—to a bar or otherwise—where you weren't running into scheming fake-ass people. Yet, for some reason, Alec stayed. Maybe it was for the money, but for Weston no amount of money would make him do something, live somewhere, or be around people he didn't like.

"We straight?" Weston asked.

"Yeah. We're good."

"How much danger do you think Silver's really in?"

"On a scale of one to ten? An eleven. Shit's adding up and what it's totaling in corruption.... Brace, brother, they think she has something. Which means they aren't done with her."

Fuck. There it was—confirmation.

Time to plan.

14

I was dying to ask Weston what he and Alec had talked about out on the back deck but I'd refrained. But now it was hours later, Alec had left to go back to DC, and we were in Weston's Jeep driving to his office.

We'd been the last to leave the house. Holden had left first saying he needed to go pack because he was leaving that afternoon for a few days. He didn't say where he was going and I wanted to ask about that, too, but Holden's schedule was really none of my business so I didn't ask about that either.

Jameson left to go home and said he'd meet us at the office in a few hours, he needed to help his woman, Kennedy, load her truck. I didn't ask what they were loading either.

Nixon and Chasin had taken off at the same time, both saying their 'laters' at the front door.

The morning had been odd. All of the men had included and openly talked in front of me like I wasn't a complete stranger. But I'd been lost for most of the conversations because I was. I didn't know who Kennedy was, but I did know Jameson's face gentled when he spoke about her. I didn't know McKenna but I knew she was a computer genius and worked with the guys. I knew she and Nixon were getting married because Nixon had said something about her planning a wedding and he didn't give a shit what she planned as long as it was exactly what she wanted.

So it was weird to be included but still on the outside. I was used to being a loner and the definition of that meant I kept to myself and didn't ask questions. But now I had a hundred of them and they were burning in my chest, not because I was being nosy but because it felt good to be around people who openly cared about each other.

"You got a lot going on in your head, babe," Weston noted.

"What?"

"You're sitting there staring off into space, quiet. What's on your mind?"

It shouldn't have been surprising how much

Weston paid attention, yet it still was. It was a little disconcerting I couldn't seem to hide my mood from him, but more than that, it felt nice to be noticed.

"What did Alec need to talk to you about outside?"

"You."

"Me?"

"He was checking to see where my head's at."

"Where your head's at?"

"Babe, I'm speakin' English."

Okay, that was funny, but mostly annoying.

"I know you are," I snapped. "But obviously, I don't understand why Alec was asking you about me. And I really don't know what it means when you say where your head's at."

"He wanted to make sure I wasn't getting ready to go off the rails leaving a trail of bodies in my wake."

"Why would he ask that?"

"Because he knows me. He knows you mean something to me. So he needed to ask."

There was a lot there to sift through. I wasn't ready to discuss how Alec knew I meant something to Weston, or how he didn't deny the accusation. Instead, I went straight to the trail of dead bodies.

"That's ridiculous. You wouldn't kill anyone."

"I wouldn't?" he asked and stopped at a red light, one of the very few in Cliff City. "You sat through the meetings at Homeland. You know what I did before I left the Navy. So you gotta know, your statement is false."

He was right, I had sat through those meetings. I also bickered with him about the planning of the operation. I'd also been adamant I should stay on the team and be the one to recon the suspected boats carrying drugs. He'd been vehemently against that plan. Then he'd straight out said I should be removed completely. It was old news and there was no point rehashing it when I knew he meant that during those meetings they discussed him being a former SEAL.

"You being an ex-SEAL is—"

"Former," he cut me off.

"What?"

"I'm a former SEAL. Not an ex-SEAL. When I left the Navy I didn't give up my Trident."

I knew what a Trident was. I'd seen enough TV shows and movies to know it's what the gold pin the SEALs wear on their uniforms, but I didn't understand what the distinction was between former and ex. Both meant he wasn't one anymore.

"I don't understand. Just because you still have it doesn't mean you can use it. Is there really a difference?"

"Babe, it's not a badge. I didn't flash it before I

made an arrest. I earned it with my blood. It's a part of who I am, not what I was. I am a SEAL, always will be. But I am no longer in the Navy, therefore I'm former. Never ex. Ex implies you've given up the right to be something."

"Was it hard becoming a SEAL?"

"Hard doesn't begin to describe it. But when your eye's on the prize it's amazing what your body can endure."

I found that to be interesting and wanted to talk more about what he had to do to become a SEAL but I had a point to make.

"Okay. You being a former SEAL is much different than you killing someone."

"You can call it whatever name you want, but the result's the same—in the end, someone's not breathin'."

He was right about that. In the end, someone was dead. But there is a huge difference between murdering someone and killing them.

"Fine. But it's not like you'd kill someone because I was in danger. If Alec knows you then he shouldn't have had to ask."

"I wouldn't?"

There was that question again, only this time it seemed loaded and I was afraid of the answer. Not because what he said would scare me, but what that said about how he felt about me. Which meant, I must've misunderstood what he was asking.

"Weston—"

"Straight up, Silver, and you need to understand this. Do not think because I wasn't the one on that boat taking the shots that I would've had an issue taking them. Because I wouldn't've. But at that moment, I was more concerned about getting to you and making sure you were okay. Any other time, it would've been me topside taking those fuckers out. And that's something you're gonna have to figure out if you're okay with." I was getting ready to ask why it would matter how I felt about anything he did when he answered my silent question. "I've been honest with you, I've told you I want to get to know you better. I want you to get to know me. I was clear when I told you while you're figuring your shit out I was gonna push forward and work to convince you to take a chance. So this is me doing that—giving you something about me you're gonna have to deal with. My job's my job and it's not going anywhere. Which means, as much as it sucks, the possibility is high, I will have to take a life."

It seemed even though I didn't want to think about why Alec thought I meant something to Weston, I couldn't steer clear of the topic. It was front and center in everything Weston did for me, everything he said, all the ways he was honest with me. He just put it out there.

What guy did that?

Why wasn't he hiding his feelings?

Why wasn't he playing it cool, acting aloof, making me walk on eggshells trying to figure out if he liked me? Why wasn't he avoiding topics that had to do with feelings or emotions?

"Don't most guys try to keep how they feel about a woman a secret?"

"Wouldn't know. What I do know is, I'm not most guys."

"No, you're not," I grumbled.

"And that pisses you off, why?"

"Because it confuses me that you're just telling me straight out how you feel and what you want."

"That confuses you?" He chuckled.

I stopped watching him pulling into a parking space and gave him my best dirty look.

Again, he didn't wilt under it, he just laughed harder.

"What's funny?" I unhappily muttered.

"Only you would think me being straight with you is confusing."

"Well, I don't know. The last guy I went on a date with kept me guessing if he was going to try to kiss me goodnight. Not that I was going to let him, but I couldn't get a read all night. One minute hot, the next cold. That's always been my experience, I never know because they never say anything."

"That's fucked."

"That's just the way it is. So you being honest about everything, even your feelings, is really damn confusing."

"Alright, Silver, how 'bout this?" Weston started and turned in his seat to face me. "Just to clear up any possible confusion in the future, there will never be a time you'll have to wonder if I want to or if I will kiss you. The answer to that is, yes. I'm not like most men, and I'd venture to say you've never known anyone like me. Pleased about that. I don't have the time nor am I stupid enough to fuck around with you. I'm a man who knows what he wants. I know what I like, how I like it, and I want to be surrounded by it. Does that make it easy for you?"

No. No, it didn't. Not even a little bit easier.

"Silver," he sighed, clearly running out of patience. "You may not get it now, but you will."

"When?" I blurted out.

"When you decide to take a chance and believe you're safe with me."

There it was again—take a chance.

"I've never had anything good happen to me," I told him.

"I don't believe that, but if it's true, then your luck's changed. You take a chance on us and I promise you'll have it good."

"But—"

"Take a chance," he whispered, leaning closer.

"I'm telling—"

"Take a chance, babe."

What the hell, why not? What's the worst that could happen? My heart shatters into a trillion pieces and I'm forever ruined and live a life full of cats and misery? I was already destined for that anyway, so what difference did it make? At least I'd have a few good memories.

"Okay."

Before I could take a full breath and grasp the gravity of my acceptance, Weston's hand was in my hair, his lips were on mine, and his other hand was on my cheek.

All of that felt nice, but when his tongue pushed in my mouth and he took the kiss straight to hungry, it went from nice to really fucking great.

Scary-great.

Crazy-great.

Desperate-great.

I should've played it cool, held something back but I couldn't. I didn't know how not to show him how into him I was. How into our kiss. How much I wanted to believe he wouldn't hurt me.

So I showed him all of those things and I knew he understood them when he growled against my lips and pulled away.

"Just stick with me, Silver, and you'll see."

"See what?" I muttered, my lips moving against his, the way his had against mine when he'd spoken.

"You'll see that I'm right."

"About what?"

"All of it, sweetheart."

My heart was beating triple time and I stopped asking questions. I knew what he thought he was right about. He thought I was worth something. He thought I was treasure.

And I wanted to be that, I wanted him to be right. But I wasn't ready to believe.

15

Weston was damn near giddy when he'd walked Silver across the street to the office. And that was a first. The first time he'd ever felt that and the first time he'd ever thought a pussy word like giddy.

But that's what he was. He was dizzy with lust, off-balance with what he was feeling for Silver, and happy she'd said she was going to take a chance.

He was on limited time getting her to trust him and Weston knew it was going to be a hard-won battle, but he knew she was worth the effort. Looking back, he'd known for months the woman was under his skin, even denied it when Nixon had called him out on it. But thinking back, he'd enjoyed every bit of their banter—even the arguments.

Most people didn't stand up to Weston. While he

was in the Navy, even men who were higher up in rank cowed under his stare, and didn't dare question him while in the field. And the women he'd been with were all too happy to take a SEAL home for the night just to say they fucked him. There was no challenge, no arguments, no backbone.

But Silver wanted not one thing to do with him when they'd met and she'd called him an asshole within the first ten minutes they'd been in each other's company. He should've known right then, it was love at first sight.

Maybe not romantic love, but he'd certainly fallen in love with her toughness and spirit.

Weston stopped to unlock the door and saw Silver shiver, reminding him fall had arrived and it was time to put the doors and top back on his Jeep. Not that he minded the cold, preferred it, actually. But if Silver was going to have her ass planted in his Wrangler, and he planned on having her in it frequently, he didn't want her cold.

She was also looking around and not doing a very good job at hiding that she was searching the area.

"No one's gonna hurt you," Weston reminded her.

"I know. I was just looking around. The first time I was here I wasn't paying attention." Silver's cheeks flushed and Weston fought back a chuckle.

The first time she'd been to the office was to bust his balls. Silver had been madder than a hornet and had let him have it. After she'd said her piece and got her pound of flesh, she'd turned and stomped out of the office without allowing Weston to respond. That scene had played out in front of Nixon, McKenna, Jameson, and Kennedy. As soon as Silver had slammed the door behind her all eyes were on Weston waiting for an explanation. He didn't give them one, he was too ticked off. He also hadn't gone after Silver, something he should've done. Instead, he allowed her to walk out and drive away. That had been a mistake.

"It's beautiful," she continued.

Weston agreed, it was. The small downtown area, as the locals called it, even though it was really only one main road and a side street, looked like a movie set. Old brick-paved sidewalks and the storefronts looked like they hadn't been renovated since they were built in the eighteen-hundreds. Mature trees lined Fountain Park. A brick courthouse with an ornate cast-iron fence surrounding its well-kept lawn. An old firehouse in the middle of the block had even been converted into a hair salon with apartments above. And at the end of the street was a dock and to the right of that a small marina.

"When we're done, I'll take you for a tour. We'll walk down to the water and grab some dinner."

"I'd like that."

And the way Silver said it he knew she would. Her response was breathy with a hint of excitement. Maybe he wasn't as far away from earning her trust as he'd thought.

Weston opened the door and offered for her to precede him up the stairs.

"These are steep," she noted.

"Yeah, they are. It was a bitch getting all the office furniture up here. Nixon found a bigger space and was thinking about buying it and moving offices but then he remembered we'd have to lug everything back out and now he's dragging his feet."

"I don't blame him. Though maybe it'd be worth it not having to climb these every day."

Weston had to agree with that, too. He was in good shape, worked out every day but he could admit he was over climbing the stairs every day.

They walked into the reception area, which was really a large room with nothing in it but two wingback chairs by the three large windows overlooking the park and a small table between them. Other than that the space was empty, and so it was the perfect place for two German Shepherd puppies to tear around. So they'd walked into the room and the moment they had, they'd been accosted.

"Oh my God. How cute are these two?" Silver dropped to her knees and was rewarded with licks to her face and jaw.

"Killer! Down," Jameson demanded.

"Stop calling him that," McKenna scolded. "You know you're confusing him."

Jameson and Kennedy's dog's name was not Killer, it was Tank. And it drove Kennedy batshit crazy when Jameson called the puppy Killer. Which was precisely why Jameson did it.

"Axel! Settle," Nix commanded, and much to Weston's surprise the puppy halted for a second, looking at his owner before he went back to attacking Silver.

There were more puppy scratches behind the ears, more cuddles as she picked up Tank first and gave him a squeeze, then she moved to Axel and did the same.

"How old are they?" Silver asked, still on her knees.

"Fourteen weeks," Micky answered, then went on. "I totally got suckered. Jameson and Kennedy brought Tank in and I fell in love. It's like when you see a friend with their newborn baby and you think to yourself you want one because they're so cute and tiny, but you don't think about all the crying, sleepless nights, and diapers. That's Axel. A cute little furball with the crying, sleepless nights, and potty breaks."

"I could see how it would happen. They're both crazy-cute," Silver returned and smiled. "I'm Silver by the way."

"McKenna."

The two women smiled at each other and something settled over Weston. He'd been a little nervous about the two meeting. Micky had been in the office when Silver had come in to hand him shit. And even though McKenna was Nix's woman, she was close to all of them. Loyal, protective, like a little sister to the whole team. And Silver had made a great first impression by bitching Weston out.

He was realizing he shouldn't have been worried. Pure McKenna. Open, friendly, welcoming.

"Nice to meet you. I've heard a lot about your mad computer skills," Silver told Micky and stood.

"Weston exaggerates." Micky shook her head. "Did you get everything you needed? Weston said he was taking you shopping."

"Pretty much."

"Well, Kennedy and I are making a Target run later. We're also hitting the mall. We'd love it if you went with us."

Silver turned to look at Weston and warmth hit his chest, bounced around, then settled. He didn't need her to ask his permission to go out with the girls, and that's not what she was doing. Silver knew she was in danger. Knew he'd promised to keep her safe. And she was looking to him for direction, because she trusted him to keep his promise.

Fuck, yeah.

"Not a good idea," Nixon said before Weston could.

And as much as it made him a pussy, he was happy his friend was going to be the one to explain why Silver couldn't go. And when Micky's smile fell and Silver's shoulders hunched forward, Weston was more than pleased it hadn't been him who had derailed their plans.

"He's right," Silver mumbled. "I really want to go, but I don't want to put either of you in danger."

Weston was happy Silver was taking the threats against her seriously but he hated it all the same. Hated that she was in danger to begin with, hated that her life was disrupted, and hated even more that she looked scared again.

"Next time," McKenna continued.

"Next time," Silver confirmed.

"Rumor has it you're a maritime expert." McKenna

changed the subject. "While I'm waiting for my searches into your coworkers to finish I started looking at the maps and waterways more closely. I could use some help if you're up to it."

Once again Silver glanced in his direction, but this time warmth didn't take over—it had already settled deep. It was something more. Something Weston would have to ponder to figure out, but it felt a lot like tranquility.

He came out of his stupor and nodded. "We'll be here at least a few hours. Nix and I will be in the conference room working."

"I'd love to help," Silver said and followed McKenna down the short hall toward the back stairs.

Weston wished they were at a place where he could call Silver back and demand a kiss before she left his side. But they weren't—not yet. However as soon as they were, he was making that a rule.

"It looks good on you," Nix said when the women disappeared.

"What does?"

"Her under your skin."

Weston wasn't sure if it looked good, but it sure as fuck felt good. So damn good he planned on keeping her there.

"Right," Weston mumbled.

Weston didn't wait for his friend to follow or for his laughter to die down, he left Nix in the reception area to deal with the puppies and made his way into the conference room.

By the time Nix had contained Tank and Axel, Weston already had the thick file Alec had brought with him that morning opened and its contents spread over the table.

"What'd Alec say to you outside?"

"Head check."

Weston didn't need to say more, his friend would know exactly what that meant.

"I'm concerned the DHS is jacking him around," Nixon said, settling his large form into a chair. "If they pull the plug, the contract's void and we'll get the stand-down order."

"Yep," Weston returned.

"You got no intention of standing down?" Nix surmised.

"Fuck, no."

Homeland could scratch the operation but it wouldn't hinder Weston's investigation. He wouldn't stop until Silver was safe.

"Could get sticky," Nix noted.

"Probably."

"If they pull the contract we'll deal. You know we'll have your back."

"I know."

Nixon chuckled at Weston's curt response. But really, what else was there to say? Weston knew his team would be at his side. Never doubted it.

"She the one?"

Weston wanted to tell Nix it was too soon. Maybe deny he was feeling what he was feeling. Tell his friend to mind his own business and worry about his own woman marrying him and stay out of his personal business.

But he didn't do any of those things. Weston had already denied it once, he figured it was a futile endeavor to do it twice.

So instead he told the truth.

"Yep."

Nixon nodded and changed the subject. "Should we talk about Holden or continue to ignore what's going on?"

Weston thought about the question and wasn't sure which way the team should lean. Holden was obviously going through something. Had been for a long time. They all knew he was hung up on a woman who he'd deemed untouchable. A woman who Holden had avoided for years. That evasion started long before one of their teammates had died in combat, leaving Charleigh a widow and her daughter without a father.

It had started when Holden had fucked around too long, Charleigh got fed up, gave Holden a choice, Holden chose wrong, and Charleigh gave up the dream of a life with Holden. She married Paul and left Holden broken. The man hadn't taken a full breath since.

The fuck of it was, Holden went to their wedding. He went to barbeques at their house. Get-togethers when the team came home from deployment. The type of man Holden was, he'd never poach another man's woman. Especially a man who was a friend and team-mate. He pushed what he felt for Charleigh aside and went through the motions of being happy for them.

But Paul was not stupid. He'd known before he started his thing with Charleigh that she'd loved Holden. Yet he still married her. Maybe he thought he could love her in a way she'd forget about Holden. And maybe he had. Paul and Charleigh had a daughter, they looked happy, they looked like they were in love, and Weston hoped for Paul's sake he hadn't lived under the cloud of Holden. Though Weston suspected he had.

Paul's last words to Holden had been to look after Charleigh. Words that had fucked with Holden's head and a promise Holden hadn't kept. He'd spent years dodging Charleigh and Faith. But recently, that had changed.

"Give him his play."

"But—"

"Seriously, Nix. We give him what he needs to sort his head. And what he needs is to go at this alone without any of us getting involved. We'll know when we need to step up and take his back, but now's not the time."

"I wish he'd pull his head out of his ass when it comes to her."

"Me, too. But right now, I need to focus on Silver."

Nixon nodded and Weston got to work.

Ten minutes later Weston knew the players.

Fifteen minutes later he knew they were fucked.

Twenty minutes later he knew Silver was in more danger than they thought.

16

Three great days.

Three nights of torture.

Three days of getting to know Weston and the guys, save Holden who was still gone. Three days working with McKenna going over the different routes the drug runners could use and combing through background checks of the people I worked with.

Weston, Nixon, Jameson, and Chasin had kept me away from what they were working on. I knew they were investigating the names Alec had given them, but the men had refused my help. Which was fine because my time was better used going over maps.

My days were busy, but my nights were agony. This was because I'd climbed into Weston's bed with

Weston at the end of each day. He kissed me. He teased me. He gave me terrific orgasms. But he refused to allow me to touch him the way I wanted. I knew he liked my hands on his chest—he groaned and his muscles flexed and bunched under my palms. I knew he loved it when I kissed his neck and throat but wouldn't allow me any lower.

Further, I knew he was supremely good with his mouth because last night, not only had he kissed me until I was dizzy but he'd used his mouth other places. Private places no one else's mouth had ever been. And it was brilliant—everything he did was.

But I wanted more and was starting to get uneasy about why Weston was refusing.

This was where experience would've been a good thing. I thought all men wanted to move to the main event as soon as possible. And just like every time Weston's hands were on me, I'd lost my mind and begged him to take me. All three nights I got "not yet" or "patience" and sometimes I got that combined or a variation, but the end was the same—no sex.

I'd slept in his arms, cuddled close, sated after terrific orgasms. I should've been happy. I'd never had orgasms three—actually four nights—in a row. But being the hussy Weston made me, I wanted more. I wanted everything. I wanted sex.

"Babe?" Weston called from the doorway.

I was in his office, it was early, and we were the only ones there.

"Yeah?"

"You want anything from Sam's?"

Sam's was the coffee shop around the corner. It was fabulous. The coffee was great, the croissants were buttery and flaky, and their raspberry Danish was to die for. In the last few days, I'd tried them all but decided the Danish was my favorite.

"A Danish and a spiced chai latte," I answered then added. "Please."

"A latte?"

"Thought I'd change it up a bit."

"Right." He smiled.

Weston smiled a lot. But when it was aimed in my direction it was different than when he smiled at McKenna. Not softer, but it reached his eyes and changed the meaning. I was quickly becoming addicted. Yesterday, I'd found myself saying silly things just to hear him chuckle or see him smile and shake his head at me like he thought I was amusing.

It was safe to say I was in the danger zone. The warnings were sounding all around me but I was ignoring them. I was no longer close to being in over my head, I was simply there. The pain would be immense and I knew it and was choosing to pretend I was living in a bubble.

It was working. I was open and honest with Weston, he was the same with me, and I was fast forgetting this was temporary.

"You gonna be okay here by yourself?" he asked and I glanced around the office I'd taken over.

Luckily he and Nix had been working downstairs in the conference room because all of my files were spread out over his desk, even yesterday's to-go cup was still in the corner. Guilt at my inconsiderate takeover assailed me.

"I'm sorry your desk is such a mess," I blurted out.

"What?"

"Your desk. I've moved all of your stuff. I wasn't thinking."

"Sweetheart, I could give a shit you moved my stuff aside."

"Well, I do. It was rude. I didn't even ask, I just came in here and took over your space."

Weston pushed off the doorframe and stalked into the room, stopped next to me, swiveled the chair, then crouched so we were eye-to-eye.

God, I loved it when he did stuff like that. Anytime he had something to say, something important, he always made sure he was looking right at me.

"I like you in here," he said. "I like knowing you're up here working at my desk, surrounded by my things."

And I was totally surrounded by him. His office was full of his Navy SEAL memorabilia. There was a handsome SEAL Trident carved out of wood that had pride of place on the wall. Next to that was a framed image of a group of bearded men all dressed in camouflage fatigues, holding rifles. The background was nondescript though it looked to be in the desert. One man, standing in the middle, was proudly holding a US flag. And among the warriors was none other than the President of the United States—Tom Anderson.

It was an awesome picture. Other pictures, similar but different, scattered the walls with other mementos mixed in.

I wouldn't call it a shrine to Weston's time in the Navy, but it was a reminder of how proud he was of his service. How much the men in those pictures meant to him.

"I like being in here, too," I whispered.

"Good." His hand went to the back of my neck and he gave it a squeeze before he put pressure there and mumbled, "Kiss me before I go."

I didn't think about denying his request, I couldn't. I simply leaned forward and gave him what he wanted. Then he gave me what I wanted. A scorching kiss with lots of tongue and a fair amount of moaning. The sounds may've come from me, but the way Weston deepened the kiss I knew he liked them.

"Damn, you can fuckin' kiss. Makes me lose my mind," he murmured before he stood. "Be back."

I watched his jean-covered ass as he moved across the space then disappeared. I did this thinking I obviously didn't make him lose his mind enough—not like he made me lose mine—or at least not enough to make him want to have sex with me.

MY EYES WERE CROSSING. I'd spent hours going over a month's worth of the canal roster and schedules. Every ship that went through the canal was documented: time, date, crew, shipping manifests. Personal crafts were the same, save the cargo lists.

I'd flagged the ships I thought were worth looking into. But one stuck out. It was a personal craft, one that did not require a pilot to board to captain the boat. It was a sixty-foot Hatteras power cruiser. I was familiar with the vessel, I'd lived on one similar. The main deck was the salon, galley, and a head. The lower deck had two staterooms and a head. The sky deck had a lounge and a sky bridge.

In other words, it was a nice motor yacht. Not just luxury but mega-luxury. There was also no reason for the vessel to travel the C&D Canal four times a month. It wasn't that kind of boat. It was meant for cruising. Fuel was expensive, there was nothing especially beautiful about the canal, and further, no one who had a one-point-eight-million-dollar yacht would waste their time cruising the canal. Even if they had the money to blow.

I gathered the papers I needed and headed down to the conference room to show Weston what I'd found, briefly stopping to poke my head in McKenna's office asking her if she was ready for lunch. After ascertaining she was and what she wanted me to have the guys order, I went downstairs.

I was wondering how in the world I'd missed the *Serafina*'s numerous trips, when I walked into the conference room and was surprised to find Holden back.

The look on his face stopped me dead. He didn't look like a man who'd just had a three-day vacation, he looked like a man who just found out his dog was run over.

"Everything okay?" I asked.

"Yeah. Come in," Nixon offered.

Everything was not okay. And I wasn't sure I

wanted to interrupt whatever conversation had put that kind of devastation in Holden's eyes.

"Hey. Welcome home," I chirped.

"Yep."

Oh, boy, I was right. Something had happened. Though it wasn't my place to ask, so instead I went about telling the guys what I found.

Weston was looking over the logs when Nixon's phone rang.

"Swagger," he clipped, and not for the first time I thought about how cool his last name was. "What the fuck?" His question to whoever was on the other end of the line had Weston standing. "Christ. How big of an issue is this gonna be?" There was a pause then. "Right. I'll tell her."

Nixon disconnected and Weston immediately started, "What happened?"

"That was Alec. Silver's dad filed a missing persons report."

"What?" I screeched.

"And went to the media," Nixon finished.

"Fuck," Weston growled. "Babe, there a reason your dad would freak out and file a report?"

"No," I answered. "I barely speak to my dad. He wouldn't have any idea if I was missing or not. Sometimes we go months without connecting."

Why would my father think I was missing? Last I spoke to him he was setting off for the Galapagos Islands. That was almost four months ago. He said he'd be gone five and not to expect any calls. That was my dad—always on the move, always out of communication, always thinking of himself and the adventures he could take.

"You need to call him," Nixon instructed.

"I can try. But last I heard he was in the middle of the Pacific. Can I use someone's phone?"

My phone was not in my purse—the only thing that had been stolen out of it. My cash had been untouched, my credit cards, I'd even had my expensive watch tucked in the inside zipper and that was still there, too.

When I'd been taken captive the first thing the men did was take my work phone and toss it overboard.

We hadn't replaced my phone, mainly because there was no reason. I didn't need one when I was never without Weston and we were either at his house or the office.

"Sure." Weston pulled his phone out of his back pocket and handed it to me.

Still remembering his code, I unlocked his phone and dialed my dad.

Surprisingly it rang—normally it would go to voicemail when it was out of range. And more shocking, he answered.

"Dad?"

"Silver? Oh, thank God. Where are you? Are you okay?"

"What? Why wouldn't I be?" I asked, ignoring the panic in my dad's voice.

"I tried to call you when I got to Florida. A man answered, said he worked with you and you were missing. Just vanished and no one could find you."

"Someone answered my phone?" I asked, and my gaze went to Weston. His spine snapped straight and his features went to stone. "Hold on, Dad." I took the phone from my ear and found the speakerphone icon. "I'm back. Start from the beginning. Tell me exactly what happened."

"Two days ago, I pulled into Florida and called you to tell you I was back early. When I called, a man answered and told me that no one could find you. You'd missed work, you weren't at your apartment, and your car was in the parking lot at the yard."

"Did the man tell you his name?" Weston asked.

"Who is that?" my dad asked, anger sliding into his tone.

"A friend," I told him. "As you can see, I'm fine. Someone lied to you. Did they tell you a name?"

"No. I can't see anything. Where are you?"

"Dad. Really, I'm fine."

"Silver. Where are you? Tell me now or I call the police and have them track this phone call so they can come and bust you out."

I glanced back at Weston with wide eyes. My dad was nuts. He'd call the police. He was also dramatic and used words like "bust out" like he was in some cop show.

Weston shook his head and mouthed the words 'he can't track the call.' At least there was that, but he'd still call the police.

"Don't call the police, Dad. I'm fine. I ate something bad, got sick at work, now I'm staying with a friend while I recuperate from food poisoning. My work knows, they've been notified. So whoever you spoke to is pullin' a prank and I'd like to know who. It wasn't cool getting you all upset. But I need you to make whatever calls you have to make and stop the manhunt for your not-so-missing daughter. And the media, Dad, really?"

"Not until I see you."

"Well, considering you're in Florida and I'm in Maryland that's gonna be hard. But seriously, it's not cool the cops are wasting resources on finding someone who is fine."

"I'm in Delaware. Meet me at your apartment in twenty minutes."

"What? Why are you in Delaware?"

"Because my goddamned daughter is missing. Where else would I be?"

Okay. That made me feel good. I didn't know my dad had it in him to travel on dry land even if his only child was missing. But as nice as that felt, we now had a big problem.

"Fuck," Nixon muttered.

"Mr. Coyle. Silver isn't going back to her apartment. If you want to see her you'll have to come to her."

"I'll come there and you let her go. Trade me for her."

What the hell?

"Dad, this isn't a hostage situation. I've told you I'm with my friends. Jeez, you've been watching too much Blue Bloods while out to sea."

"I don't know that. It sounds like a trap."

"Mr. Coyle, it is not a trap. But if you'd feel better, I'll meet you at the Kent County, Maryland Sheriff's station," Nixon entered the conversation. "As a matter of fact, that's where I want to meet you."

"Why?"

Great, now my dad was going to argue about where to meet even though Nixon was actually giving him what he wanted by involving the police.

"Because I want to make sure you weren't followed."

"Why would someone follow me if my daughter was safe?"

"Didn't say she was safe," Nixon told him and I braced for the theatrics.

"I knew it. How much do you want? Name your price—"

"Dad!" I shouted. "Just meet Nixon at the sheriff's station and I'll explain everything when I see you. But please be careful, and whatever you do, when you meet him, try and be normal. Just once, do not embarrass me."

"I embarrass you?" he whispered and pain sliced through me.

"That's not what I meant, Dad," I sighed. "But you tend to lean toward drama worthy of an Academy Award. These are my friends, they're going out of their way to keep me safe, and I don't want to repay that with you going all Colombo on them."

"Fine. I'll meet them at the sheriff's station."

"Do you need directions?" I asked.

"No, I'll find it."

"Bye, Dad, see you soon."

"If there is one hair on my daughter's head that's hurt, no one will have to worry about Colombo. I'll go all Clint Eastwood and paint the town red and you can take that to the bank."

My dad disconnected and I rolled my eyes.

"Something we should worry about?" Nixon asked with his lips twitching. "Him going all Clint Eastwood?"

"If he has a harpoon, possibly. But other than that I think the only thing you're gonna have to worry about is his flair for crazy."

"You okay?" Weston asked.

My eyes swung to him and he wasn't smiling—unlike Nixon, he didn't find anything funny about my dad calling the police then acting like he was living out a scene from the movie *Taken*. He looked concerned. And once again, I liked it. I liked that he cared and showed it. I liked that he was worried how my dad's unexpected appearance would make me feel.

I liked all of that so much, I did what I always did when Weston asked me something. I answered with one hundred percent honesty.

"I don't know."

"Right." He moved around the table, walked right to me, and pulled me into his arms. "Whatever happens, I have your back."

"I know," I mumbled against his chest.

And I did know. Weston would never let me swing.

17

Dale Coyle was fucking nuts.

Weston was thrilled Nixon had met him at the sheriff's station with Holden and that he'd stayed behind with Silver. She'd tried her best to cover up how nervous she was her dad was in town. But she was open about how freaked she was someone had answered her phone. And Weston had to admit that was fucked.

The only good news was, whoever was playing this game was an amateur. They couldn't find Silver, therefore they were willing to use whatever they could—even the police and media—to get her out of hiding.

While Nix and Holden had been gone, Silver warned the rest of them about her father. She'd looked embarrassed when she told them he was a little over-the-top—which was an understatement—and he tended to lean on the side of drama—again, understatement.

They'd decided to meet back at the house and it was a good thing they had. Dale was loud, he was drama, and it had taken a solid hour to get him to understand they were not in some fucked-up action adventure Hollywood movie. And the only reason he finally stopped accusing the team of kidnapping and brainwashing his daughter was because Silver had stopped sugar-coating what had happened to her and laid it out.

After that, the man had looked freaked and pissed. Then he looked impressed his daughter had single-handedly figured out the C&D canal was being used to run drugs. Then he'd gone back to freaked.

And that brought them to now—Dale trying to convince Silver to go back to Florida with him, get on his boat, and sail off to parts unknown.

"Dad, that's not gonna happen," Silver told him after the fifth time Dale had asked her to leave with him.

"You know I have room. And I've been waiting for you to take over," Dale returned.

"And I've told you, I don't want to take over."

"Come on, Scout, it's time. Give your old man a break. I want to retire."

Something in Silver changed. It was subtle, but it was there. She lost the exasperated but friendly look and it went straight to stubborn.

"Then retire. But I am not taking over your business and I am not going to Florida with you to jump on your boat and run away from my problems. I'm staying right here."

"Scout—"

"Enough, Dad. Weston has everything under control. I'm safe right here."

Weston has everything under control.

The single sentence echoed in his head like an invocation. A spell that tethered around his heart and squeezed until the organ damn near stopped beating.

"Are you? Do you even know these people?" Dale inquired.

The new change in Silver wasn't subtle, it was immediate and fierce.

Weston didn't have time to look around the room at his teammates, nor did he need to, to know they were just as annoyed as he was. But before he could speak, Silver beat him to it.

"You are unbelievable," she seethed. "You've been gone for four months. During that time I haven't heard hide nor hair from you. Not a call. Not an email. Not a text. Dale Coyle comes and goes as he pleases. Been that way my whole life, Dad. Only when I was a kid you had no choice but to drag me along. Now suddenly you're here and worried about my safety? But you don't pull me aside and have a rational, caring conversation. Instead, you do what you always do, make it about you. Me coming with you to take over your business so you can retire, making it not about me and whether or not I'm safe. And in the process of trying to get me to do what you want, you insult my friends. The very men who saved your daughter's life. But do you thank them for that? No. You throw your drama, pitch a fit, and *insult* them."

Time to shut this shit down.

"Dale," Weston started and waited for the man to look at him before he continued. "Not only is Silver safer with us, but she's also needed. Her knowledge and insight is invaluable."

"So you're using my daughter to help you find these drug dealers and you want me to believe she'd be safer in Maryland than on a boat in the middle of the Caribbean far away from all of this?"

Weston wasn't about to explain himself or the operation to the man. He was irrational, selfish, and now Weston fully understood where Silver had learned to be stubborn. Only when she did it, it took very little to talk her around. And once she saw the truth she backed down. Not in a spineless, helpless way—in a rational, intelligent sense.

"Straight up, Dale, I don't care what you believe. My only concern is Silver. Bottom line, we can't make you keep quiet about what Silver has explained. But I can promise you if you run your mouth and tell anyone where she is, the threat level that is already high, goes up exponentially. That doesn't mean I can't and won't keep her safe, it just means you will have made my job harder. That's your choice. What isn't, is forcing Silver to do something she's repeatedly told you she's not going to do. I couldn't give the first fuck, you want to question my or my team's motives. Again, your opinion doesn't matter. What does is Silver's. And to that end, if you wanna stand here and argue with her, upsetting her more, then you're done and you can leave."

Dale's face turned a shade of red Weston had never seen. And for a moment he hoped the man didn't have high blood pressure. But as soon as Dale opened his mouth, all worries about the man having a stroke vanished.

"After everything I've done for you, Scout, you're gonna let some man you barely know speak to your father that way? I should've known—"

"You're done. No more talking." Weston turned to Silver. "Babe, do me a favor, yeah? Go on upstairs and give me a minute with your dad."

"Sure."

Easy.

No argument.

Defeat.

That was when Weston knew the blow her father had dealt was painful. Not only that but it sliced deep. Which made what was going to come next all that much easier.

"Scout—"

"Do not speak," Weston growled and waited until Silver hit the top of the stairs then disappeared out of sight. "There's a hotel in town. I suggest you find it, check in, and spend some time reflecting on what you just did to your daughter. If you come back here tomorrow and you haven't sorted your shit, I'll put you out again."

"You have no right to tell me what to do with my daughter. And I'm not leaving here without her. I don't know what you've done to her, but you've turned her against me and I don't—"

"You're wrong. As the man who sleeps next to her, I have every right to protect her. And if you think anyone can make Silver do anything she doesn't want to do, you don't know your daughter. Silver's in danger, she's stressed, she's worried, she's lost damn near everything she owns, yet she's still standing strong, doing her part to take millions of dollars of drugs off the street. She is brave beyond belief. Yet in twenty minutes you've successfully brought her more stress, more worry, and laid your bullshit on her shoulders. And just to point out, for a man who was so worried his child had supposedly been missing, worried enough he high-tailed his ass all the way up to Delaware, you have to know what you just did to her was jacked. And the icing on that is, you didn't even touch her. Not even when she told you she'd been held against her will did you pull her into your arms and hold her. Not when she told you her apartment was trashed, did you hug her. That's not jacked—that's plain fucked-up."

"So, that's it. You're sleeping with my daughter—"

"Christ," Weston bit out. "Listen to yourself. Out of everything I just told you that's what you want to latch on to? You have two minutes to walk out that door on your own, before I put you out. Go sort your shit and we'll see you tomorrow."

"If you think you threatening me with physical violence makes me want to leave my daughter with you, you're wrong. Obviously, you're a dangerous man."

Weston was trying to draw from every reserve he had. But he was fresh out of patience. Couldn't find an ounce of care. And couldn't muster any consideration for the man. He had nothing. Dale was selfish, inconsiderate, and a dick.

It was a miracle Silver had survived her mother's verbal attacks, but if Dale's current behavior was how he'd treated his daughter when she was growing up, Silver wasn't a miracle—she was a goddamned phenomenon.

Treasure.

"You're right, I am dangerous. And you should be thrilled I'm the man standing by your daughter. You should go home and rest easy, safe in the knowledge I will protect her—even from you. I don't threaten physical violence, I'll enact it. And the only reason why I gave you two minutes to walk out on your own was out of respect for Silver. But you're down to sixty seconds and I suggest you use your time wisely."

And the standoff ensued. Weston unmoving, arms crossed over his chest. Dale Coyle stubbornly staring at him. The whole scene was as ridiculous as it could be. So ridiculous Weston would've laughed if he wasn't so angry. How the fuck could a father be so callous? How could a man who was supposed to love his child be so selfish?

Questions Weston knew he wouldn't get the answers to, so he gave up, broke the standoff, and turned to Nixon.

"Your house, your call. I'm going up to check on my woman. Neither of us is coming down until he's gone."

Giving Dale not a second more of his time, Weston moved to the stairs.

"I'm calling the police." That was Dale. Weston didn't know who he was talking to and didn't give a fuck.

He was done.

He'd said what he had to say and now it was up to Dale to clue in or not. If he didn't, Weston would make it so the man wasn't around Silver until the op was over —and even after that, he'd wade in when it was necessary. Weston wasn't stupid, he also wasn't a dick so he'd never dream of trying to keep father and daughter apart. But what he would do and planned on doing was making sure Silver didn't get cut up in the process.

That was the last time he'd watch Silver take a hit that put sadness in her eyes.

18

I heard.

Everything.

Every word Weston had said to my father after he'd asked me to go upstairs.

I didn't question him or put up a fight mainly because I was so embarrassed by my dad's antics. I wanted to run away and disappear or hit my dad over the head with a lamp. I couldn't believe he'd behaved like that, and that was saying something because my dad was pretty melodramatic and over-the-top. There'd never been a time where he wasn't.

When he and my mom argued it got dirty, but Dad was normally the one to back down because there was no winning with my mother.

"Hey." Weston's voice filled the room and my eyes closed.

"I'm sorry."

"You got nothing to be sorry for."

"Yeah, I do. That was embarrassing."

"I agree. For him, not for you."

That was nice of Weston to say, but we both knew that wasn't true. Dale was my father. My blood. The man who made me and raised me. I was a direct reflection of him, and him of me. Either way, it said nothing good about me.

"Is he still down there?"

"He was when I came up," Weston told me and shut the door to his bedroom. "You all right?"

"No."

My honest answer did something funny. His lips tipped up but the gesture died before it turned into a smile. Warmth and understanding swept over him and I wasn't sure how I knew that's what he was feeling, but I did.

Not only did I know it but I could feel it. The crackle in the air, the unconcealed concern, the anger on my behalf.

Weston didn't wait, he didn't stop to ask more questions, he didn't tell me everything was going to be okay, he didn't tell me not to be upset or I had nothing to worry about. He simply closed the space between us and pulled me into his arms. Something he'd pointed out my father hadn't done.

Once my cheek was resting on his chest and his big arms went around my shoulders, I wrapped mine around his middle and held on. And for the first time since Nixon's call from Alec about my dad calling the police, I felt safe. Protected. Cocooned. Nothing could touch me if Weston was around.

"Do you think I'm desperate?" I blurted out, and when Weston stiffened I regretted my outburst. "That didn't come out right."

"I sure as fuck hope it didn't. Wanna explain what you meant?"

"I don't want you to be mad at me."

"Then don't say stupid shit."

That had me stiffening and a little pissed.

"I'm not saying stupid shit, I'm telling you how I feel. How is that stupid?"

"It's stupid if you're getting ready to try and convince me you're desperate."

The 'little' went out of the little pissed and I moved straight to pissed.

"Well, I'm kinda acting like I am don't you think? I mean, here I am latched onto you like some desperate, lonely fool, thinking that as long as you're around no one can hurt me when I should be standing up for myself."

Some of the stiffness from his body waned but the hardness of his voice remained.

"First, pleased you recognize that you *are* always safe when you're with me. Can't tell you how happy it makes me that you trust me to do that for you. Second, even more satisfied you've latched on, because, sweetheart, I wasn't gonna give you a choice about that. And, Silver, you are no fool. Not when it comes to me, not when it comes to your dad. You knew he was diggin' in, you know he's stubborn, and you saw the wisdom in extraditing yourself from the situation. That is not weak, that is not desperate, that is you being smart and strong and knowing when to cut your losses and walk the fuck away before shit gets worse. So no, I do not think you're desperate. I don't think you're easy. I don't think you're a lonely fool. But I do think you are a beautiful, intelligent woman, who had the misfortune of having two assholes for parents."

I was silent because I was savoring what Weston said but at the same time, I found it annoying he could make me feel like I was all the things he said I was when I was angry at him. Not that I remembered why I was pissed to begin with. Which was annoying as well.

"Why is he so hell-bent on you taking over his business?"

"He wants to retire," I semi-lied.

"No masks, Silver."

"How do you do that?" I fumed. "It's exasperating.'

"What is? That I know when you're trying to hide from me by giving me partial truths?"

"Yeah, that."

"It's a gift," he joked.

"Annoying."

With his arms still firmly wrapped around me, I felt his body shaking with laughter and I really wished I could see his face. I bet he was smiling. Not one of his soft smiles that I loved, but the one I arguably liked better. The one that was full of humor and amusement. Because that one was also soft and sweet but a different soft, and he only smiled that one at me.

"Noted. So why is he pushing you?"

At his question, all the good and fuzzy feelings I was enjoying vanished. I didn't want to talk about my dad and I didn't want to have to explain the dysfunction.

"Can we—?"

"Tell me."

"But—"

"Just get it over with so we can move on."

Annoying.

"Fine," I snapped. "He wants me to take over because my mother would hate it."

"Thought they didn't talk."

"They don't. But it doesn't mean she isn't up in his business and that he doesn't keep tabs on hers."

"What does that even mean, babe?"

"It means my mother's remarried. And I heard that from my dad, not from her. Apparently, he's some wealthy yacht broker who also dips into headhunting for crew and captains. That means he knows the business and knows what my dad's doing. My dad has a lot of friends, again all in the business. He knew the second my mom got engaged and to whom. So if I took over my dad's charter business my mother would know and it would crawl under her skin. He'd win. It's ridiculous, but there you have it."

"Win?"

"Yes, win in the battle of who was right and who was wrong when it came to all things Silver. Though my dad's forgetting something. If I take over, my mom will be right."

"How's that?"

"Because she always said I'd turn into him, a loser with nothing to my name but a pocket full adventures that didn't amount to shit."

"She said that?"

This time when I felt Weston's body shaking, it definitely wasn't from humor.

"My dad is at the top of the list of what she hates most. I think I'm number two but only because there is a lot she hates about my dad. When they divorced, she told him he could keep me because he'd already ruined me and there was no hope of turning me into anything more than what I already was."

"Silver, that is so fucked-up I'm at a loss. Actually, that's a lie. However, since beating the hell out of a woman isn't an option, all I can say is—she shows up, I will not go as gentle on her as I did your father."

"That's just her."

"No, sweetheart, it's not just her. Everything she ever said to you was the ramblings of a vile, jealous bitch. There is no excuse for her behavior. None. But the problem is, all her nasty poison is still inside of you. It's simmering below the surface, smoldering, just waiting to detonate. That's what she gave you—toxic waste."

"I agree. It is inside of me. It is toxic and I don't want it to spill over onto you. I told you that. I told you I wasn't good for you, I told you I didn't know how to do this without my poison leaking into your life. And it has."

"And I told you, Silver, now I see I need to remind you of something. It is not lost on me, that viper who carried you in her body, only to give life to a stunning, strong woman, then did her best to feed you shit, left you with scars. I'm now seeing your father did his own damage. But I told you, I'm gonna unravel that. And I wasn't lying then and I'm not lying now—you give me your time and your trust and I'll dig it out. All of it."

And that was when it hit me—everything. It all came crumbling down, the shaky hold I had on my sanity. The tears started, and once they did, I didn't know how to turn them off. I hadn't cried over my mother since the day she took off for good. She didn't say she wouldn't be back, but I knew. It was the way she'd said goodbye. I'd gone down to my stateroom, hid from my dad, and cried.

But after that, no more. I'd set out to prove I was not what she said I was. But Weston was right, her poison was simmering. It came out a hundred times a day in a hundred different ways. Every decision I'd made my whole life was with her in mind.

Suddenly Weston's arms were no longer around me. He bent, his arm went under my legs, he scooped me up, and carried me to the bed. I was still trying to process how he'd pulled off the fireman's hold when he settled himself on the mattress, his back to the headboard, and me in his lap. Through all of this, he said nothing. But he didn't need to—his actions, the way he was holding me, the kiss he'd placed on the top of my head—told me more than any words ever could.

"Why does she hate me so much?" I whispered.

"She doesn't."

"Did you not hear what I just told you?"

"Every. Single. Fucked-up. Word. But she doesn't hate *you*. She hates herself. She hates her life. She hates the woman she sees in the mirror. She hates the choices she made. She hates that something so precious and beautiful came out of those choices. Instead of setting aside her self-loathing and learning to be a good mom, she set out to destroy that beauty. But she failed, Silver."

I sat quietly, my head against Weston's shoulder, and thought about what he said. I'd never considered my mother's issues were her own. When I was younger, my dad had told me stories, he would smile and laugh and tell me how much fun he and my mom used to have. He'd say, "Scout, you wouldn't believe it, your mom, so beautiful. Always smiling and having a good time." That was not the woman I remembered. She was always hyper-critical. Always scowling. Always complaining.

"Maybe," I whispered.

"Why does your dad call you Scout?"

I smiled hearing Weston say my dad's silly nick-name for me. He used to say it with a smile, pride and happiness, not like he had downstairs.

"My dad's not normally that bad," I started to explain. "Well, he's always dramatic and irritating when he wants his way. But mostly growing up he showed me love. I think I was about five when he started teaching me to read charts. Dad was searching for an old Portuguese merchant vessel that had sunk in the Strait of Malacca. He was plotting the next day's dive and I off-handily—because I was five—told him to move his dive to a new location. He humored me and found the wreck and the five coffers of jewels and silver. After that, he called me his good luck charm and nicknamed me Scout."

"I take it from that, you traveled a lot."

"I've motored around the world more than once. More like six times, and been to every continent and most islands."

Weston's arms tightened around me. "Interesting childhood you had. More adventures than most people could dream of."

It's funny. What some would consider adventures I'd considered mundane, boring, torture. Being stuck on a boat for days, sometimes weeks, with no dry land in sight. Scary storms where I thought we were going to die, rationing food because we had to take a detour, no friends, no TV, no normalcy. There were times I'd loved it, but mostly I'd hated it.

I wanted to go to school like a normal teenager. I wanted a boyfriend. I wanted girls I could gossip with. When you grow up in a bubble, you have a skewed sense of reality. When your only insight into high school was watching old episodes of 90210 or *Saved by the Bell* you believe that Brenda Walsh's and Dylan McKay's really exist. You long to have a friendship like Brenda, Kelly, and Donna. You dream of walking into the Peach Pit or The Max.

I never had that.

"It was lonely," I admitted. "And when I got to college, I didn't fit in. I had no social skills, I didn't know how to make friends, and I was too trusting. I didn't know that people were so mean to each other. Everything was new and shocking. I was a new kind of lonely. Lost in a sea of people and I was invisible."

"You're not invisible anymore." Weston's gruff voice made me smile.

"Well, duh. I now have multiple people all looking for me trying to kill me. If there was ever a time I wished I really was invisible it is now."

"No, that's not what I mean." Weston tilted my

chin up, bringing my face level with his. So close I could see the brown and gold flecks in his eyes. My belly did a somersault at his proximity and I wondered again how it was possible I was where I was—in Weston Beil's bed. Not only that, I was in his lap. I'd slept next to him and done other stuff in that bed besides.

"I see you," he murmured. "I see all of you."

I was blinking back tears when his lips touched mine. My mouth opened for him, and Weston's tongue swept in and off I went—straight to paradise. The kiss was different, he was giving me gentle, giving me what I needed, telling me he meant those words—he saw me. And I poured everything I had into that kiss, giving him back what he was giving me because he deserved it.

No, he'd earned it.

19

Weston was in the kitchen a mug of coffee—his first of the day—halfway to his mouth when Chasin walked in.

"Where's Silver?"

The way in which his friend asked, the ease, the normalcy, hit Weston. It was like the woman had been with them months or years—not just days. It was a given she was in the house somewhere and when it hit, Weston liked the tightness in his chest. He liked that Silver was in the house, in his bed where he'd left her sleeping. He liked it enough to know he was going to do his best to convince her that not only did she like it, too, but she wanted to stay.

Weston didn't know how that was going to work with her job—the commute would suck—but the two-week rotation would suck more. Something he knew he had to prepare for now that Silver was in his life and he was keeping her in it.

"Sleeping," Weston answered before taking a drink.

"She okay after what went down with her dad?"

Putting the mug on the counter next to his hip, Weston took in his friend. Totally disheveled, track pants on, and shirtless. That was Chasin every morning when he came down for coffee. Something that was going to have to change with Silver in the house.

"You gotta shirt you could put on?"

The smug bastard smiled and shook his head.

"Not one handy."

"You think maybe you could find one?"

"I could, but I'm not feelin' the necessity seein' as I'm in my kitchen first thing in the morning and I haven't even had a cup a joe a' yet."

Weston watched his friend move around the space, pulling bagels from the cabinet before setting them on the counter, pulling one out, splitting it open, then popping it in the toaster. He did that thinking about what he'd done to Silver on that counter. Then Weston smiled and decided he didn't give a fuck if Chasin walked around with his shirt off. Silver was his in a way that he knew she wouldn't stray.

"No, she's not," Weston answered the other man's earlier question.

Chasin's mouth got tight before he said, "That man's an ass. Totally clueless. His daughter was standing right in front of him and he missed it. And the fuck of it was, she wasn't hiding what he was doing to her. And if he couldn't see it, he should've been able to hear it."

"Agreed. Family dynamics are fucked and that's putting it mildly. Her mother is a total bitch, pure poison."

"Gotta say, watching that shit yesterday, I get that stubborn streak she has. Bet she learned that attitude early on or she'd get railroaded."

"She learned a lot of things early on, and none of them good."

"Alec still coming down today?" Chasin asked, thankfully changing the subject. It was too early to think about Silver's fucked-up parents, a subject that was sure to piss him off. And that was the last thing he wanted to be when he went back upstairs to wake up his woman.

"Far's I know. He said his team's made good progress and they're close to getting us what we need."

"Good. I'll be happy when this shit's over."

Chasin's bagel popped up and he scowled at the toaster.

"Why?"

"Why?" Chasin repeated, pulling the hot bread from the appliance and dropping it on the counter.

"You have a problem with Silver staying here?"

"Fuck, no." His friend turned his attention to Weston. "The obvious reason I want this shit done is because your woman's in danger. I'd like that to be over for her, and for you as well. The other reason is someone needs to sort Holden's shit."

Hell, not Holden's issues again.

"Listen, I already talked to Nix about this. I think we need to give Holden space to work this out on his own. The situation is seriously screwed up and he doesn't need us in his business. He needs time—"

"Fuck that. Would you give me time if I was purposely hurting myself?"

Goddamn it, Chasin had a point. Weston wouldn't stand around with his thumb up his ass while his friend tortured himself. But still, things were complicated. Very complicated, and there was more than Holden to think about.

"If you get in Holden's face about this and he retreats, that could fuck Charleigh and Faith. As far as I see it, they just got him back. You say something about that guilt he's been carrying around, it comes back ten-fold and he may never recover. We hang back and watch. If he needs it, we take his back. But you know Holden, you know the love he has for Charleigh, you know what her choosing Paul over him did to him, and you know he's never recovered. It's time for him to move on."

"And if he moves on with Charleigh? You gotta problem with that?"

Weston didn't, but by the look on Chasin's face, not to mention the anger in his voice, he had an issue with it.

"I got no problem with a man loving a woman and finally doing what he should've done more than ten years ago."

"That's Paul's wife."

"No, Chasin, that's Paul's widow. Paul's gone, has been for a long time. He was a good friend, a good teammate, father, but a shit husband. And if you dig deep and take off the rose-colored lens, you'll see it, too. Paul married a woman because he got her pregnant. He did that knowing she loved someone else. He tried to make her love him, but he failed, mainly because he kept throwing Holden in her face. And you know that to be true, too, because he admitted it to us, and you were the one that told him that shit was jacked."

"Fuck," Chasin growled. "He fucks her around, I'm gonna be pissed."

"He won't."

"Yeah? And you know that how?"

"Because he fuckin' loves her."

"He loved her before and still let her walk."

"And he's lived with the consequences of that. He stopped livin' the day she left. He stopped taking a full breath the day she married Paul, and he's been punishing himself since the day Faith was born."

Chasin was staring at his feet and Weston decided he was done with a conversation he didn't want to have —but seriously didn't want to have while his woman was upstairs in his bed.

"I'll leave you with this, Holden is dying inside. If Charleigh and Faith can heal that, they'd have my gratitude."

Weston left his half-empty cup on the counter and decided he'd come back down and make a fresh pot after he woke up Silver. He left his friend in the kitchen to ponder alone, hoping Chasin didn't talk to Holden. Weston walked back into his room. His eyes hit Silver's long, shiny hair fanning over his pillow, and all thoughts about Holden, Chasin, and Charleigh were gone.

He took his time studying the beauty in his bed.

Then his mind went back to last night and the way she writhed under him when his tongue was in her mouth and his hand in her panties playing with her clit. She stopped writhing and started bucking as soon as his fingers slid into her pussy. When her orgasm broke loose and her pussy convulsed, all he could think about was how badly he wished it was his cock and not his fingers feeling her spasm.

It was becoming increasingly harder to hold back and go slow. Giving her more of him every night but stopping before he lost control. Silver was getting bolder—her hands freely roamed, her tongue licked and nipped his throat and chest. As dangerous as that was, allowing her to go any lower in her exploration would be catastrophic. His only recourse when she begged to take things further was to kiss her. And that was problematic in its own right, the woman could fucking kiss, every time their lips touched it was like she was drinking from his soul.

Silver shifted, rolling from her side to her back, the sheet only covering her lower half. She was in his tee and a pair of silky lavender panties with black lace trim. The image of them seared into his memory, the way his hand looked disappearing under the material, the look of them when he'd yanked them down her legs and tossed them on the sheets so he could fuck her with his fingers without the obstruction. And finally when he'd put them back on her. There was something supremely sexy helping his woman dress, sliding the panties back up her long legs and smoothing them around her hips, knowing he'd taken them off and now he was putting them back on. Same with his tee, though last night, he'd left it on and pulled it up, leaving it bunched under her chin. If her pleading and moaning were anything to go by, Silver hadn't minded he hadn't taken the time.

The longer he stood staring at her, the harder his cock became until it was throbbing in jeans, imploring him to give up his quest to give her time. Three times he'd jerked off in the shower, all three had taken no more than wrapping his hand around his cock and squeezing for the urge to hit, a few strokes later come was pulsing from his cock, with the way Silver looked, sounded, and tasted on his mind.

He was still enjoying watching her when her eyes opened and she smiled.

"Morning," she mumbled, and he wondered if he'd ever get used to her sleepy, soft voice.

He hoped like fuck he didn't. He liked she came awake slowly, taking her time, to let the sleepy shift from her. He loved the little mews she made when she stretched. Though, there wasn't much he didn't like about Silver.

"Morning, babe."

Weston made his way to the bed and sat on the edge, brushing the hair off her neck so he could lean in and kiss her there. Smelling the faint smell of the lotion she used did nothing to calm his dick. It smelled like summer, flowers, and the crisp scent of champagne. The bottle called it "A Thousand Wishes". He had no idea how the name came to be, but he'd wished more than a thousand times that fragrance would never leave his bed.

His mouth hit her soft skin, and he smiled when Silver moaned. Foolishly deciding she needed more, his tongue came out and he tasted her from the bottom of her ear down to her throat. That earned him more groaning, and Silver's hand making its way under his shirt and gliding up his back.

Foolish.

He knew better. The simplest touch, even an innocent one meant to say good morning, was lethal.

Silver's head tipped back, wordlessly asking for more, and like the idiot he was, he gave it to her, starting something he knew would end with his cock in extreme pain.

"Weston."

The sound of his name falling from her lips on a moan made his cock throb and he lifted his face from her neck.

"Time to get up, sleeping beauty," he muttered against Silver's forehead, and unable to move until he did, he pressed a kiss there.

"Why do you keep doing that?"

"Doing what?"

"Pulling away from me."

He hated she sounded so unsure. Hated her voice was just above a whisper and she wasn't looking at him.

"The last thing I'm doing is pulling away. Silver, you have all of me."

"No, I don't."

"Babe?" he prompted when she didn't continue.

Her eyes came to his and all Weston could see was hurt and uncertainty.

What the fuck?

"You keep stopping. You won't let me touch you."

Realization hit but it still didn't explain the hurt. Each time they'd been together Weston knew she'd wanted more, thought he was doing the right thing taking it slow and not allowing her to get caught up in the moment. Not wanting her to regret being with him, or her going into her head thinking she was easy. Nowhere in any of that had he meant to hurt her.

"You got today," Weston told her. "Think on it when we're not in this bed, when your head's clear. Tonight if you still want me to take what you're offering, we'll go from there."

"I don't need to think on it. I know what I want. I keep telling you."

"Take the day, Silver—for me. I need it. I need to know you're sure, *really* sure. I'm in deep, sweetheart. We take it to the next level and you regretting it will gut me. I'm taking things slow, giving you time. But what I need you to understand is I want you so fuckin' bad I literally ache. Me not fucking you has nothing to do with you and everything with me wanting to do right by you."

Silver's eyes lost the hurt, they went soft and lazy before she said, "I'll take the day."

There it was, his girl, she wasn't as stubborn as she wanted everyone to think. Deep down she was agreeable with the important stuff.

"I want you naked, babe."

"What?" The lazy went out of her face and was replaced with hunger.

Fuck, yeah.

"Naked. Now. I'm gonna fuck you with my tongue before I take you downstairs to feed you."

Silver didn't answer, not with words. She tore the

tee up over her head, exposing her tits, making Weston's cock jump. Silver caught the way he was staring at her and shivered.

"Hurry, Silver, I'm hungry."

And Weston did his second favorite thing and removed his woman's panties. Though he supposed after tonight that action would move down the list and be replaced with something else.

After her panties were on the floor, Weston set about fucking Silver. When she started bucking her hips and grinding her pussy on his face, he decided to add his fingers. When she came on his tongue, calling out his name, he decided tonight he'd eat her again right before he filled her full of cock and made her come a different way.

20

If anyone could ruin the high of an early morning orgasm, it was my dad. Even after a good night's sleep, he was still acting like a lunatic. Only now, he was doing it in front of Alec Hall.

Alec had shown up not even a minute after my dad had been banging on the door demanding to see me. He did this at barely eight AM, Chasin letting him. Weston and I were still upstairs but we heard Chasin's booming demand for my dad to be quiet all the way in Weston's bedroom.

Then as we were walking down the stairs a second knock came at the door, annoying Chasin. I knew that because he'd not-so-quietly muttered, "Christ, it's goddamn Grand Central Station around here." Then he opened the door and in walked a very irate Alec.

Next came Holden. He didn't knock, he just walked in, looked around the room, his eyes landing on my dad, and he, too, looked pissed.

That was when the high started to fade and it had gone downhill quickly.

Dad being Dad, meaning he was a drama-king thinking he was playing the role of some smart guy in a movie who had everything figured out, that being his daughter was being held hostage and brainwashed and no one could be believed—including said daughter—because they were all in on the deed.

This necessitated Dad looking up the Department of Homeland Security's phone number on the internet, because the business card Alec had given him could be fake, and after ten minutes of him being transferred and being placed on hold, finally confirmed Alec Hall indeed worked for DHS.

That's when Dad fucking finally admitted everything could possibly be on the up-and-up. But he did this by saying, "You can never be too careful."

God, my dad.

But it had taken a man named Jonny Spenser, who was a Kent County sheriff, showing up and talking to my dad before he agreed to call the police in Florida and tell them I wasn't missing. Jonny had spoken to them as well, explaining he was looking right at me and I was fine.

With all of that done, my high was no longer a high —it was a memory. Albeit a fantastic memory as any memory of Weston between my legs was, but now I was pissed and embarrassed.

Through all of that, Weston never left my side. He'd led me into the kitchen, fixed me a cup of coffee, made me toast after I declined eggs and bacon, then he stood next to me while I ate and my dad was having his drama in the living room.

I'd apologized profusely, offered to try to calm Dad down, but Weston had refused and told me Chasin, Holden, Alec, and Jonny would deal with him. Then he ordered me to enjoy my coffee and not worry about what was going on in the other room.

That proved to be impossible. Not the enjoying my coffee part, the not worrying. Dad was making himself look like an idiot, and by extension, me.

If that wasn't enough, Jameson was now walking through the door with Nixon and McKenna on his heels.

Fucking perfect.

"Good morning," McKenna said, coming directly to Weston and me in the kitchen, ignoring my crazy father.

"It's something.... but what it isn't, is good," I grouched, and McKenna smiled.

"Well, I have some good news."

"Awesome. I need something good."

"Actually, I have two things. Both good."

I waited for McKenna to continue but I did this looking at her smile. It was huge, it was blinding, and it was full of love.

"Nix and I set a date," she told me. "We both wanted something small so that made it easy." Understanding dawned. She and Nix had been going back and forth about their wedding. They'd finally decided. "We're gonna do it here on the farm. In four weeks."

"That's not good news, that's *great* news," I told her, and Weston's arm around me squeezed.

"Yeah, it is," she whispered.

I didn't know McKenna all that well, but I knew she loved Nixon beyond reason. Her face lit every time she talked about him. And when he walked into the room it was that times ten. She'd told me about her ordeal, how she and Nixon met, then how she'd found herself in a tight spot and Nix had saved her from something really horrible. I was happy my new friend was happy.

Genuinely happy, maybe for the first time in my

life, even with my dad acting like a fool and someone after me wanting to silence me—permanently, I was truly pleased McKenna was getting what she wanted. Which was to become McKenna Swagger, however, that might come.

"The other good news is, I found out Leonard is in debt up to his eyeballs, but with a sick child that was expected. But the medical bills are staggering," McKenna shared.

Damn. I felt bad for Leonard—he was a nice guy. No parent should have to be worried about mounting debt while they're scared shitless about their sick child.

"But other than that, he was clean," she went on. "It took some digging, but I found some hefty deposits in an account in Gary Goldbloom's mother's name. Six months ago the account had three-hundred dollars in it and was inactive. Now it has more than five-hundred thousand."

"Did you trace the deposits?" Weston took over.

I was still in shock at the amount of money that had been deposited. Half a million dollars was huge.

"Yep. Shell companies," McKenna answered. "I'm still sifting through everything but I think it's safe to say we found our guy. Now we just have to find who's paying him off."

McKenna's gaze came back to me and I hated that all the joy had melted away. "You okay?"

"I don't know. I'm pissed. Super-pissed. I wanted you guys to be wrong but you weren't, and I'm really angry that someone I work with, a man who sits next to me in the boathouse, who sleeps in the next room for two weeks at a time while we're on rotation, would not only stoop so fucking low he'd take dirty payoffs, but he'd sell me out."

"I get that," she returned.

"Babe?" Weston called as I tipped my head back so I could look at him. "Know it sucks, but this is good news. Now we can come up with a plan. This will be over soon. But we still have to talk about why he suspected you. No one else has had any break-ins. Which means Gary was watching you and doing it close."

That freaked me out. All of it—from it will be over soon, to Gary watching me.

I was on edge about what came next. When this was over and Weston took me back to my apartment. Or as it were, since my car was outside in the driveway, when I got in and drove away, where did that leave us? Weston wouldn't *need* to protect me anymore. I wouldn't *need* to be in his bed every night. Did that mean that would be the end of us? And was there an *us?* Weston acted like it, but I had no points of reference. I had no idea what was going on, even though Weston had been forthcoming, I still didn't know.

Then there was Gary. What the hell was that about? He must've been watching me carefully because I couldn't think of a single thing I'd done that would make him suspect me. I hadn't kept written records, I hadn't taken pictures, I hadn't talked to anyone, taken phone calls—nothing.

"He had to follow me," I blurted out. "It's the only thing that makes sense. I went to the Coast Guard, then I went to Washington to meet with you and Alec. Gary had to have been following me," I repeated. "It's the only way. Everyone involved knew my schedule and knew not to call while I was on rotation. We were careful about that. And I deleted the call history, so even if someone got my phone and unlocked it, they'd never see the calls. Alec's number is saved as Bonnie and no one would know that either."

"That'd be my guess, too," Nixon said, joining the conversation. "Gary was probably watching the whole crew, but Silver's the only one who went off-routine."

"What's this about someone following my daughter?" Dad asked as he stormed into the kitchen.

I stopped looking at Nixon. I stopped being freaked out and I started being extremely pissed.

"Enough!" I barked and my dad jerked. I would've felt bad speaking to my dad like that if I wasn't so angry he'd been such an ass. I would've felt guilty if he hadn't pulled me back into his shit with my mother. Something I'd tried very hard to separate myself from.

"Scout—"

"No, Dad. No more. You hauled your ass up here and I appreciate you being worried. That was nice of you. But now you know I'm safe so you can haul your ass back to Florida and go back to your life."

"You're far from safe."

"You're right. But Weston's seeing to it that I get that way. Alec and the rest of the team are working on it, too. You blew in here like a maniac, refused to listen to me when I repeatedly told you what was going on. You embarrassed yourself, you sure as hell embarrassed me. And because of all that, I want you to go home. I want to concentrate on what I need to be doing to play my part in taking these men down. This is serious. We're not scouting grids for sunken treasure, we're trying to stop drugs from hitting the streets. Millions of dollars' worth of drugs that will harm a lot of people."

"I embarrassed you?" My dad's face paled and I would've felt bad about that, too, except I was too far gone.

I was remembering all the times my dad hadn't

listened to me in the past. All the times I had to play peacekeeper between my parents. All of the times I was pressured to live a life I didn't want because my dad was too selfish to see how miserable I was.

"You're seriously asking that? You were so insane yesterday, Weston had to tell you to leave. Today you grilled Alec like he was some terrorist holding me hostage. If Jonny hadn't come in, you were still going to refuse calling the police to tell them I was okay. Which meant I was going to have to do it."

"I'm worried about my daughter," he snapped.

"Really? And were you worried about me when you were gone for four months and didn't once check in with me? Did I cross your mind while you were diving off the Galapagos? Were you thinking about me when you were going through the Panama Canal? Rounding Cuba, passing Cancun, Belize? Did you think to call me when you refueled in Honduras? Maybe as you hugged Nicaragua, Costa Rica? No, you didn't. You never do. Dale Coyle thinks of no one but himself and the next great thrill. I'm done, Dad. Over it. I don't care what stupid game you're still playing with my mother. I don't care the only reason you want me to take over your business is so you can rub it in her face. And you know that's the reason. It's not because it is what would make me happy. It's never about me. It's always about you and Silvia and all the ways the two of you can piss on each other. I'm simply the tool you both use. Done. Way done. So done, I want you to leave and after that leave me alone."

My dad stood speechless. He also looked like I'd smacked him. *That* made me feel bad. Weston's arm around my waist tightened just for a second, giving me the support I needed.

"Dad—"

"I'm sorry, Scout."

Then my dad turned to leave and guilt slammed into my chest. I'd never spoken to my father like that, never in anger, never with malintent, proving I was the worst, absolute *worst* daughter in the world.

"Wait."

"I deserved that," my dad started. "But you're always on my mind. Doesn't matter where I am in the world, I'm always thinking about you. Always loving you. Be well, Silver."

And with that parting shot, he was out the door. I stood frozen in Weston's arms replaying my dad's last words. He called me Silver. Not since I was five had I heard him call me by my name. That hurt worse than the look on his face.

"Babe?" When my eyes didn't move from the door, Weston's hand cupped my jaw and gently lifted my chin to look to him. "We'll give him a few hours and if you want, we'll go to his hotel and the two of you can sit down and talk."

"I can't believe I said all of that to him."

"You keeping all of that bottled up inside is not good—it needed to be said. Now that it has, we'll give him some time to think on it and I'll take you over there later."

My face planted on his chest and my eyes closed. Sure my dad was flighty, he was always on the lookout for the next best thing, the next good time to be had, but I knew he loved me. Something ugly was building inside of me, so ugly I wanted to throw up. I'd turned into my mother. I'd said hateful things on purpose because I wanted my dad to hurt the way I did. I wanted him to feel the pain his abandonment had caused me.

My worst fear—I was my mother's daughter.

———

"Got a minute?" My head came up to see Alec standing in the doorway.

I was in Weston's office. After that craptastic scene with my dad, Jonny went back to the station, and soon after, the rest of us went into the office, including Alec.

No one had said anything about me squaring off with my dad, or about what a bitch I had been. At some point, I'd have to apologize, but I was too ashamed and embarrassed to bring it up yet.

Weston had also taken me by the hotel, at which time we'd been informed my dad had checked out. At Weston's urging, I'd called him and the call had gone to voicemail. It was official—I was a bitch and a horrible daughter.

Weston being Weston, gently reminded me I had a right to my feelings and I said what I'd needed to say and my dad would have to deal. I didn't agree, but I hadn't argued. I didn't think I had any fight left in me, not after I'd hurt my dad so badly—the only parent I had who gave a shit about me.

"Of course," I told Alec, trying my best to hide my foul mood. "Come in."

Alec prowled to the only extra chair in the office and that's what he did—prowled. Alec didn't walk anywhere, he was too big, too intense to merely walk. The first time I'd met the man he scared the shit out of me, and each time I'd been around him since hadn't lessened the fear. He looked like he could snap a grown man in half, which meant it would take very little effort on his part to crack me in two.

"We're going over the canal roster looking into the vessels you've highlighted."

"Find anything?" I asked hopefully.

"Howard Sposato," Alec announced.

"Don't know who that is."

"He owns the *Serafina*. The Hatteras you flagged."

"Okay. I take it that's good news?"

"Far from good news. The Honorable Howard Sposato was the associate judge for the first district court before he became the chief judge for the district court of Maryland."

"Oh, no."

"Sposato also has strong ties to Avon Chapman, as in Sposato was Chapman's attorney before his crooked ass took his seat on the bench."

"Crooked?"

"McKenna found the money trail. They're all fucked."

"What does that mean?"

"It means Chapman paid your buddy Gary, but the money came from Sposato. It also means Jason Scott is fucked because he's a dumbfuck who thinks he's untouchable, therefore he uses his phone way too much. He made a call to Avon Chapman last night and he didn't hide the fact he was pissed they lost the product from the *Dora B*. He bitched for twenty minutes how his guys were getting antsy, because no product means they got nothing to sell. If his soldiers got nothing to sell they're not making money. Low-level scumbags have no loyalty, they'll find another crew that will keep them supplied so the money's not cut off."

"So it's over?" I asked even though I didn't want to hear the answer.

Over could mean heartbreak.

"It's over," he confirmed and my heart sank. "You did good, Silver."

"Thanks," I muttered.

"You didn't have to get involved. You could've kept your suspicions to yourself. You could've turned a blind eye. And after what happened on the *Dora B* you could've walked away. But you didn't. You stayed the course, pushed through. And because of you, two very powerful men are gonna go down. You saved lives. So when I say you did good, Silver, I mean you did *good*."

He was right, I could've ignored all of those things, but then I wouldn't have been able to live with myself. No way I'd be able to look in the mirror every day knowing I was a coward.

"See something—say something."

Alec's lips twitched before they tipped into a smile and I was momentarily mesmerized. I'd never seen the man smile. But when he did, it transformed his whole demeanor. He was handsome even when he scowled, but when his features softened and his eyes crinkled he didn't look so scary, therefore he looked approachable and really good-looking.

"You should smile more."

The words had barely left my mouth when his smile faded.

"How are you doing with everything?" Alec asked and I wished I kept my mouth shut. I had a feeling the DHS agent didn't smile all that often—if ever.

"Great. As you said, two powerful drug dealers disguised as upstanding citizens will be—"

"I'm talking about your dad," he cut me off.

"Oh." My eyes slid to the wall behind Alec. "Well..."

I had no idea what to say and I wasn't sure how I felt. Sure, I'd told my dad to leave and I'd said some pretty shitty things to him. but he was my dad—shouldn't he have at least stuck around to try to talk to me again? But he didn't. He gave up and went home. That hurt. I couldn't imagine giving up on my child, especially after an outburst like I had. Wouldn't he want to try to get to the bottom of my verbal attack? Find out what was eating at me that I would say such awful things?

"Not my business, but the way I see it, you had a

lot of shit built up. The problem with burying shit is when the cork pops, it boils over. And what fizzes out is never pretty. Now it's out in the open and you and your dad can start repairing the hurt."

"Not sure he'll be receptive to repairing anything. He took off."

"Don't have kids, which means I'm not a father, but I suspect he needs a minute to lick his wounds. He knows now he did you wrong, and that has to kill. Give it some time."

"I behaved like my mother this morning. I was nasty and bitchy. Worse, I did it on purpose."

"You need to give that to Weston, let him help you dig that load of shit out before it festers."

Weston. Right. I'd already piled enough of my psychosis on him. He didn't need anymore of my crazy.

"Like you said, this is over. I'm no longer in danger—"

"What does that have to do with anything?"

"Well—"

"Silver." Alec stood, not letting me finish my explanation. "Straight up, now that this is over, if you turn your back on Weston, you are not the woman I thought you were."

That felt like a punch to the gut.

"I think you have it backward. Now that I'm safe,

he has no reason to put up with me. There's no reason for me to be in Maryland. There's no reason—"

"For someone who's fuckin' smart, you're not too bright." His insult didn't sting—it sliced through me. "Let me tell you a secret about Weston, he doesn't *put up* with anything. And if you think he let you into his life, he wound you up with his team, with McKenna, put you in his bed, only to cut you loose when this shit was over, you're seriously not the woman I thought you were."

"You don't understand," I bit out, getting super-pissed Alec was being so mean.

"I damn well do. I get you're scared. I get you were thrust into an extreme situation. I get things around you are moving fast. But mostly, I get you're insecure as fuck. I know, Silver, because it's written all over you. I know because, while you are damn good at your job, smart as hell, beautiful, and courageous you still hide. I know because when I look at you I see myself. I also know what it means to lose something because you can't see what the other person sees. Clue in, Silver, before *you* push away a good man."

Alec didn't allow me to respond before he stalked out, leaving me sitting behind Weston's desk surrounded by the things that meant the most to Weston. I didn't move mainly because I couldn't.

Alec's accusation stunned me. But his admission did, too. He saw himself in me. And that sucked for him. And sitting there frozen, I began to realize just how much it truly sucked to be paralyzed by your past. I *was* insecure.

And if I wasn't careful, I'd lose Weston.

21

Something had happened, and whatever it was had Silver pulling into herself.

Weston had come back from picking up lunch and found out in the thirty minutes he'd been gone, McKenna had wrapped up their case in a tidy bow, and Alec had taken the intel and gone back to DC.

He was also told that Alec had informed Silver. Instead of being happy that Alec was making the necessary arrangements for Howard Sposato, Avon Chapman, Jason Scott, and Gary Goldbloom to be picked up, she seemed upset.

While Weston was contemplating what to do about Silver, a bond skip had been punted to Gemini Group, taking his attention. The skip was believed to be in Montgomery, Alabama. As he read the details of the case an idea came to him. It was a federal case, meaning the Marshals Service would pick up the skip and take him back to New York. It was a low-risk corporate case, the skip was not thought to be a danger to himself or the community.

The more Weston thought about his idea, the more he wanted to give this to Silver. The more he wanted to give it to himself. Now all he had to do was convince her to take off a little more time from work and come with him.

Thirteen hours in the car with Silver alone sounded perfect. Getting her away from all the shit that had infiltrated her life, even better. The added benefit was while they were in Alabama, she could meet his parents.

So with all of that going on in his head, he hadn't had a chance to suss out what was bothering her. But now they were home—alone. Holden was at his place and Chasin out doing whatever it was Chasin did. Probably hanging with Jonny. The two of them did that a lot, met up for a beer, which meant they were carousing. Weston knew, because he'd gone out with the two of them a few times and that was exactly what they'd been doing.

It was time to figure out what was wrong, even if Weston was fairly certain he knew.

"You ready to talk now?" he asked.

Silver was sitting on the couch in front of him, eyes on the TV, Weston behind her with his arm over her resting on her hip. They'd eaten dinner then settled in the living room to chill. When he felt her body go solid, he figured the time he'd allowed for her to unwind hadn't been enough.

"Babe?" he encouraged.

"I'm insecure," she whispered.

"Didn't miss that, sweetheart."

His answer in no way made her relax.

"I have a temper."

He knew that, too, so he remained silent.

"I'm stubborn, not because I want to be right, but because I'm tired of people walking on me."

"People...or Dale and Silvia?"

"Dale and Silvia," she admitted.

His hand flexed on her hip, encouraging her to continue.

"My mom was nasty and mean. I've turned into her."

"You haven't," Weston returned.

"She'd say stuff just to hurt my dad. Like I did today."

"You are not her."

"She knew what buttons to push, the perfect thing to say for maximum damage."

"You're not her, Silver," he repeated.

"But I am. I did that to my dad today. I was a bitch and I knew what I was saying when I was saying it and I knew it'd hurt him. That makes me her."

"Not even close. You said what you said to your dad, not because you wanted to hurt him. You said it as a daughter reaching out to her father. A man who, while he loved her, didn't do right by her. You bottled all of that up for so long it was bound to explode. And when it did, you finally gave him what he needed to hear."

"That's kind of what Alec said."

In a moment of weakness, jealousy crept in. Weston knew Alec was not the sort of man to move in on another man's woman, but that didn't mean he wasn't wary of the reasons Silver had opened up to Alec.

"What else did Alec say?" Weston inquired, trying to keep his tone even and his body still.

"He said, I needed to give you that."

"Give me what?"

"How I was feeling about my behavior. He said I needed to give it to you before it festers. He said if I didn't stop being insecure I was gonna lose you."

Relief washed over him—she was giving it to him. She wasn't hiding, wasn't pushing him away, and wasn't being stubborn. Straight-out she was giving Weston everything he wanted—all of her laid bare.

The feeling was heady. It was warm and it slid over him, making him even more certain. Treasure. He'd found it.

"You're not gonna lose me."

"I will if I don't stop holding back because I'm scared."

"What are you scared of, sweetheart?"

"I'm scared that now that I'm no longer in danger you won't want me."

Fuck. She believed that. Truly and deeply down to her bones she felt that fear.

Totally unacceptable.

He was done having this conversation on the couch where someone could walk in at any moment. But more importantly, Weston wanted to look at her while they were having it. He knifed up, taking her with him. Brought them to their feet and headed for the stairs. Uncaring the front door was unlocked and the TV was still on, he guided them and didn't stop until he was in their room.

Theirs.

Silver stood motionless as he yanked her tee over

her head, tossed it on the floor, pulled off his, and dropped it. He did the same with both of their jeans, her panties, and his boxers. And finally, he unclipped her black lacy bra and let that fall to the floor.

Weston wasted no time pulling the covers back and helping Silver into the bed. She remained silent, her big pretty hazel eyes trained on him, no looking away, no hiding, no bullshit.

He settled in over her, his hips in the cradle of her thighs. Weston took a moment to marvel in the moment. The first time he had her fully under him, with only one last thing between them. Something he planned to obliterate.

"Tell me why you're scared," Weston demanded.

Silver's eyes widened at his question, her mouth opened and closed a few times before her brows pinched together and she finally muttered, "What?"

"Why do you think I wouldn't want you?"

"You wanna talk about this now?" The shock on her beautiful face was clear.

"Tell me."

"I can't think when you're on top of me and I'm naked."

Weston smiled at her candor.

"Try, Silver, it's important."

"Maybe we should put on clothes if you want to

talk about this." Silver squirmed under him brushing her sex against his half-hard cock.

"Please stay still," he groaned. It took a full ten seconds before he had himself under control and could continue. "No hiding," he reminded her.

"Putting on clothes isn't hiding."

"I want nothing between us when we're having this particular conversation. Completely bare. Stripped of everything. Both of us, Silver. Tell me why you're scared so I can return the favor."

"You're scared?" Her face scrunched like it was beyond the realm of possibilities he'd be scared, too.

"Scared shitless. Scared that I found something so precious and all I want to do is keep hold of it but I'm afraid of it slipping away. I'm scared because I've never met a woman that meant something to me and now that I have I'm worried I'll do something to fuck it up. I'm scared because I'm falling in love and it's unknown and uncertain. So, yeah, Silver, I'm fucking terrified you'll rip my heart out. But, baby, none of that is gonna stop me from continuing to take us to a place where neither of us will be scared anymore."

"I don't think I'm scared anymore," Silver blurted out and Weston jerked in surprise.

"You wanna explain that?"

"I was scared that once you didn't have to protect

me we'd be over. I'd go back to Delaware. You'd stay here and all of this would just be a really great memory."

"I told you that wasn't gonna happen. I told you I wanted to explore what was between us."

"I know you did. But I was still scared." Silver's long lashes brushed under her eyes and Weston gave her the time she needed to gather herself. When she opened her eyes they came to his—clear, unguarded, open. "I'm insecure."

"But you're not scared anymore?" he asked for clarification.

This was really fucking important—the last thing between them, her fear. And Weston knew he needed to get this right, needed to make sure the path was clear to take them where he wanted. He couldn't have her holding back, and he didn't want to. He wanted her to fall, and when she did, he needed her to know she'd have a safe place to land. That when she was ready to give him her heart, he'd take care of it.

"Knowing that you're scared, too, makes me not scared. Knowing you feel the same way I do, takes away the uncertainty. Knowing I'm not alone in the fear, settles me." Silver shrugged and continued. "I was scared I was falling in love with you but afraid you'd figure out I was more trouble than I'm worth."

He fucking hated when she said shit like that. Hated her mother with a burning passion. Hated even more that Silver had lived with it her whole life.

"Sweetheart, your mother's shit didn't cause scars on your beautiful flesh, she injected that shit deep. So deep, I know I got some time before you believe me, and I'll keep saying it until you do. You are not Silvia. You're not what she said you were. I see you, Silver. I see how strong you are. How wicked smart. How accomplished. How beautiful. How caring. How loving. How funny. How stubborn. And when you puzzle all of that together, all the pieces that make you, you. What you get is so blinding, so fucking gorgeous, so priceless, you are worth more than any sunken treasure your dad could ever unearth. And you are mine. My Silver. My treasure. All of you, mine."

"Does that mean you're mine?"

"Fuck yeah, it does."

Her full lips tipped up into a smile and her green-ish-brown eyes danced. Goddamn, the woman was crazy-beautiful. And his. Silver shifted under him, her hands going to his ass and her nails dug in. That was when Weston's thoughts turned carnal. Gone was the heartfelt conversation, though it would make what came next even better.

His eyes dipped to her pink lips and he figured he

deserved a gold medal for the best control known to man. Lips that were made not only for kissing but for wrapping around his cock. Something he thought about a lot.

"Are you gonna keep staring at me or are you gonna kiss me?" she whispered.

"I'm gonna kiss you, then you're gonna watch me when I go down on you. After that, I'm gonna watch as you take my cock."

That earned Weston a full-body shiver, something that his cock hadn't missed. Weston's mouth was on hers when she muttered, "Finally." Weston didn't take the time to smile. He had more important business to see to.

22

I was dizzy.

Weston's lips and hands had been everywhere. He'd started with a bruising kiss that would've melted my panties had I been wearing any. Then his lips moved to my neck, then both of his hands came to my breasts, pushing them together, paying close attention to my nipples, sucking and nibbling until I was wiggling and begging him for more. Then he'd moved lower, dragging his tongue down my stomach and finally much lower. He'd tossed my legs over his shoulders and feasted.

He was relentless in his pursuit. Mouth, tongue, fingers. He'd engaged all three and I was helpless to hold back. It would've been embarrassing if it hadn't been so fucking glorious at the speed in which he brought me to a screaming orgasm.

But he didn't relent, not when my hands tugged at his hair, not when my hips bucked, not when I pleaded with him to fuck me. He kept going, torturing me, building me back up.

I couldn't take it.

I was dizzy with it. I needed him and I needed him right then.

"Weston," I panted between moans. "Please, honey. I'm ready." He flicked my clit and I jolted. "Now, Weston. I need you, right fucking now."

He pushed up, forcing my legs to fall from his shoulders, and before I could beg anymore, he was looming over me, mouth on mine, his hand working between us. Then I felt it—the head of his cock pushing through my wetness.

My back arched and my hips tipped up in invitation. He slowly rocked into me, still kissing me rough. The mix of the sensations kept me on the edge. So opposite, I didn't know what to concentrate on. Both felt great, both made me dizzy.

I tore my mouth from his and begged, "More."

"No, baby. I don't want to hurt you."

He sounded hungry and suddenly I felt brave. The

sound of his voice, knowing he wanted me as much as I wanted him, empowering.

"More," I demanded, and locked my legs around his hips using all the strength I could muster to bring him closer.

"Silver," he growled and surged forward.

The force of his thrust taking my breath, I was full of him, so full I thought I'd burst. His hand came to my breast, thumb and forefinger to my nipple and pinched. The pain turned into a sizzle and my clit pulsed.

"Oh my God," I panted.

Weston slid out to the tip and asked, "Can you take it?"

"Yes. More."

He drove home, but this time didn't wait, he pulled out, pushed in, and plucked and played with my nipple. I lost track of time, lost track of everything but what Weston was doing. I felt it all. The way his thick cock stretched me, the way the engorged head of his cock rubbed inside of me, a place so wondrous, every time he bumped it I screamed out in ecstasy.

"More?" he grunted and the sound made me shiver —from my toes to my fingertips. "Yeah, my baby wants more. I want your hands on me, Silver."

Momentarily I felt stupid, I'd been lamely fisting the

sheets. But when my hands went to his back, the strain of his muscles under my palms, all the power I knew he was keeping under control—suddenly I wanted him to lose it.

Unleash it.

"Harder, honey."

Weston rocked into me harder, driving faster, rougher, stealing the oxygen from my lungs, building something so big I knew when it broke I'd fly apart.

I wanted it.

I wanted him to have it.

"You need my finger on your clit?"

"No. Harder, Weston. Fuck me harder."

"Get there, baby, I'm close," he grunted.

My pussy spasmed, clutching his cock, I felt a gush of wetness, and then with four limbs wrapped around Weston, I flew apart.

Millions of tiny pieces.

"Fuck," he growled, and shoved his face in my neck.

He was still fucking me rough, my orgasm still pulsing through me, not letting up, or maybe a new one was building, maybe I was floating or dreaming, because nothing could feel this good.

"Please," I moaned. So delirious I wasn't sure what I wanted or needed.

His hand moved under my ass, lifting it off the bed,

tilting it, the new angle making him go deeper and my body locked tight and something so magnificent tore through me it couldn't be called an orgasm, it was something else, something more. I didn't just feel it in my pussy, or my womb, or my belly, I felt it all over. A full-body experience that left my hair tingling and the rest of me on fire.

"Weston!" I screamed, unable to hold back. I shook, my hips bucked, trying to prolong the sensation.

As the orgasm started to leave I couldn't stop the whimper. Weston heard it, squeezed my ass, and planted deep, groaning his orgasm.

"Silver, baby." His words sounded painful, like they were ripped from his soul as he spilled into me.

I felt that, too. Every shot of come as his cock twitched and pulsated.

It might have been seconds, or minutes, or an hour later. However long it was, I wished it had been forever. Me lying under Weston, both of us catching our breath, coming down from a high so high, even in my limited experience I knew it was not normal.

Weston started to slowly stroke in and out, his hand that had been on my ass now on my thigh, gently rubbing his thumb back and forth.

"Goddamn," he muttered against my neck. "Knew you'd be perfect. Knew it before I even kissed you,

you'd be wild. Knew we'd be good together. Never been more wrong."

I went stiff wondering how I could've felt something so wonderful and he didn't. I was so stupid to think I'd be enough for Weston. He was used to women who didn't have to be told what to do with their hands. Who would know how to please him.

My heart sank.

"I'm..."

Shit. What was I? Sorry I'm bad in bed. Sorry I didn't know what I was doing.

"So goddamn tight and wet I was fighting, getting you there first."

"What?"

"Knew it'd be a struggle, knew it the first time I had my fingers inside you and your pussy so tight I had to work to get two in. Knew the way you got wet, your excitement dripping down my chin how hot you were. But, babe, I had no clue the feel of your pussy squeezin' my cock would be so goddamn good that within seconds I'd be ready to blow. No idea how fucking good it would be when your come coated my cock I'd have to fight off the need to fuck you so hard you'd be feeling me for a month."

Through all of this, Weston kept gliding, giving me sweet strokes. And then I stopped thinking about the sweet he was giving me and started to get excited again. Wondering what "so hard you'd feel me for a month" would be like. Then I was thinking he'd gone at me pretty hard and was shocked he could go harder. But I knew I wanted to know what that felt like.

"You doing okay?" His head lifted and his fabulous brown eyes were sated and lazy.

"Yeah."

"Did I hurt you?"

"No."

"I was rough." He was and I loved every minute of it. "You like rough."

It wasn't a question, it was an observation and my face heated.

Then even though he already knew what I was going to tell him, I admitted, "I don't know enough to know what I like. But I loved what you gave me."

Something big happened. Weston's eyes heated, his hand on my thigh tightened, and the pulse in his neck started to throb. Being as I was already slightly embarrassed reminding him of my lack of experience, I went whole hog and continued.

"And I'd like to know what 'fuck you so hard you feel me for a month' is like."

A lascivious smile graced his handsome face, one that made my pussy spasm and my clit throb. Holy smokes, he was hot, and hotter when his still-hard dick jerked inside of me.

"Then we'll explore that. But now I want you soft and slow."

"What?"

"I gave it to you rough, sweetheart. Should've given you sweet our first time. Fucked that up when I slid into your warm pussy and lost my mind. I'm gonna rectify that now, and give soft and slow."

I guess I was wrong, he didn't care I didn't know what to do with my hands.

"Now? But you finished."

"Finished?"

"You...um... you..."

"Shot my load?"

My face was on fire and Weston noticed because his smile widened.

"Yeah, that."

"Babe, my dick is still inside of your sleek pussy, hard and ready for more. You up for that?" Was I up for it? Hell, yeah. "You're up for it." He answered his own question and adjusted his hips, losing some of the slow but somehow keeping the gentle.

"How do you know?"

"Legs tight around my back, Silver."

I did what he asked and locked my ankles. His

hand went into my hair, keeping me where he wanted me as he lowered his head.

"How did you know?" I whispered.

"Because you're so tight, I can feel every twitch. I know you liked it when I told you I had to fight to keep control. I know you loved it when I told you it was sexy as fuck when your orgasm coated my cock. I know because I can feel your pussy convulse."

"Oh."

"And make no mistake, I fucking love it."

Weston's mouth came to mine, his tongue pushed in and he got down to the business of giving me slow and gentle while his mouth gave me hard and rough.

It was no less good. My orgasm was no less earth-shattering. The only difference was when I shouted my pleasure I did it with Weston's mouth on mine, meaning I got to experience his as he groaned it against my lips.

When he was done rocking my world, he gave more sweet, this time in the form of kisses—my jaw, my throat, the side of my neck, my lips. After that, he rolled off the bed, went into the attached bathroom, and came back with a wet washcloth.

He sat on the bed next to me, tapped my thigh and my eyes went to him.

"Open your legs, sweetheart."

"Huh?"

"I need to clean you up."

I clenched my thighs together as hard as I could and shook my head.

"That's okay. I can do it."

"Babe." He grinned. "I've had my face between your legs, my tongue in your pussy." My face flamed. I knew it because I felt it and because he chuckled. "I know you down there better than you know yourself. Every fold, every—"

"Stop," I groaned. "I get it."

"Then spread for me, babe."

"I'll do it," I repeated. Thankfully Weston was silent and didn't give me another detailed description of where he'd been and what he'd seen. But he wasn't moving so I continued. "This is different."

"Different how?"

"I don't know. But it feels personal, just different."

"Doesn't get more personal than me inside of you," he started. "How 'bout this? Let me do it this time. If you hate it, I won't do it again. But this time, I want to take care of you."

There was something in the way he asked that made me spread my legs. This meant something to him —cleaning me after he'd taken me. And he was right, there was nothing more personal than what we'd done.

If I hated it, I'd tell him. But this time, I'd let him do what he wanted.

He pulled my leg wider and gently started to swipe the warm cloth against my sex. My eyes fluttered closed, not because I was embarrassed, I wasn't. His ministrations were soothing, I felt cared for.

"Didn't use protection, Silver."

My eyes popped open and I stared at him staring at the space between my thighs.

Shit. *Shit.* Shit.

"I'm not on birth control."

He nodded and his gaze came to mine. "I'll glove up next time. If you want to go on the pill and are cool with no condoms we'll do that. If not, I've got us covered."

There was a lot there, all of it good, mainly the fact he didn't look panicked we'd just had sex twice without protection and pregnancy was a possibility. A real one, considering it was about ten days until my next period. *Fuck.*

"You wouldn't mind if I didn't want to go on birth control?"

"Your body, your choice. I'm certainly not gonna complain about a condom if that what's needed."

"I'll go on the pill."

"Right." He chuckled. "Your choice."

My choice. I loved that.

"What if...I mean, I'm supposed to start my period soon. I'm not entirely sure but I think this is about the time in my cycle where I can get pregnant. I could get the morning-after pill."

No sooner had the suggestion left my mouth Weston's entire body strung tight, his hand stopped wiping me clean, and his eyes became guarded.

What the hell?

"Is that what you want?"

"I'm just saying it's an option—if you want."

"Your choice."

That felt awesome, too, but it kind of wasn't only my choice.

"It's not only mine when we're talking about something that would be yours, too. I appreciate the sentiment but you have a choice in this."

Weston was quiet for a long time. He finished between my legs and tossed the cloth on the nightstand. Still deep in thought, he tapped my leg and I was grateful he was done. I felt exposed and vulnerable as I waited for his answer, not sure how I felt. Either option was life-changing. One answer and there would be a very real possibility a baby would be a result of our lovemaking. The other would mean, there wouldn't be. It was too soon to be thinking about babies and the future, so I knew the thundering in my chest was ridiculous. But it was there and I couldn't stop it. What if he told me to take the pill? Would that mean he wasn't ready now, or did it mean he didn't want kids in general, or just not with me?

"I don't want you to take the morning-after pill." The breath I was holding whooshed out. "But the choice is yours and whichever decision you make I support a hundred percent."

I didn't want to take it and I knew I'd only offered because I had to give him that option.

"I don't want to either."

"Right. Then we deal when the time comes."

"You seem awfully calm about this," I told him. "Isn't this something most men would freak out about? I mean, I'll be honest, I'm kinda freaked out."

"Why?"

Was he nuts?

"Well, let's see. I just had phenomenal sex—times two—with the hottest man I've ever seen. We didn't use protection, which means there's a chance I could be pregnant and it's been less than a week since we stopped throwing barbs at one another. I think if there was ever a time to freak out it would be now."

"Then it's a good thing by the time we find out if

you're pregnant we'll have been together going on a month."

Yep, he was nuts. Arguably crazier than I was and that was saying something, because since all of this started with Weston, I'd questioned my sanity a million times.

"I think you're missing the point."

"Silver, I want kids. Lots of them. And if they came out with your pretty hazel eyes, all your beauty, your intelligence, and your strength, I would not complain."

Okay, all of that felt good. So good, I let the warmth of his crazy declaration settle over me. But he was still nuts.

"Um, Weston, I like all of what you said—a lot. But don't you think maybe you should be freaking out, too? It's really soon to be having this conversation. It would seriously make me feel better if I wasn't alone in this."

"You're not alone," he returned. "And this might freak you out more than you already are, but not only does the thought of you carrying my baby *not* freak me out, but it fills me with so much fuckin' joy it hammers home what I've known all along."

I was afraid to ask, I really was, but I needed to know. "What have you known all along?"

"That you're it for me. You're the one. I knew it, I was sure. But hearing there's a chance that what we just shared created a life and the fact that I am elated should tell you I know what I've found and I'm not ever letting it go."

I stared up at Weston, calm as he could be, no fear, no regret, no second thoughts.

How did this happen? How did it happen so fast? How did Weston Beil know exactly what I needed to hear to ease my fear? But the best part was, he wasn't just saying those words, he felt them.

"Okay." I drew in a deep breath. "We'll deal with it in a few weeks."

His face lit and his sexy smile appeared. And when it did I prayed that if I was pregnant, our baby got his smile, and maybe his warm brown eyes, too.

23

The call came just before dawn, and Weston rolled to grab his phone off the nightstand. Silver was tucked to his side, the same place she'd been when they'd gone to sleep. Something Weston liked a fuckuva lot. His woman liked maximum body contact when they slept.

"Lo," he muttered when he placed the phone to his ear.

Silver started to move away but Weston tightened his grip, not wanting to lose her bare tits, bare thigh, and hand resting on his chest.

"Just got word from Alec," Nixon started, sounding like he, too, had been woken up. "Takedown was successful. Three are in custody. No casualties."

"So it's done?"

"It's done. Silver's safe."

Weston let that settle before he continued. "What's next?"

"Chasin will work with Alec to see who else they can bring in. You're after the skip. Holden and Jameson are working a case with Jonny and I'm left to enjoy my future wife."

"Fucker." Weston chuckled. "I'll let you go so you can get on that."

"Right. See you in a few hours."

Nixon disconnected and Weston tossed his phone back on the nightstand and wrapped his arm back around Silver.

"Everything okay?" she mumbled.

Fuck yeah, everything was perfect.

"All your hard work paid off. Takedown was a success."

"That's good news."

"It is."

Silver's hand started moving. No longer shy and timid, she knew exactly where she was going and didn't delay. Her dainty fingers wrapped around his cock and she started stroking.

"You want more?" he asked, his cock already getting hard.

"Yeah," she whispered.

He rolled them so they were on their sides, her

back to his front, his arm snaked around, and he found her puckered nipple.

"You have great tits," he said to the back of Silver's neck and she wiggled her ass against his hard-on. "You ready for me or do you want me to eat you first?"

A full-body shiver. Fuck yeah, his woman was responsive. Not only to his touch but to his words. She couldn't hide anything.

"I'm ready," Silver moaned as he kept playing with her nipple.

"You sure, baby? I could roll to my back and have you ride my face."

This time Silver didn't shiver, she quaked, and she wasn't hiding her needy little mews. So fucking sexy, his Silver.

His hand moved lower and she automatically opened her legs to give him room. His fingers toyed with her clit before they circled her opening and teased.

"So fucking wet for me, baby. You want my cock or my fingers?"

He played with her pussy—not penetrating, just gathering wetness as it leaked.

"Your cock."

Weston nearly shot off.

"Honey, I need you." Silver punctuated that need

by reaching between her legs, knocking his hand away and grabbing his dick.

"Take what you need, Silver," he said through gritted teeth.

She was struggling to get him where she needed him, her sighs of frustration not only cute as hell but hot as fuck. Weston tilted her ass back, lined himself up, and in one thrust drove home. Silver's fingers still between her legs and Weston not being a man to ever let a golden opportunity slip by, covered her hand with his.

"I'm gonna ride you hard, Silver, you ready?"

"Yeah." Her moan filled the room and he wondered how it was possible after two really great back-to-back orgasms he was ready to blow so fast.

"You're gonna play with yourself while I fuck you."

Her pussy convulsed and it was Weston's turn to groan. "Goddamn, Silver. Nothing better. Not in my whole life has anything felt as good as your pussy huggin' my cock."

Weston adjusted his angle and gave her a few short, sharp thrusts.

"Rub yourself, baby. I wanna feel your fingers playing with your clit."

Silver did as she was told and just as Weston had expected she went wild. Her ass snug against him, his cock pounding deep, her fingers moving fast. She bucked, moaned, and fucked herself the best she could with the limited movement Weston allowed.

"Next time you play with yourself, you're doing it while you're riding my cock so I can watch."

"Whatever you want," she moaned.

Whatever he wanted. Christ.

"You want me to watch?" he asked, though her pussy had quivered so he knew the answer.

"Yeah, I want to ride your cock while you watch."

Jesus.

He took his hand off of hers, moved it back to her tits, and honed in on her nipple rolling between his fingers.

"More," Silver panted and he smiled.

Yeah, his woman liked him rough.

"You gonna be able to find it or you need my fingers to help?"

She rubbed her clit harder and bucked back. "I can find it. Hurry, Weston, I'm almost there. Harder."

Weston stopped holding back and gave his woman what she wanted. He powered into her, hard, rough, and unrelenting. He did it bare, he did it until she shouted her release calling his name, then he fucked her until he found it and returned the favor moaning hers, spilling himself inside of her. And when he did, he knew with crystal clarity that whether it happened the first time, the second time, or the third time, or if it happened five years from now, one day Silver would carry his children.

And that didn't freak him out. Not one single bit.

It was a long time before Silver finally spoke. It was after he'd given her slow strokes, bringing them both down from their orgasms. It was after he kissed her neck, her cheek, and when she turned her head he claimed her mouth.

"Who knew," she muttered.

"Who knew what?"

"Who knew an orgasm could be that good."

Weston smiled and buried his face into her hair, inhaling deeply, loving the floral scent of her shampoo.

"Pleased it was just as good for you as it was for me."

"That wasn't good—that was awesome." His body started shaking with silent laughter. "Seriously."

"I agree, baby. You good sleeping like this?"

"With you still inside of me?"

"Yeah."

Silver's ass pressed closer and he figured that was his answer, but was happy when she added. "Yeah, I'm great just like this."

It wasn't what she said that made him happy, it was

the breathy wonder. Like she was more than okay to keep their connection for as long as she could.

"Go back to sleep, baby."

"Okay, honey."

Silver's breath evened out and within minutes she was out. Weston did not find sleep right away. He laid awake behind her, not wanting to close his eyes, not wanting to miss a single moment of her in his arms. He spent his time memorizing the feel and smell of her. He knew he wanted this for the rest of his life, hoped he got it, and if he did, he wouldn't need the memory. But he still took the time.

"I'M NOT sure this is a good idea." That was Silver. She and Weston were in the Suburban Gemini Group owned on their way to Alabama.

It had taken Weston five minutes to tell Nixon he was taking Silver with him. Then it had taken him thirty minutes to convince Silver to come with him. The second she'd agreed, he'd taken her upstairs to pack, then shuffled her out to the SUV, and loaded her up.

"Do you think I'd ever put you in a situation that was dangerous?" he returned.

"No. And like you said, I'll be in the hotel waiting for you. It's not like I'm going to apprehend the skip with you. Though that might be fun."

Weston did his best to keep his groan silent—maybe this hadn't been a good idea. Silver was fearless, and he could see how she'd think it was fun. Hell, the woman had thought tracking drug runners by herself was a good idea, too.

"Silver," he growled. "You're not coming with me to pick up the skip."

"Jeez, keep your pants on. I just said it sounded like fun."

"Then what aren't you sure about?"

"Meeting your parents."

Taking one hand off the steering wheel, Weston reached over and laid the back of his palm on her thigh and waited for Silver to take it. When she did, he threaded their fingers and brought their combined hands to his mouth, kissing the back of Silver's.

"Never brought a woman home to meet my parents," he told her.

"Never? Really?"

"Not a woman. They met a few girls in high school but not one after I graduated."

"Why not?"

"Never had one that mattered." They went back to

silence for a beat, then Weston went on. "My parents are good people. Hard-working. Average. Normal. You have nothing to worry about."

"I've never met anyone's parents before. And as you know, I'm not accustomed to normal, average, good people. I was raised by Dale and Silvia."

Weston hated that shit for her, hated it was a constant in her life.

"Trust me. You got nothing to worry about."

"Okay," she mumbled, not sounding convinced.

"Do you think I'd bring you to meet them if I thought there'd be a problem?"

"No."

"Right. So stop worrying."

Weston felt Silver glaring, and when he glanced in her direction, he found he was correct. Her puffy, full lips pursed together, her eyes narrowed. It was a cute look but Weston knew her, therefore he knew she was gearing up for a snit.

"You know," she said conversationally. "Just because you tell me not to worry doesn't actually mean I'll stop worrying."

"It should."

"It should?"

"Yep. I told you, you have nothing to worry about so just stop."

"It doesn't work that way," she snapped.

Weston scanned the traffic in front of him trying his best not to laugh. The woman could argue about anything. And when she tried to snatch her hand from his, he held fast.

"Why not? You don't know my parents. I do. I'm telling you they're cool. They'll treat you with kindness and respect. So again, babe, you're working yourself up for no reason. Relax, enjoy the road trip. And hopefully, by tomorrow night we'll be sitting at my mom's table and she'll pull out all the stops. Then you'll see you were worrying for nothing."

"You can say that because *you* do know them. I don't, so between now and then I'm gonna worry."

"Suit yourself," he conceded.

"What?"

He tried, really he did, but the shock in her voice was too much. It started as a chuckle but when Silver grunted and unsuccessfully tried again to pull her hand from his, Weston erupted into laughter.

"I don't see what's so funny."

"I know you don't," he said through his hilarity. "That's what makes it funny."

"So it's funny because I'm nervous about meeting your parents? It's funny I want them to like me? But more importantly, I want them to like me for you? It's funny because I'm scared if they don't like me then that means you'll stop liking me, because they're important to you? All of that is funny, Weston?"

He sobered immediately. There it was—the root of her concern. No bullshit. No hiding.

"Babe, I don't know how to make this any clearer to you. I know they'll love you simply because I do. But also, it will take them all of five minutes to figure out all the reasons I do, and see you for exactly who you are. A beautiful, challenging, intelligent woman who makes their son happy. They'll get it and they'll like that for me. They'll like it for you. Neither are dumb and it takes less time than you think to see the hurt you guard. Both will see that and both will move in to give you what you need to stop guarding it and start healing it. That's the type of people my parents are."

"Love me?"

It took Weston a moment to understand what she was asking. And when he did he smiled. Of course that was what Silver would hone in on and he wondered if she'd heard anything else he'd said after that.

"What exactly do you think's going on between us?"

"Um...I...well..."

Damn, his Silver was cute when she was clueless.

"Straight up. We had a conversation less than

twenty-four hours ago about there being a possibility I planted my kid inside of you. Not long after that, I took you again bare. No protection. I spilled inside of you, uncaring that if I hadn't knocked you up the first two times, I could've that time. During that conversation, I thought I made myself pretty damn clear I wasn't freaking out because there was nothing to freak out about. I thought I was also clear that I wanted kids, and I wanted those kids to look like you. So with all of that, you're seriously asking me if I love you?"

"Well, you never said you did, so how was I supposed to know?" she shrieked.

"I don't got a bunch of kids roaming the streets and baby mamas I pay child support to, so I think it's a pretty safe bet, I'm damn careful. And the fact that I was not careful with you, should be a pretty fucking big indication you mean something to me. But if that wasn't, me taking you again after I knew you weren't on birth control and still let loose inside of you should've been a huge, flashing, red neon sign that said I loved you."

"That's crazy. And you having sex with me without a condom doesn't say I love you, it says you're a man and wants himself some and doesn't have time to roll on a condom."

"Never in my life have I been so turned on I didn't have time for a condom."

"Well, maybe I'm just special that way, you were more turned on with me."

"You're special all right," Weston blurted through his amusement.

"You're laughing again," she angrily noted.

And he was, his body shook with it, the sound filled the SUV, and try as he might he couldn't stop it.

"I am," he unnecessarily confirmed.

Silver made a strangled sound and muttered, "You're an ass."

"Stubborn," Weston returned.

"I'm not being stubborn, Weston Beil, but if you don't stop laughing when I'm having a mild freak-out you're gonna see stubborn in a way you've never seen it."

"Right." He chuckled.

"And don't you even wanna know if I love you?"

It took Herculean effort not to bust a gut at her annoyed question. Only Silver could fight about them loving each other.

"I know you do," he told her.

Silver's hand in his spasmed before she growled, "Arrogant much?"

"Nothing arrogant about it."

"It totally is. You just assume because you're good-looking and have superpowers in the bedroom I'd fall madly in love with you."

He let the good-looking and superpowers comments go, though he was keeping those in his back pocket for a later date. Something he'd use to tease her with.

"You were madly in love with me before you had my cock and I know it."

"You're crass."

"Maybe."

"And annoying."

"Probably."

"And infuriating."

"Yet you still love me."

"Whatever. How much longer until we stop?"

Weston checked the road signs and was calculating when their next stop would be when Silver broke the silence.

"You're shaking with it again. I swear if you laugh at me again I'm gonna be pissed."

"Can't help it, babe, you're hilarious."

Then he laughed again. And Silver pretended to be pissed. It lasted all of fifteen minutes. Then Weston caught her smiling.

24

"Hands and knees," Weston growled against my pussy.

We were in the hotel room. He'd just finished licking me clean after he'd feasted between my legs. I scrambled to the position he wanted and waited.

His big hand spanned my hips, holding me steady as he plunged into me.

"Fuck, yeah," he groaned and my pussy spasmed around his thick cock.

His body curved around mine, one hand playing between my legs, the other rolling my nipple, his mouth at my neck.

"How rough you want my cock, babe?"

"Rough."

"Hold on, baby."

I was holding on.

"You're gonna feel me next week, Silver."

Yes! I wanted that.

"You're gonna feel me and know how much I love your pussy."

I wanted that, too.

"Fuck, you're wet, baby, it's coating my cock and dripping down my balls."

I probably was—that was how turned-on he made me.

"Tight, sleek, and hot."

Through all of this, Weston wasn't giving me rough, he was giving me slow, gentle glides. I loved it, all of it, but I wanted him wild. Out of control. Mindless.

I pushed my hips back as he thrust forward and moaned when he pressed deeper.

"Harder, honey."

"Fuck," he groaned and pulled himself upright. His hands going back to my hips, the pads of his fingers digging in, he was gonna leave a mark, and I was looking forward to that, too. "You need my hand to get you there?"

I knew what he was asking, and miraculously I didn't think I'd need either of us touching my clit to get me off.

"No. Just your cock."

"Fucking love it when you talk dirty, baby."

I didn't have time to say more. He left me speechless as he pounded into me.

Breathless. His cock created magic. Rough, hard, bliss.

By the time I shattered—which was quick, no clitoral stimulation needed—I was boneless. Weston was not, he was energetic and finished with me on my back, his face shoved in my neck, and my legs locked around his hips.

Then like always, he gave me sweet.

He barely had me settled, pressed close, my head on his chest, our legs tangled, and his hand resting over mine on his chest when he spoke.

"Too rough?"

"Perfect."

"Need you to tell me if I'm taking you too hard."

I'd gone from boneless, sated, relaxed to high alert in a millisecond. Weston was always concerned about me, but there was something different in the way he was asking.

"I'm the one who begged you to go harder," I reminded him.

Weston fell silent and I did, too. I was lost in the feel of his heart beating under my palm, enjoying the rhythm, the warmth, the way he cuddled me close.

My mind drifted back to the car ride and our ridiculous argument over him knowing I was in love with him. How he knew, I still didn't know, but I was glad he did. It helped that he'd told me, without actually telling me, that he loved me, too. The more I thought about it—the silliness of me being able to turn anything into a fight—the less I could stop the giggle.

"Babe?" Weston's hand on my hip tightened and I laughed harder.

"I love you," I announced through my giggles. Weston went stiff under me and I couldn't help it, that was funny, too. He probably thought I'd finally cracked. "I love you and you love me and I..." I had to stop speaking because my entire body was vibrating with humor. I could barely breathe through it. Tears had started to form and threatened to spill. "Fight about it." I finally got out.

Weston said nothing, he held on tight until I finally burned myself out and stopped laughing.

"I love you, Silver."

My breath caught and now the tears that were rolling down my cheeks were different—not from the mirth of my stupidity but from happiness Weston said straight out he loved me.

"I love you, too," I whispered.

That earned me another squeeze. But something still wasn't sitting right. Something I couldn't let go.

"Why'd you ask me if you were too rough?"

"Because I don't want to hurt you."

"You wouldn't hurt me," I gaffed at the absurdity.

"Not intentionally," he conceded. "But I..."

"You what?"

"Tend to lose control when we're together. I don't ever want to do something you don't want to do, or hurt you, or make you uncomfortable."

"You don't. Where's this coming from?"

He blew out a breath and I didn't like my big, strong Weston sounding unsure. He was never unsure, he was always in control. Always strong.

"I'm sure it's not lost on you I know what I like. I have no problem asking for it, demanding it even." I nodded against his chest because it wasn't lost on me he was bossy in the bedroom and I loved it. "I don't want to talk about my past but to say, I'm finding I'm different with you."

"Different how?" I asked, but hoped he didn't give me examples because I really didn't want to hear about the women he'd been with.

"Different in a way, that when I'm demanding, I seriously get off on it."

It was safe to say, I was not understanding.

"What does that mean?"

"Babe, when you are naked, my mouth on you, my cock inside of you, something deep inside of me clicks into place. When I tell you to spread your legs for me and you look at me and all I see is trust staring back, and you open yourself up to me, it fills something I didn't know was missing. But then I want to demand more. I want to push you and see how far that trust extends. Every time I ask something of you and you do it, swear to God it's a gift, but I want to take more. I want my hands fisting your hair while I fuck your mouth. I want to hear the crack of my palm when it rains down on your ass. I want shit I never thought I did, and moreover, I want it so fucking badly, it scares the shit out of me. I don't ever want to lose control and hurt you."

I took a moment and waited for the mini-orgasm from his words to subside while I tried and failed to find the words I needed in order to explain—not only wasn't I worried he'd ever hurt me, but I was turned way the hell on.

In the end, I found I couldn't find the words, so I did something bold. Something that before Weston, before he showed me he liked—no, loved—me for who I was, I'd never be able to do.

I climbed atop him, my hands going to his chest, and I kept my center off his lap.

"Touch me." His head tilted to the side in question and I sucked in a breath preparing to say something I'd never said outside of making love to Weston. "Take your fingers and touch my pussy."

Immediately. Instantly. His brown eyes heated and he was gonna miss my point if he didn't hurry because that look alone was turning me on more.

Weston's hand moved, his finger teased my opening, and his heat turned into hunger.

"Fucking drenched," he growled and I shivered.

I nodded.

"You trust me to take you where I want to go?"

I nodded again.

"I need the words, Silver."

"Yes. I trust you."

"Grab my cock, and guide me inside."

With my hand shaking and my body trembling I did what Weston asked. His hands clamped onto my hips, stopping me from slamming down.

"Slow, baby."

He didn't let go as I slid onto his cock slowly. His eyes flashed approval when I waited for him to tell me what he wanted next.

"I want you to ride me nice and slow, with your fingers on your clit."

My pussy spasmed and his face got tight. "Fuck, but I love that."

I knew he did, I did, too. I loved more that he told me he did. Every time it happened he didn't hide his appreciation.

His hands squeezed my hips and I started to move on his lap, my finger going between my legs. I waited a long time for his eyes to leave mine, for him to look down and watch me play with myself, but he never did. Our eyes stayed locked. Between his cock filling me, my finger teasing my clit, and his eyes on me, I was ready to explode. It was frustrating as hell, Weston refused to allow me to go faster. My orgasm was dancing just out of reach.

"Faster," I panted, not above begging. Not that I ever was with Weston.

"Slow."

"Weston, please. I need more."

"Move your hand and lean forward."

Yes!

His mouth brushed against mine and his hands went from my hips to my ass. One hand moved between us and I felt him touching where we were connected, then it was gone and his finger was circling my hole. My body locked and I froze. No one had ever touched me there. Not ever. And that was by choice.

"One day I wanna take you here." He kept circling. "Keep riding me, Silver."

I came out of my stupor and started moving, still very unsure of what was happening. He kept adding pressure but my orgasm was no longer dancing—it was barreling fast and furious.

"Faster, baby," he demanded. "You gonna let me take you here?" He pressed in the tiniest of fractions and my hips bucked, my orgasm *right* there. "I get you on all fours, eat your pussy first, get you wild for me, you'll let me take your ass."

I pressed my face into the crook of his neck and I don't know what came over me. I bit down as my world exploded. He gave me more of his finger in my ass, thrust up into me as I slammed down, prolonging my orgasm. It was dirty. Naughty. Forbidden. But I knew I was going to let Weston take my ass.

"*Fuck*, baby. Grind down harder."

With my teeth still sunk into his shoulder, blinding flashes of light behind my eyelids, I fucked him harder.

"Goddamn, treasure. My treasure," Weston grunted and held me to him.

That time I didn't get to feel his cock swell, or the ropes of come throb from his dick. I couldn't feel anything because I was in shambles. Broken apart. But I wasn't worried. I trusted Weston would put me back together.

———

THE NEXT MORNING I awoke in a fog. Sun was shining into the room through unfamiliar sheer curtains, lighting unfamiliar cream walls.

"Babe?"

"Sorry. Took me a minute to remember where I was."

We were still in the same position Weston had put us in last night. Naked. Me on my side, my back to his front, his heavy arm around my waist. I loved that Weston cuddled. That he wanted me close even in sleep.

His arm tightened around me and I wiggled my bare ass against his lap.

"Took you rough last night," he weirdly started.

"Yeah."

"That means this morning I take care of you. We'll take a shower, get you something to eat, then before I go, I'll run you a warm bath."

That seemed odd, that I'd need a shower and bath so I told him so.

"Don't think I'll need a bath after we shower."

"The shower's because I need one before I head out and I want you with me. The bath is for you to relax."

That was sweet. I liked he wanted me to relax, though I wouldn't because if all went well today and he caught his man, we were headed to his parents' house. Though I wouldn't bring that up and start another argument. Not only because it was silly, it didn't matter how many times Weston told me not to worry, I was still going to. But also because he had to get on the road and catch a bad guy.

"Okay."

"It's a miracle she's agreeable," he muttered to himself.

"*She* won't be for long if *he* continues to be an arrogant ass about it."

"Wouldn't want that, now would we?" He chuckled.

"I don't know, would we?"

Weston's face pressed into my hair and I heard him inhale.

"Are you smelling me?"

"Yep."

"That's weird."

"Nothing weird about smelling my woman.

Nothing like waking up to the smell of sex and flowers."

"Are you saying I stink?"

Weston's big body started shaking so hard my body had no choice but to quake with his. It felt nice—so nice I forgot I was gearing up for an argument.

"No, baby, I'm saying you smell fucking great."

"Sex doesn't smell good."

"Says who?"

That was a good question. I didn't know exactly who says that, I just knew that it was said. At least I thought people said that. But now I wasn't so sure.

"I don't know. But sex is sweaty and there's an exchange of bodily fluids."

"Bodily...fluids." Suddenly Weston wasn't pressed against my back, he was on his, roaring with laughter. Now not only was *he* shaking, making *me* shake, but the whole bed was moving with it.

"Weston!" I shrieked.

"Babe, give me a minute."

I didn't give him a minute. I sat up and stared down at him.

His hair was messy and I knew part of that was because my fingers had been in it. And I knew my fingers had been in it because his mouth had been between my legs, but also because he'd been on top of me. Then my eyes traveled over his smiling face and my heart squeezed. But it was when my gaze traveled over his chest that my insides clenched.

The shock of it all, big, strong, hot, Weston loved me. *He* loved *me*. Months and months of hiding I had some weird crush on him fueled by frustration and anger. Sometime during my perusal, the bed had stopped moving and my eyes went back to Weston's face.

"Good morning," I whispered.

"Indeed. Shower."

I wasn't ready to get up but had no choice when Weston rolled off the bed, reached back in, and yanked me to my feet.

"Bossy," I mumbled as he guided us to the bathroom.

Ten minutes later I was standing under the warm spray, Weston's soapy hands roaming my body. From top to toe he gently washed me. He shampooed my hair, ran conditioner through it, and rinsed it. Never had anyone taken care of me, the way he was.

"You feeling okay?" Weston asked, turning me so we were face-to-face, his hands on my hips, mine went to his shoulders.

"Better than okay," I answered but my concentration was on the bruise my teeth had left on the skin above his collarbone.

"I meant here." Weston's hand went to my booty and tapped my cheek. If it was possible to burst into flames I would've.

"I marked you." I felt my face heat further.

"Wild," he muttered.

"Did I hurt you?"

"It would suck, baby, if you weren't into as much as I was. You letting go, with my finger in your ass, sinking your teeth into my skin, was hot as fuck. So, no, you didn't hurt me. But you didn't answer my question. You okay with what I did?"

"Yeah."

"Is that a yeah because you know it pleased me, or is it a yeah because it felt good?"

"Because it felt good," I whispered.

Weston hauled me closer, our fronts touching, his thick erection trapped between us, resting on my stomach.

"I was serious about taking you there. I want that, Silver, but I want you to want it just as bad."

Until that moment I wasn't sure if it was possible for me to want it as bad as Weston did, but when his dick jerked between us I couldn't deny my pussy trembled thinking about his reaction.

"Have you ever—?" I started.

"No. Never had the desire."

"Me either," I told him.

I liked the thought of Weston and me sharing something that neither of us had done. A first for both of us. I knew he'd make it good, and I wanted to try it.

"I want it just as bad."

His mouth crashed onto mine, his tongue plunged in, and by the time he was done taking what he wanted it was a good thing I was getting a bath because the area between my legs was drenched.

25

_____

Silver was quiet and Weston knew why.

She was no longer anxious about meeting his parents even though they were in the SUV after checking out of the hotel and on their way.

It was because it had taken Weston very little time to track the fugitive, but the man had decided to put up a fight. A fight that included using a gun. Luckily for Weston, the other man was a high paid executive who wore a suit to work—that was, before the man lost his job for embezzling money—and had no knowledge of how to actually aim the gun he'd pointed at Weston.

The man fired one shot before Weston tackled him. The unfortunate part was Weston now had a bullet graze to his hip. The low caliber weapon barely kissed his skin, leaving only an abrasion that did not require stitches and looked more like a burn. Which was exactly what it was.

But Silver was tweaked.

He knew it not because she'd freaked out when he'd gotten back to the hotel, taken off his clothes to take a shower, and she saw the injury. No, it was because she'd grown quiet.

"You know I'm okay, right? It doesn't even hurt."

"I know," she mumbled, staring at the passenger window.

"Babe?"

"Yeah?"

"Look at me."

He felt her gaze on him and glanced in her direction before his eyes went back to the road. This was not the ideal time or place, while he was driving and couldn't give her his full attention, but it also couldn't wait. And not because they'd be to his parents' house in ten minutes. Silver had started to revert back to the closed-off woman he'd first met and there was zero chance Weston was going to allow it.

"Drop the mask and tell me what you're thinking."

"I'm not thinking about anything."

"Bullshit."

"What do you mean, bullshit? You're not in my head. You don't know what I'm thinking about."

Here we go.

"You're hiding, Silver. The mask is firmly in place. Drop it and tell me what's got you freaked out."

"You know, it's supremely annoying when you say shit like that. I'm not hiding. There *was* nothing wrong. Now there is because you're acting like an ass."

Stubborn.

"Drop the fucking mask, Silver," he barked.

Weston felt the air in the cab crackle and he did not need to look at her to know she was pissed.

"I'm scared," she blurted out.

Relief washed over him. He was getting somewhere.

"What are you scared of?"

"Of you."

What the fuck? Weston's relief was short-lived, his gut twisted and his chest hurt.

"Baby." He softened his tone, no longer annoyed now but extremely concerned he'd done or said something that would frighten her. "I'd never hurt you."

"Your job is dangerous."

"Sometimes."

"Not sometimes, all of the time, Weston. It's always dangerous."

He was confused. Silver had had a front-row seat to everything his job detailed the day he'd rescued her from the *Dora B.* And before that, she'd sat through briefings where the dangers of the operation had been laid out for her, all of the reasons he'd recommended her being sidelined. It was no secret what Weston did for a living and it had never seemed to bother her. As a matter of fact, she hadn't batted an eye when they'd discussed the deaths of three drug dealers who'd held her captive.

"Where's this coming from? None of this is new."

Weston waited. Knowing they were running out of time, he pulled into the next gas station and parked, needing to get this straight before they showed at his parents' place.

"Silver?"

Her head snapped toward him, eyes squinted, anger clear.

"Why can't you leave this alone? Why do you always have to push? I don't want to talk about this right now. Just let it be."

"I wouldn't have to push if you'd stop fuckin' hiding and start being honest with me. When shit's eating at you, we talk about it."

"I don't want to talk."

Her arms crossed over her chest and she set her eyes toward the windshield and huffed.

Jesus Christ, the woman drove him crazy when she was being hard-headed.

"I take it you didn't learn a damn thing about keeping shit bottled up. So I'll remind you, Silver, you lock it down, it festers. And when it finally makes its way out, it's too late. It's eaten a hole inside you. That's not a place I'll allow us to go. Straight up, shit's bothering you, we talk. Whether you want to or not, I'll dig and I'll dig until your stubborn ass caves."

"So it doesn't matter what I want? It's Weston's way or no way?"

"With this? Yes. Because my way means you get pissed, you burn hot, then we work it out. Your way means you sweep it under the rug, it burns for a long fucking time, making you miserable and making my job a fuckuva lot harder when you finally break and tell me what's wrong. And, sweetheart, we haven't scratched the surface of fixing all the poison your bitch of a mother left inside of you and now I see we got some work to do in regard to your dad. What we do not need is you having issues with my job. Which leads to you telling me you're fucking scared of me."

"So you think of me as what, a project? Poor broken Silver, trying to piece her back together."

"What the fuck?"

Weston's insides were boiling. Never had he insinuated or even hinted he thought she was broken.

"That's what it feels like. Perfect Weston riding in to save the day."

"That's fuckin' jacked and you know it. Take a minute, check the attitude, stop being a bitch, and remember who you're sitting next to."

Silver's door flew open and she jumped out. *Fuck.* It took Weston two seconds before he was out of the SUV and making his way to her side. It took another ten seconds to have her back pressed against the passenger door, her eyes on his, and shock clear on her face.

"Step back," she demanded.

"No fucking way. You had space when we were sitting in the truck. You jumped out, now you get none. Tell me what the hell had your head so fucked-up you're spewing venom."

"You called me a bitch."

"I did."

"That's not cool."

"You're right it's not. And I'll apologize for it after you tell me what the fuck is going on inside your head."

"I can't do this."

Weston reared back, Silver's verbal strike hitting center mass, causing a painful explosion in his chest.

"Come again?"

"I can't do this. I wasn't thinking. I was so caught up in you, I forgot."

"Forgot what?"

His hands itched to reach out and shake the words out of her. However, the anguish her words caused rooted him in place, too afraid to move. There was no way he'd been wrong. Not about any of it. He'd known Silver loved him before she'd said it. He'd felt it, the knowledge had settled deep in his soul, and he wasn't going to let this take it away. It didn't matter how fucking stubborn she was, he would fight her, fight *for* her, until she broke.

"Forgot about your job. Forgot how dangerous it was. Forgot that you'll leave me, just like everyone else. Only with you, it's gonna hurt worse. It's gonna kill. I can get over my mother leaving me because she never loved me. I get past my dad always wanting to chase some stupid adventure, leaving me behind because he never showed me half of what you have. But when you abandon me, when you leave, it will destroy me. I forget everything when I'm with you."

Weston was no longer frozen in place, he moved fast and when he did, he yanked Silver to his chest and wrapped his arms around her.

There it was, entrenched deep into her soul—*when you abandon me.*

He'd missed it, the root of everything. He'd been wrong thinking her mother's constant belittling had left Silver with insecurities. That was only part of the issue, the surface scars.

"Baby, I will not abandon you," he whispered.

"If something happens to you, you will."

"Nothing's gonna happen to me."

"It did today. Something happened. You were shot and—"

"I wasn't shot. It's a graze and I'm not leaving you."

"You can't promise that."

Silver was trembling. Straight up shaking like she was breaking apart in his arms. He drew in a breath and took a moment to calm down. All the anger had ebbed, leaving him with extreme concern.

"Sweetheart, I cannot predict the future. I can't promise I won't be hit by a bus tomorrow. I can't promise you that my job won't put me in another situation that's dangerous. What I can promise you, is I will not *ever* leave you of my own free will. I will not walk out on you. I will not chase some stupid adventure without you by my side. I will not abandon you. I will not take my love away from you. I swear it, Silver. I swear on my life—you're stuck with me. Stuck, baby, glued to me, tied so tight that if you stop a minute and think, you'll remember."

"I'm scared to lose you."

Weston's eyes closed as her painful admission scored his flesh but at the same time made him feel like he was on the top of the world.

"I'm not gonna leave you."

"But—"

"Never, baby."

"You can't—"

"Love you, Silver, down deep to my soul. I fucking love you so hard there's not one goddamned thing that's gonna take me from you. Believe in it, baby. Trust me— all you have to do is trust me and I swear I'll never let you down."

"I'm sorry," she sobbed. "Sorry I'm so crazy."

Sweet fucking relief. She was back, the stubborn-ness had ebbed. Thank fuck. With his arms wrapped around her, he soaked in her warmth, her love, and her pain. He'd gladly take it all if it meant he had all of her, he'd endure anything.

"You got nothing to be sorry for and you're not crazy. But we're standing in a gas station parking lot. You think you're ready to get back in the car?"

"No. I need to feel you holding me."

Thank fuck she trusted him. Believed in what they

were building and would continue to create. Layering more and more on top of the strong foundation they'd constructed.

His Silver.

His treasure.

26

Okay, so, I'd had another freakout.

This time in the parking lot of a gas station ten minutes from Weston's parents' house. Not only was the timing horrible, it was a doozy.

"When will it stop?" I asked with my face still pressed to his chest.

"Don't know, just know it will."

God, I loved him. He totally understood.

"I don't do it on purpose."

"I know you don't, baby."

Of course he knew, Weston seemed to know everything. Which reminded me, I had a huge plate of my favorite dish to eat.

"I said some pretty shitty stuff, I'm sorry. It was

totally uncool and you were right, if I would've calmed down, we could've talked about it without getting ugly."

Weston's hand moved up my back, over my shoulder, then tipped my chin up.

I would never get used to the way he looked at me. Each time it was a gift, each time told me something different. He hid nothing from me. He never withheld his concern, his love, his passion, his need, not anything. His honesty was the one thing that held me together. In some ways, it meant more to me than knowing he loved me and he'd protect me.

"Shouldn't have called you a bitch, told you I'd apologize for that, and I am sorry. But, I am not sorry I pushed you. I know we're gonna battle it out, I know there are times it's gonna get dirty, we might have to roll around in the mud a time or two. And I don't give a shit as long as when we stand back up, we do it like we are now. With you in my arms and us making progress." He dipped his head and brushed his lips against mine and I was grateful he did. It took the sting out of what he said next. "Something you said that sliced deep was that I thought of you as a project. I know you were upset, you were hurting, and you were scared, but I need to know right now if that's how you really feel."

Tears started to sting my eyes. I'd hurt him—*really* hurt him. He showed me that, too. Didn't hide that my careless, bitchy words had cut him.

"I'm sorry, Weston. I didn't mean that. I was thoughtless and bitchy, and I promise I'll try to never do it again."

His hands moved to cup my cheeks, his thumbs brushing the tears away as they fell. Through all of that, his eyes never left mine. He was studying me, reading the veracity of my statement. I didn't move—I owed him this time.

"Good, baby, let's get back on the road before my mom sends out a search party." I flinched at his statement and Weston's head tilted. "Silver—"

"I'm not gonna freak out. I just feel bad we're late. Not the first impression I wanted to make."

"I was joking. Mom and Dad understand my job is unpredictable. I didn't tell them an exact time."

I nodded because that was a good thing. Weston hadn't planned on the detour to the florist, nor had he budgeted time for a second stop to the liquor store. And he certainly hadn't taken into consideration at both stops I'd pitch a fit when he refused to allow me to pay for his mother's flowers or the bottle of his father's favorite bourbon.

I'd given in both times, if him pushing my hand

away and thrusting his card at the cashier was considered giving in. After the bourbon debacle, I would've let him have it and was fully prepared to demand he stop acting like a macho, alpha asshole, when he calmly explained I was taking an unpaid leave of absence from work. I also had all new household wares and furniture to buy in the near feature and I didn't need to be wasting a hundred dollars on a bottle of liquor.

That meant I'd spent the next hour thinking about my apartment and what I was going to do with its contents and where I wanted to live instead of thinking about who drank bourbon that costs a hundred dollars a bottle. In that hour I was no closer to figuring out where I wanted to live or how I was going to start my life over—buying everything new—but I did come to the conclusion I couldn't ever live in that apartment again. Not after someone had been in there, totally violating my privacy and security.

"Yeah, I'm ready," I finally answered.

With a gentle lip touch, Weston pulled away and helped me back into the Suburban. Why I'd jumped out in the first place was a mystery. What, was I going to make a mad dash and run home? *So embarrassing.*

Weston pulled back onto the highway and immediately my nerves started. I wanted to drill him about his parents, ask if there were any topics I should avoid. I had a hundred questions but I didn't ask. I figured I'd made myself look crazy enough for one day. Instead, I decided on a safe topic, like my job.

"I only have four days left until I'm back on rotation." I told him something he knew, considering not only had I used his phone to call my boss, but I'd already talked to him about what was said.

"Yep."

His clipped reply had my head snapping in his direction. He didn't sound all that happy about me going back to work, less so now than he had when I first told him.

"I was thinking on our way back, we could stop and get me a phone. Work will issue me a new one, but I still need to replace my personal one."

"We'll stop."

"Everything all right?"

He didn't answer and every second that stretched made my stomach uneasy.

"Weston?"

"We're here."

Weston parked at the curb and I glanced out the windshield wondering which house belonged to the Beils. The neighborhood was beautiful, all of the homes well-kept, with perfectly manicured lawns and colorful flowers still in full bloom.

I didn't have to wait long before a stunning, older woman stepped out onto a porch, a beautiful, broad smile I'd seen plenty of times when Weston grinned at me.

"Ready?"

"You're sure they're gonna like me?"

Weston's lips twitched and he nodded. "Positive." His hand shot out, hooked me around the back of the neck, and his mouth met mine halfway. "Everything's gonna be fine," he murmured before his lips were on mine.

The kiss was hot, involved tongue, but short. I wasn't sure if I was disappointed as I always was when Weston pulled his lips from mine, or thankful he had the self-control not to make out with me while his mother was watching from the porch.

When his eyes danced with knowing humor, fully understanding my dilemma, he winked. And it was then I decided I was totally disappointed.

"Later," he mumbled, and righted himself in the seat before he cut the engine and pulled the keys from the ignition. "Wait until I come around."

This wasn't the first time he'd opened the door for

me. He'd done it each time we'd stopped and if I thought about it, he always came to my side of his Jeep. Even if there wasn't a door to open, he still helped me down. I liked that, liked that he was always considerate.

We were halfway to the porch, walking hand-in-hand, Weston's mom now rocking on her heels excited to see her son, when Weston leaned down and whispered in my ear, "Brace, babe."

"What?"

"Didn't want to freak you out more than you already were but my mom's a hugger."

"What's that mean?"

"Brace."

That was all he said as his mom practically skipped down the two steps off the porch and threw her arms around Weston's shoulders. His hand in mine squeezed before he let go to return the embrace.

"My boy's home!" she exclaimed.

"Jeez, Ma, you're acting like you haven't seen me in a decade."

"It's been almost a year, Weston Francis," she scolded, and I couldn't stop the giggle from slipping out.

Weston Francis.

It was downright hilarious—my big, bad, former Navy SEAL was getting the full-name reprimand from his mother.

"Now you're embarrassing me in front of my woman."

Mrs. Beil pulled back ignoring Weston completely and smiled up at her son.

"You look good. Happy."

There was no missing the excitement in her tone.

"I am."

"I'm glad." Her hand came to his cheek and gently gave it a pat. "So glad."

"You think maybe I can introduce you to Silver now?"

Mrs. Beil didn't move. She simply stared up at her son smiling. So much love shone it hurt to see. There was so much adoration pouring from that one look, my insides soured and something ugly started to roil. My mother's poison churned and slopped in my belly.

That was how a mother looked at her child. That was what parental love felt like. That was what I'd been missing.

I knew it was big, I knew I'd gone without something important growing up, but until that moment standing in Mr. and Mrs. Beil's front yard, I hadn't known exactly how huge it was.

Weston's hand was suddenly on my cheek, something he'd done so many times I'd lost count. A touch I treasured, but until then I didn't know the depths of its meaning. It was tender, loving, something his mother had done to him probably a million times over his lifetime, now a gift he gave to me.

"Babe?" Warm, sweet, brown eyes bore into mine. "You good?"

I nodded and gave him what I hoped was my biggest, brightest, reassuring smile, even though I wasn't sure I was good.

"Yeah."

And just to prove I was all right, even though I really wasn't because I'd just been punched in the gut with something so profound I could not breathe, I turned to Weston's mother before he could make the introductions and I took over.

"Hi, Mrs. Beil. I'm Silver. It's a pleasure to meet you."

I extended my hand, she glanced at it, shook her head, and then yanked me forward with jarring force and wrapped her arms around me.

Her hug was almost as good as her son's. But just almost, because no one's arms felt better than Weston's.

Then she pulled back, her hand went to my cheek —exactly like she'd done to her son—exactly like her son had done to me moments before—and she smiled at me. Her look soft, friendly, motherly—not the same but close to what she'd given Weston. Tears pricked my eyes. I thought it was beautiful watching her give that to her son. I was wrong. Now that I had all of it pointed at me, I realized it wasn't beauty, it was so remarkable there wasn't a word in the dictionary to describe it.

"Silver," she breathed my name like she was testing the sound, found she liked it and smiled brighter. "Of course it would be an ardent beauty, a precious treasure, that would bring my boy home."

I sucked in an audible breath, trying to fill my lungs with oxygen to stop the painful burning.

"And please call me Margie," she finished as if she just had shaken me to my core.

Treasure.

With another sharp embrace, she let me go and Weston was there to claim me. And thank God he was. My knees were weak, my legs jelly, my heart hammering, and my world rocked, I couldn't stand on my own.

"Jeez, woman, you just couldn't stop yourself, could you? The poor boy hasn't even gotten his girl in the house!" a voice boomed from the porch.

"Quiet, Len. I haven't seen my son in ages."

"Well, now you have. So how 'bout you let them in so I can say hello to *my* son?"

"Bossy," Margie mumbled and I giggled.

Weston's arm around my shoulders tightened and I looked up at his smiling face.

"Now I understand where you get it from."

"Right." Weston's lip twitched. "You ain't seen nothing yet, sweetheart."

I wasn't sure if he meant him or his father's bossiness but I didn't have time to ask because we were moving up the steps, across the porch, then into the house.

I also didn't have time to look around the beautiful interior before Weston's father pulled me from Weston, held both of my hands in his, gave me a once-over from top to toe before he loudly declared. "Passed all the right genes down to my boy."

"Um..." I didn't know what to say to that because I had no clue what the man was talking about.

"Len!" Margie snapped. "That is rude. And sexist."

"Woman, how is a man complimenting a pretty lady, sexist?" Len returned.

It's important to note that during this exchange, Len was still holding my hands and he hadn't stopped looking me dead in the eyes. *Dead on.* It was hard not to squirm, he looked so much like Weston, save being thirty years older. But the intensity in his gaze was the same. Searching. Knowing. So I gave Len the only thing I could give him—all of me. I let go of my social mask, the one that Weston hated so much, and let Len see the real me.

I knew it worked when Len's brown eyes, the ones he'd given his son gentled. He saw me and for once in my life, I wasn't afraid he'd exploit the pain. I wasn't scared he'd walk over me. I knew Len, like his son, would protect the soft spot.

"There is more to a woman than her looks," Margie continued.

"Know that. I gave that to my boy, too, great taste in women. That means the woman standing before me is not only beautiful but smart. Bet she doesn't put up with his shit, either."

"Mouth!" Margie shrieked and I pressed my lips together to stifle a laugh.

"Jesus. Can we not freak my woman out? Dad, give me Silver."

Len ignored Weston's request and jerked me to his broad chest and wrapped his arms around me in what was an arguably better hug than his wife's. But only because when he held me, I felt the same umbrella of protection I did when I was in Weston's arms.

"Mighty pleased you're here, Silver."

"Pleased to be here, Mr. Beil."

"Len," he corrected.

"Len," I whispered.

Needless to say, I wasn't freaking out anymore, worried Weston's parents would hate me. Now I was in a panic, because they seemed to like me, and I really loved that they did.

27

Weston watched as Silver charmed the hell out of his parents. Margie Beil wasn't easily impressed, but Silver had the older woman eating out of her hand. He'd never doubted his parents wouldn't welcome Silver and see exactly who she was to him. However, it had taken his father less time than he'd thought it would for Len to see the pain Silver tried to hide from the world.

Though it had shocked the shit out of him, Silver hadn't hidden it. Not from his mother when she'd cradled Silver's face and tears had formed from the foreignness of motherly affection, and certainly not from his father when he was openly studying her. Silver had let it all hang out. And just as Weston had suspected, his father saw it, didn't like the pain in her eyes, and had already moved in to do his part in eradicating it.

Damn, but he loved his folks. They'd been good parents, patient and supportive when he was growing up, but what they were giving Silver proved they were straight-up good people.

"Are you sure you don't want to stay the night?" Margie inquired for the hundredth time.

"'Preciate the offer, Mom, but I told you, we need to get a few hours in tonight before we stop. Silver goes back to work in a few days. We need to get back," Weston reminded his mom for the *hundredth* time.

"But—"

"Woman, they need to get back. And even if they didn't, do you think they really wanna sleep in the room next to us?"

"Len!" Margie snapped.

"Well? Do you? I may be old, but I can still remember courting you and if I had my choice between the room next door to your parents and a hotel room, your hair would've been on fire I'd pull you from the house so fast."

"Len Beil, I swear on a stack of Bibles if you don't stop being such a tactless fool, I'm gonna throw a lamp at your head."

Silver's hand in his flexed before she crumbled into a fit of laughter.

Weston sat motionless enjoying the sound, but mostly he was just enjoying her—carefree, happy, open, unguarded.

In all of the time he'd known Silver, Weston had never seen her so relaxed and at ease. She was always stunning, but seeing her like this was beyond compare. Totally effortless, and he knew if he hadn't already fallen in love with her, watching her laugh at his parents' antics would've done it.

Weston caught his father's smile from across the room, and he knew his old man was feeling it, too. The beauty that was Silver filled the space. It couldn't be missed. A glance at his mother's soft face watching his woman laugh had his chest tight and his heart near bursting.

"Try that, woman, and I'll bend—"

"Don't finish that sentence, Dad." Silver rested her head on his shoulder, her body still shaking with humor.

"It's not funny," he grouched.

"It kinda is," Silver returned.

"We're leaving," Weston announced and Silver wrapped her arms around him, keeping him on the couch as another wave of giggles tore through her.

Weston let that settle in, too. Her tits pressed against his side, her warmth all around him, his parents' laughter joining Silver's. Life was good. The only thing that would make it better was if he'd indeed planted his kid inside of Silver.

———

IT HAD TAKEN APPROXIMATELY an hour to say good-bye, three-thousand promises that they'd be back soon, a hundred hugs, and Silver thanking both his parents five million times before they'd been able to exit the home Weston had grown up in and get on the road.

By that time, Weston had grown impatient—they weren't going to try to drive a few hours tonight. They were hitting the hotel they'd stayed in last night.

"We should've just stayed at your parents'," Silver said.

That was not going to happen. He loved his parents, loved spending time with them, loved how they'd treated Silver. However, he was not staying in his childhood bedroom with his woman.

"You heard what my dad said," was the only explanation Weston had to give.

"I like your parents."

"That's good, baby, seeing as they loved you."

And they did, all it had taken was a few hours with her and the Beils were head-over-heels for her.

"You were right. I had—"

"Say again?"

"You were right."

Weston was happy he was stopped at a red light so he didn't miss the roll of her pretty hazel eyes nor the shake of her head.

"Thought that's what you said. But I wanted to make sure."

"Arrogant," she muttered. "I feel like I say that to you a lot."

"You do, so I'm not sure why you still doubt me."

"If you plan on making good use of the hotel bed tonight, I suggest you stop rubbing it in my face and learn now, I don't doubt you when you say things, I just prefer to learn things on my own."

Weston's grip on the steering wheel tightened as he dissolved into laughter.

"Babe," he said through his chuckles. "That's called stubborn."

"No, what it's called is: Weston's sleeping alone on his side of the bed tonight."

He tried but he couldn't hold back, his head tipped and a roar of hilarity rumbled from his chest.

"That would last all of two seconds before you'd be rolling over to my side keeping me warm."

"We'll see," she taunted.

"Yeah, sweetheart, we will."

"Weston!" Silver panted, yanking on a handful of his hair. "Harder."

He moved his hands from her hips, shoving them under her ass, bringing her higher as he pounded into her sleek, wet, pussy.

Heaven.

"You need my fingers?" Weston asked, knowing the answer—she never did.

"No. I'm almost there."

"Let go, baby."

"Weston!"

Weston had been wrong, it didn't take two seconds for Silver to roll to his side of the bed. It hadn't even taken two seconds for the hotel room door to close before she attacked. Two seconds after that she went wild.

Silver was right—but Weston still won huge.

Absolute heaven.

"Thanks for stopping so I could pick up a new phone."

They were back in Kent County, close to home, and Silver's face had been glued to her phone for the last hour as she set it up.

"And thanks for not arguing about who was gonna pay for it."

"You're welcome." He chuckled.

"Now I have your phone number. I was starting to feel funny having all this ridiculously great sex with a hot guy and I didn't even have his number. At least I knew your last name before we got down to business," Silver teased.

"Yeah, baby, good thing you knew my last name before we got down to the business of ridiculously hot sex."

"So what now?" Gone was the playful woman who'd been joking moments before.

"What do you mean?"

"Real life. We're back in Maryland. I go back to work in a few days. I have an apartment to sort out. The bad guys have been caught. So what now?"

"We haven't been living in make-believe, Silver."

"I know that, *Weston*. What I'm asking is, are you gonna take me home tonight—"

"No."

"No?"

"There's nothing for you to go back to. You'll stay at the farmhouse until you go back to work, and while you're on rotation, the guys and I will sort your place. After it's cleaned out, you can decide what you want to do."

"Well, that's nice of you," she snapped. "I mean, *letting* me decide what I want to do."

"Silver—"

"Do not 'Silver' me. I get that you're bossy. I get that you want to help me and that's nice of you. But you don't get to take over my life."

"Nice of me?"

Weston was keeping a loose hold on his irritation, and by the biting tone of her voice, so was Silver.

"Maybe we shouldn't talk about this right now," she suggested.

He could see the logic in her thinking, it was a smart play, however, he wasn't going to give it to her. They were just outside of town and had thirty minutes to hammer this shit out before they hit the house. And after being on the road for thirteen hours, all Weston wanted was a shower and a bed. He didn't want to hash shit out before he got either of those things.

"You got five minutes to explain to me how I'm taking over your life," he told her.

"I do? Really? I have five minutes? How accommodating of you."

"Serious as shit, right now. I'm too tired for this. Just explain to me how I'm taking over your life and lose the attitude."

"You're an ass."

"You're a fucking pain in mine."

Silence hit the cab of the truck and Weston didn't try to break it. If she wanted to be unreasonable, so be it. It was time Silver learned he could be just as pig-headed as she could be.

28

"I'm going home," I announced as soon as Weston parked the SUV in front of the farmhouse.

He hadn't even cut the engine before I was jumping out of the vehicle and making a mad dash to the back of the Suburban to get my bag. Unfortunately, I wasn't fast enough and Weston's hand shot out and caught mine as I attempted to open the back hatch.

"What are you doing?"

"Quiet!"

I was already pissed, but at Weston's rude demand, I went straight to seeing-red-pissed, the kind of mad that made your blood boil and all rational thoughts flee. Therefore, I also went straight to bitch.

"Don't tell me to be quiet. I'm going home."

Weston stopped dragging me toward the house,

bent and planted his shoulder to my stomach and hefted me up.

That was familiar. It was also infuriating.

"Put me down, Weston!" I screeched and struggled against his hold. "I'm fucking serious."

Weston didn't answer verbally, he didn't need to, not when his big hand came down on my ass with a thud and shocked me into silence.

The door slammed behind us and Weston continued stomping through the living room toward the stairs.

A raucous peal of laughter came from the couch and Chasin glanced over at us and mumbled. "It's like déjà vu."

"Screw off," I returned.

The shock of Weston's slap on my ass now thankfully wearing off, I doubled my efforts and was met with a steel band around my back pressing my belly into his shoulder as he held me in place.

"You're seriously an asshole, Weston. I cannot believe you're doing this."

Silence.

"I'm really, *really*, fucking mad at you."

His bedroom door opened, then it slammed, then I was on my feet face-to-face with a really, *really*, pissed off Weston.

That was precisely the moment I should've checked my attitude and caught on to the feel of the room. But stupidly I didn't.

I was Silver Coyle, stupid, stubborn, and thoughtless.

"You're not the only one, sweetheart," he snarled.

"But I am the only one with a sore ass."

Weston's head cocked to the side, his eyes narrowing. But I didn't stop to take that in either.

"We're done," I announced.

"We're far from done."

"We so are, Weston, you *hit* me." It was safe to say, Weston's eyes were now burning but I ignored that, too. "I'm not even stupid enough to be with a man who puts his hands on me in anger."

"Did I hurt you, Silver?" Not even Weston's voice vibrating with anger pulled me from my snit.

I'd set the course and I was fully prepared to follow through. Though it was safe to say, I wasn't sure what the course was or why I was willing to follow it. My insides were burning, warning me I was pushing too far about something that meant nothing. And it meant nothing because currently I couldn't even remember why I was mad in the first place. I just knew I was and I was stubborn.

"Yes," I blurted out even though it was a partial lie. He didn't hurt me as much as he'd stunned me.

Weston's body jerked like I'd landed a physical blow. "You're a piece of work. You just can't help yourself, can you? You get pissed, and all reasonable, coherent thoughts fly from your head. Straight up, I smacked your ass with the intention of making you stop wiggling before you successfully made me drop you resulting in you hurting yourself. I got your attention, you stopped thrashing. So you cannot stand here in front of me, with a straight fucking face and tell me I *hit* you in *anger* with the intention of *hurting* you. And if you try to, you're a goddamned liar and you know it."

"You shouldn't—"

"Second thing," Weston spoke over me. "In the car, when you suggested we stop talking, I should've listened. I should've remembered that when you get something twisted in your head, there's no untwisting it while you're pissed. I was wrong then and I was wrong when we got home. I should've let you leave."

At that, I flinched and my stomach dropped. I'd pushed too far, I didn't listen to that voice inside my head that told me to calm down and think about what I was saying before I just let words I didn't mean fly out of my mouth and now I was going to pay a hefty price.

I knew it.

I could feel it.

"I didn't want you to leave pissed. I wanted to talk it out and explain what I was thinking about your apartment. But you're all fired up to leave. You're pissed. I'm tired as fuck-all. So there's the door, Silver. Use it."

And with that, Weston went into the bathroom and calmly shut the door behind him.

It was that calm that worried me. He didn't stomp, he casually walked across the room. He didn't slam the door like he had the other two, he simply shut it quietly.

Shit.

Why did I push?

I felt like the world had dropped out from under my feet and I was at a loss. I'd been angry and prepared to battle it out. I wasn't, however, prepared for Weston to give up and walk away.

I started the conversation in the car because I didn't want to go back to my apartment alone but something ugly had bubbled to the surface when he told me what we were going to do. The hell of it was, it was what I wanted. I wanted to stay with him. I wanted the help cleaning out my old apartment. And I wanted help finding a new one. I hadn't even talked to him about not wanting to stay in the place where I now felt scared to be in and felt violated. But even so, he wasn't going to allow me to go at it alone.

What was wrong with me?

I'd gone too far telling him he was taking over my life. And I'd gone way too far accusing him of hitting me and hurting me. When even in my altered state of over-the-top crazy I'd known damn good and well he'd never hurt me.

Talk about getting myself in a pickle I had no idea how to get myself out of.

Somehow I didn't think admitting I was wrong was gonna cut it this time. I thought I seriously fucked up. No, scratch that, I *knew* I did. If I hadn't felt it deep in my soul, Weston telling me to use the door would've sealed it. But I did feel it and it felt like shit.

The door opened and Weston's angry gaze came to mine. I'd hadn't realized I'd stood there rooted in the exact spot he'd left me in long enough for him to take a shower and come out with a towel wrapped around his waist. But I did know I had to try to make this right before I left.

"I'm sorry—"

"Not now."

"Please. I need—"

"I see you've calmed down, but we're not at the part where you apologize, I apologize, and then we move on. But honestly, Silver, I'm not just tired. I'm just plain tired of saying I'm sorry." Good night, that hurt. "Only for the same shit to happen. And I'm not talking weeks or even days later, I'm talking hours. So honest to God, I don't want an apology and I'm not offering one up until you're ready to give me more."

"Give you more?"

"What made you flip in the car?"

"Flip?"

"Flip from sweet and playful to sarcastic and nasty? What did I say that had you so pissed, made you turn so fuckin' fast I could hardly keep up?"

I didn't have an answer to his question so I remained silent, trying to think of why I'd over-reacted the way I had.

"Right," he mumbled, and moved across the room to his dresser.

The towel dropped, but I was so lost in my head trying to pinpoint exactly why I'd gone from joking with Weston to shoring up my defenses to protect myself, I didn't even enjoy the sight of his nakedness. I vaguely saw him pulling on a pair of shorts but I was frozen. Why had I felt the need to protect myself— from Weston?

Why would I fight with him about him giving me what I wanted?

What the hell was so screwed up in my head I'd pick a fight about nothing?

"I was protecting myself," I blurted out what was turning over in my head. "I don't know why. I didn't want to go home. I never want to go back to that place again. I don't think you're taking over my life. But in that moment, it felt that way. I don't know why I felt it or why I said it, I only know I was feeling it."

"I'm not Dale."

"I know you're not."

"No, baby. I. Am. Not. Dale. I'm not him. I'm not taking over your life, taking away your choices. I don't want to be in charge of you. What I want is to make sure you're not alone in a place where you feel unsafe. The easiest way for me to do that is to make sure you're not there when everything is cleaned out. After that, whether you decide to live there or not isn't up to me. What is up to me is making sure the woman I love is not bustin' her ass filling it full of new furniture and doing that shit alone. So, if you've got a problem with that, I suggest you get over it or let's hash it out now. Because what we will not be doing is fightin' about it when I move your new shit up those steep-ass stairs."

"Okay."

"Okay, what?" Weston snapped and I didn't blame him.

I'd done that, I'd made him wary. I'd taught him that when it came to moving furniture, paying for flowers, or bourbon, or anything really, I'd make it into a fight.

"I won't argue about you moving furniture."

Now it was his turn to stare at me in silence and I knew I owed him more so I gave it.

"I also won't argue about you and the guys cleaning out my apartment. You're right, I don't feel safe there. And before I freaked out in the car I was going to ask you if you'd help me find a new apartment because I'm not ever staying there again. Logically, I know you're not my dad. I know you're not selfish and self-centered. I know I don't need to protect myself against you. But I can't help it. It's habit. It's so ingrained to fight against any sort of dominance or control I can't stop it."

My insides still burned with humiliation and guilt. I'd hurt him again. I needed to do the right thing and walk away. I was too screwed up. It wasn't fair to him that I kept putting us through this. I wasn't treasure, I was toxic. Weston was a good man, he deserved better than me. So much better than the shit I kept piling up.

I was so dumb to think I could change. What was inside of me wasn't ugly shit my parents had let in, it was simply just me. I was cut from the same cloth as Dale and Silvia. I was their daughter and had inherited the worst from each of them. And my parents' selfishness mixed together was grotesque and vicious.

"Don't ever walk away from me when you're mad and especially when we're in the middle of talking about something important—no matter how heated that talk gets. And that is not me being bossy or controlling. That's me telling you exactly what I need in this relationship. I need to know you're willing to stand and fight for it. Not cower from what you're feeling."

I felt my eyes start to drift closed. I should've felt some sort of relief he was talking about the future but I didn't. My heart and my head were at war. A battle so devastating I didn't think I'd survive.

"I think—"

"I know what you're thinking, Silver, and you're wrong." My spine snapped straight but I held my tongue, remembering this was Weston and I'd inflicted enough pain. But before I could remind him he was not a mind reader, therefore he had no way of knowing what I was thinking, he proved me wrong. "I know you're planning your retreat. You've twisted an argument into the end of us. You're standing across the room from me thinking that you're not good enough. Thinking that I'm some pussy who would give up something I know is right, know is mine, because I'm so fucking stupid I don't understand what two assholes left inside of you. Further, you're thinking that because I told you to use the door, I was giving up. Which you're gonna warp into me being one more person who abandoned you."

He knew it all. Everything that had been swimming in my head. I should've been scared out of my mind how he'd figured me out down to the very last smallest detail, but I wasn't.

Finally, someone saw me.

Finally, someone cared enough to *see* me.

Finally, I wasn't walking through life invisible.

But that still didn't negate that fact I'd hurt him again. As a matter of fact, it made it worse—way worse.

His hands on my shoulders made me open my eyes and the second I did I wished I'd kept them closed. Brown, soft eyes full of so much care and love it hurt to see, hurt to feel as his adoration washed over me, warming my insides.

"I don't deserve you," I whispered.

"We've—"

"I don't, Weston. I know I don't. I'm so sorry I keep screwing up. I know I have to do better. I know I hurt you. But I can't let you go."

I stood nervous with my heart jack-hammering in my chest. His hand moved from my shoulder, slid up, curled around the back of my neck, and he brought my forehead to his lips before he tucked me under his chin.

"It's a good thing you're not letting me go because I wasn't gonna let you."

"Wes—"

"Let's get into bed, baby. I'm wiped."

"But—" My throat tingled and my body shivered.

"Bed, Silver. Everything else can wait until tomorrow."

Two minutes later, Weston had me in his tee, cuddled to his side. Five minutes after that Weston was asleep—I was not. An hour later I was still staring at the ceiling trying to figure out how I was going to get rid of all the ugly shit my parents left me. Then I realized, it wasn't ugly, it was hideous and more than that, it was dangerous. If I didn't find a way to let go, I'd lose everything.

29

_____

A week later, Weston found himself standing in Silver's bedroom shifting through the papers that were strewn about. The rest of the guys were in her living room and kitchen. He did this with his blood boiling, his gut churning, and his heart heavy. Everything Silver owned lay tattered.

He stacked the papers, probably shit she'd kept in her now demolished nightstand, when his fingers grazed a glossy four-by-six. Weston turned the picture over and his breath caught.

Silver stood smiling flanked by Dale and a woman Weston assumed was Silvia. The fact that Silver was a spitting image of the beautiful woman meant it really wasn't an assumption. Much like her daughter, Silvia had long, shiny brown hair, the same natural light streaks, same hazel eyes. But unlike Silver's bright beautiful eyes, Silvia's were dull. Even smiling, the woman looked unhappy. Lifeless.

Silver looked beautiful.

Weston hated the picture.

"How was your day?" Weston asked, lying on his bed holding his phone to his ear.

"Boring. It's fall, so it's not slow, but it's not summer," Silver answered. "How was your day?"

"Finished cleaning out your apartment. Packed up what was salvageable—mostly clothes and some papers we found. Loaded the boxes in the back of the Suburban and brought them back to the farm for you to sort through later. We tossed the rest and the dumpster we rented was hauled."

He heard Silver suck in a breath.

The day had been shit. Damn, the last week had been hell with Silver back to work and on a two-week rotation, meaning he only got scraps. Mostly at night when she bedded down and had a few minutes to call him.

He knew it was going to suck, he knew he was going to miss her sleeping next to him, seeing her every day, but he hadn't known it was going to feel like a knife to his gut.

"Thanks for doing that," she whispered and her soft voice relayed just how much she meant those words.

"Not a problem, babe."

"Seven more days until I'm home." That whisper didn't fill him with the warmth of her gratitude—it slammed into his chest, her calling his house home, and made his cock jerk thinking about her once again sharing his space and his bed. "You're still sure you're okay with me staying with you until I find an apartment?"

That was something they'd discussed before she'd left for work—her staying at the farmhouse with him, instead of a hotel. And miraculously it hadn't turned into a fight when Weston had suggested—bossily because he knew no other way—that she not bother with a hotel because she'd never actually see the inside of the room she rented.

When the topic had come up, Weston braced for the argument but it never came. He watched as her back had strung tight and she opened her mouth, but before she unleashed her attitude, Silver had clamped her mouth shut. He'd given her the time she needed to work through whatever was going on in her head. After a few questions, mainly ascertaining Chasin would be okay with her staying, and Nixon, being the owner of the house, wouldn't mind, she agreed.

"Lookin' forward to you comin' home," Weston said instead of covering ground they'd gone over.

"Me, too. This is harder than I thought it would be."

"Can't lie, Silver, it sucks. But I suspect we'll get used to the routine."

"I guess you're right." Silver paused and went back to whispering. "I miss sleeping next to you, honey."

Her admission didn't make his cock jerk, it made it throb. It'd been seven days since he had her and it'd be seven more before he'd have her under him. Seven very long fucking days.

"You someplace private, with a door that locks, where no one can hear you?"

"Weston." Her breathy voice took him by surprise. He thought he'd have to coax her into his proposal, but his name falling from her lips on a slight moan, told him he did not. She was on board.

His hand moved to his cock and he squeezed the base. "Door locked, babe?"

"Yes."

"Can anyone hear you?"

"I'm alone. Travis is on vacation and Rodger went out to get groceries."

Fuck. Perfect.

"Take off your shirt, sweetheart. Bra, too, if you're wearing one."

"I'm not."

Images of her full tits assaulted him. Dusty pink nipples that puckered at the slightest touch.

Weston waited. He heard fabric rustling, then she was back.

"It's off."

"Good, baby. I want you to slowly glide your hand up your belly and circle your nipple."

"Oh, God."

"Slowly, Silver. Tease yourself. Just your thumb, circle it around until your nipple is nice and hard."

"What...what are you doing?"

"Lying in our bed, thinking about your fantastic tits. How much I love to pinch, and lick, and bite down on your nipples. How you go fucking wild when my mouth is on you."

Weston tightened his grip on his cock, forcing himself to stay still.

"That's hot," Silver moaned.

"Yeah, it is. So fucking hot when you arch your back with your hands fisting my hair keeping my mouth on you. Goddamn, you have great tits, baby." He heard her whimper and his hips bucked. "Pinch your nipple for me, Silver. Nice and hard like I do."

Silver's whimper turned into a moan. "Weston?"

"Yeah, baby?"

"I need more."

Fuck yeah.

"Your nipples hard, baby?"

"Yes," she hissed.

"Slide your hand down into your panties."

"I'm gonna take them off."

"No, Silver." His voice took on a hard edge. "I want them on. Just slide your hand in."

"Okay."

No questions. No argument. Hell, yeah.

His eyes closed thinking about Silver doing what he'd demanded, and with a tight fist, he gave his cock a few strong pulls.

"You wet?"

"Yes."

"Tease yourself, feel how wet you are." Weston stopped talking just long enough to pump his cock a few more times, grinding his teeth, knowing it wouldn't take much more before he blew. "Can't wait until you're home, and I can bury my face between your thighs. Do you know how good you taste?"

"Yes."

He couldn't help the smile that tipped his lips up. "Yeah, baby, you do know. You know because I fucking love going down on you, eating your pussy until you come in my mouth. But you also know because you like the taste of yourself on my tongue, don't you, Silver?"

"Yes. I need more, honey."

Yeah, she did, she needed his cock or his mouth, something unfortunately he couldn't give her while she was fifty miles from him and he was alone in his bed.

"Slide two fingers in. Hard, Silver, I want you to ride your fingers hard like you do mine."

"Wes—"

"Do it, Silver. Now, baby. Rough, just like I do it when my mouth's clamped on your clit."

Weston remained still waiting for her breaths to become labored. Precome leaked from his cock, pooling around his fist. The now-constant pulsing of his cock growing to a new level of painful. As soon as he heard it, the hitch in her voice telling him she was seriously enjoying what she was doing, he gave her more.

"Baby, I'm so fucking hard for you, my cock's ready to explode."

"I'm gonna."

"Slow it down, Silver, wait for me."

"Can't, Weston. I'm too close."

Fuck. He started stroking his cock, knowing it wouldn't take much to catch up, and he was right—a few hard pulls and his hips thrust up to meet his hand. Hearing Silver's sexy whimpers, knowing she was fingering her tight pussy, knowing what it tasted like, knowing how fucking great it felt when it hugged his cock, so sweet and wet, had him fighting the urge.

"Take your fingers out and rub your clit."

"That will make it happen faster," she groaned.

"Do it, Silver. I want you with me when I come."

"Oh, God."

"Goddamn, I wish you were here watching me jerk off for you. My dick on the verge of exploding, thinking about how good it feels to be inside of you. How wild you get for me."

"Honey!"

Fuck, but he loved when she called him 'honey', loved it more when she moaned it into his neck as he fucked her hard and rough. But loved it the most when she said it after he did something she thought was sweet.

"You like knowing all it takes is me thinking about you lying next to me, your tits pressed against me and I get hard?"

"Yeah." Her answer more of a grunt than a word.

"How 'bout knowing all it takes is me thinking

about your sleek, soft pussy taking my cock and I'm close to coming, you like that?"

"Oh, yeah," she panted.

"Oh, yeah," he repeated. "Get yourself there, Silver, I'm gonna come for you."

"I'm there, honey."

"Fuck yeah, come with me."

His balls started tingling, heat raced up his spine, his fist tightened, and he stroked harder, until hot come shot from the head of his cock, and pooled on his stomach.

"Wes..." That was all Silver moaned or all Weston could comprehend as the roaring in his ears intensified before his orgasm started to shift from him.

"That was hot," Silver whispered after a few minutes of heavy breathing. "You get all growly over the phone, too." Weston's lips tipped. "I didn't know if that would really work, but seeing as it did..."

"Yeah, babe, I'd say it worked, seeing as I got the evidence of how well it worked on my stomach."

"Maybe we can do it again."

"You want that?"

"Yeah."

Weston's grin turned into an all-out smile. Good to know his girl wasn't just wild when she had his mouth, she could get wild and let loose over the phone, too. He liked that a hell of a lot.

"Anytime you want it, baby, all you gotta do is ask."

"Okay, Weston."

"You good?"

"Oh, yeah."

"Good. Gonna let you go so I can go wash up."

Silver's giggle filled his chest and he went from relaxed and sated straight to overcome with joy.

Just for a giggle.

"Is it really all over your stomach?"

Weston looked down to check, then confirmed, "Stomach, damn near hit my chest, and dripping down my hands."

"That sounds hot, wish I could see it."

"You want that, when you get home, I'll watch you play with your pussy and jerk off for you."

"Now you're turnin' me on again," she mumbled, sounding miserable. "Better let you go."

"Yeah."

"Weston?"

"Still here, baby."

"I love you."

Weston closed his eyes and let that sink in. 'Overcome' didn't come near enough to describe what he was feeling.

"Love you, Silver. Sweet dreams."

"They always are."

Fuck. He hoped that was the case.

"Night."

"Night."

Weston disconnected the call, tossed his phone on the mattress, but didn't roll out of bed. He lay there a good long while thinking how lucky he was.

30

"You got nothing to worry about," Weston told me.

We were in his Jeep on the way to Jameson and Kennedy's house for a get-together. Nixon, McKenna, her two siblings, Zack and Mandy, Chasin, Holden, and Alec were all going to be there.

I'd arrived at the farmhouse that morning after I got off rotation. Finding Weston still in bed, I stripped down and climbed in next to him. Of course he was already awake when I did this. Even though I tried to surprise him and didn't call to tell him I was leaving work a few hours early, I suspected he'd heard my car when I'd pulled up.

The first thing I noticed was Weston had grown a beard.

He looked hot. And when I told him how sexy I

thought it was, his smile broadened when he told me I'd like it even more when his mouth was between my legs. He was right of course, but I'd have to wait to find out because the second I hit the sheets, Weston commenced talking me through touching myself while I got to watch him stroke himself.

After that, he'd cleaned his stomach, but not before I got a good long look at his come coating his hand and dotting his six-pack—and I was right, it was hot—he went straight to work building me up. He did this with his mouth between my legs and holy fuck, the beard was better than I imagined. His hands roamed every inch of me and once he had me trembling and begging for more, he finally gave it to me hard and rough, yet he still managed to make it tender. How he did that, I do not know.

I just knew that while he was pounding inside of me, taking my breath from the force of his thrusts, I felt nothing but love surrounding me.

After we finished making love, showering, getting ready for the day, we'd met Chasin in the kitchen and found him in the mood to bust chops. He did that by embarrassing the hell outta me by complaining he was moving into the Airstream with Holden—either that or he was moving his room.

Weston of course couldn't stop himself from

moving in to protect me and my feelings and growled for Chasin to shut the hell up. Chasin being Chasin didn't shut the hell up, or maybe he did stop teasing me, but he further poked the bear by winking at me and telling me he was happy I was home.

I was no longer embarrassed that Chasin had obviously heard us having sex. I was too busy feeling something I'd only felt a few times in my life, all of them recently, and all of them when I'd been around Weston and his team—belonging.

So now as we were driving to Jameson and Kennedy's I wasn't worried, not even a twinge of trepidation.

"I know," I answered.

Weston glanced at me, shock clear on his handsome face.

"Fuck."

"Fuck what?"

"You're not worried."

"Nope. Why would I be? You'd never take me somewhere where I felt uncomfortable."

"Fuck," he repeated, and I didn't ask again what that meant.

I'd spent some time alone in my bed while I was at work thinking on the time I'd spent with Weston. Even way back to the first time I'd met him. I knew then, too, but I was too stubborn to admit it. Weston had always been looking out for me. And now more than ever, I trusted him. Not only with my heart but my well-being. I knew unequivocally he'd never hurt me.

And in that time I spent in my head trying to work out why I behaved the way I did, I also promised myself I'd do everything I could do to prove to Weston I was worth it.

———

IT WAS AFTER DINNER, and it's worth noting, Kennedy could cook. Not only was the roast she made the best I'd ever eaten, but all the fall vegetables she'd served were fresh out of her impressive garden. And, she had beehives. *How cool was that?* While we'd been waiting for Holden and Alec to show, Kennedy had walked me through the rows of vegetables pointing out the different varieties of lettuce and cabbage. She had beets, beans, garlic, pumpkins, and squash. Finally, we'd made it to the far end of her property and she showed me the bee boxes.

So now, it was just the four of us women in the house. The guys—plus the two cutest German Shepherd puppies I'd ever seen—had gone outside to the back deck. But not before Weston had checked to make sure I was okay with him communing with his team, thus taking him away from me.

I loved that he'd checked. I loved what it said. And I loved even more that I was right—Weston was always looking out for me. I, of course, had no problems with him going outside leaving me with the girls.

I found that Kennedy just like McKenna had been, was extremely friendly and welcoming. Mandy had been a little shy at first, but she'd quickly opened up. And Zack? Holy smokes, he was a mini-Nixon. I wasn't sure if that meant good things for McKenna having a badass and a mini-badass-in-training in the same house, but she was over-the-moon happy, so I guess it was a good thing.

"What's left to plan for the wedding?" Kennedy asked, bringing a new bottle of wine to the table.

"Nothin'," McKenna answered.

"Nothing?"

"Please," Mandy started. "This is Micky we're talking about. Not only is everything planned, but if that plan goes to hell, she'll just roll with it and not care."

I found that interesting. McKenna struck me as laid back, but I figured any bride would get freaked if the plan for her wedding day went to hell.

"It's just family." McKenna paused and zeroed in

on me. "Weston reminded you to ask for the day off, right?"

He had and so had McKenna—twice. Something that I was having a hard time processing, because as she'd said, the wedding was just family and I was included in that.

"Yeah. I'll go back to work a day late. Thankfully my boss should be back from vacation so I don't have to switch with anyone."

"Awesome. Everything is set. We're getting hitched in the back pasture then we'll go back up to the farmhouse where a tent will be set up for the reception."

"Why are you getting married on the farm and not at your place? Weston says it's beautiful," I asked, bringing my wine glass to my lips.

The cool, crisp white wine filled my mouth and I froze, unsure if I should swallow, spit it back into the glass, or rudely rush to the bathroom.

Before I could figure out what to do, McKenna started speaking, and with no other choice, I swallowed.

Shit.

"The farm is where Nix grew up. The land means something to him. He used to work up that pasture with his dad. He didn't say it, he never would because Nix wants me to have whatever I want, but I know us saying our vows there on that farm will be like having his dad with us. And I want that for Nix—for us. I want Wayne a part of our day even if it's only in spirit."

"Silver?" Kennedy called.

"Hmm?"

"You okay? You look like you've seen a ghost."

Shit. *Shit.* Shit.

I wiped my features clear of the panic bubbling inside of me, or at least I hoped I did and I answered.

"Yeah. Sorry. I just remembered something I forgot to do at work," I lied then turned back to McKenna. "I think that's beautiful, you wanting to give that to Nixon."

Her intelligent eyes bore into mine for long moments before she glanced down at my still full wine glass then back to me. "Yeah, everything's gonna be perfect."

Conversation flowed around me about the wedding but I was too busy doing mental arithmetic to pay attention. My period was due. I was regular, like clock-work, and I always started first thing in the morning. I was concentrating so hard trying to remember exactly what day I was supposed to start and if I was actually late, I didn't hear the guys come back into the house.

"Babe?" Weston called at the same time I felt his warm hand curl around the back of my neck.

"Hmm?"

"You ready?"

I craned my neck back and saw Weston gazing down at me, brown eyes full of apprehension.

"Yeah. I didn't realize how late it was."

"It's not that late. You wanna stay and finish your wine?"

Think, *think*, think. One thing about me, I sucked at lying and I super-sucked at it when I was put on the spot and needed to come up with something on the fly.

"Um. I..."

"I think lack of sleep from work has caught up to her," McKenna saved me from formulating a fib.

"Yeah," I agreed. "I'm sorry, I don't mean to be rude. I don't get much sleep while I'm on rotation and I left Delaware at five this morning. I'm beat."

That incidentally was the truth. I was tired, but that wasn't why I was distracted.

"Please." Kennedy waved her hand in front of her. "You're not being rude. Go home and get some sleep. We have the two weeks to carve out some time and get together."

"I'd like that," I told her.

"Good. Then it's a plan."

Another thing to mention about Kennedy—not

only was she friendly but she was stunning and when she smiled you knew down to your bones it was genuine.

We said our goodbyes, thankfully this endeavor took less time than it did when we'd left Weston's parents' house, and we hadn't even pulled out of Jameson and Kennedy's lane before Weston started in.

"Everything okay?"

I stayed silent for a beat wondering if now was the best time to bring up my *maybe* late period or if I should wait a few days. Deciding that Weston noticed everything and I totally sucked at hiding things from him, arguably more than I sucked at lying, I figured it was best to just get it out.

"I think I'm late," I blurted.

"Late?"

"My period."

I watched with rapt attention as Weston's lips curved up into a smile.

"Yeah?"

"I think so. I'm normally regular and I need to look at the calendar to be sure, but I think I was supposed to start yesterday."

Weston didn't say another word as he drove the back roads to the farmhouse. However, the sexy grin never faded.

Finally, I couldn't stand the silence anymore, mainly because I was seriously freaking out inside. I turned sideways in my seat and said, "Say something!"

"Hope you don't get your period."

That was what he said—straight out. No bullshit, no cushioning the declaration. Nothing. Just "hope you don't get your period".

Needless to say, I was speechless. Was he crazy? Of course he was, apparently I was, too, because I knew this could happen, we'd talked about it, yet never once had we used protection. I'd lost my damn mind.

"Wes—"

"Know that freaks you out. Know we talked about this and I think I made myself clear, it's your body, your choice, and you still gave yourself to me knowing I was going bare. You had options, you could've at any point made a different choice. Now faced with the strong possibility that we made a baby, I see you're freaking out. But I need you to take a minute and breathe, remember what we talked about. If you're pregnant, it's not you going at it alone, it's us starting our family."

I'm a fairly intelligent woman. Independent. Hard-working. Self-aware enough to know I'm a little nuts. So, intellectually I knew all of this was fast. I was smart enough to know that we should've waited, oh, say, five years before we brought a child into the world together. But I couldn't deny that while I was freaking out because, well, it was crazy, I was excited about the prospect of having a baby with Weston.

It was fast.

It was outrageous.

But I was happy.

So happy, I found myself saying, "I hope I don't start my period."

The Jeep jerked to the left, crossing over the dotted yellow line before Weston righted the vehicle and his smile went from a content grin to an outright sexy smile.

"Well, if you do, we'll just have to try harder next month."

His statement sent a thrill through my body, particularly my girly parts.

"I had two glasses of wine with dinner before I remembered," I admitted.

"Don't think that's a problem, sweetheart."

"But—"

"I'm no expert, but unless a woman's trying to have a baby, I don't think she knows she's carrying until she realizes she's missed a period. And I'm sure the majority of those women consume alcohol in the interim. So, again, I don't think that's a problem."

"Okay," I agreed, figuring he was right.

Weston's hand reached over and landed on my thigh. He wasn't shy with his affection and I loved that about him. Loved that even in front of his friends he was constantly touching me, holding me close, finding ways to show me he liked my company and liked being near me.

It totally worked for me because I loved being near him, too.

"Oh, God," I panted.

"That's it, Silver, take it."

Weston was behind me powering hard. So hard I was having a difficult time staying up on my forearms.

Then I felt it, his thumb circling, his other hand fisting my hair. Oh, God, that was hot.

"Cheek on the bed, baby. I want your ass tipped higher."

He put pressure on my head and I went down to the mattress and my ass tipped high, giving him what he wanted.

"Goddamn, you're sexy as hell," he growled.

Weston was building it, I could feel it happening.

"More," I begged and his thumb stopped teasing and pressed in.

Forbidden. Erotic. Lewd.

My hips bucked, my thighs shook, and I exploded.

"Fucking hell," Weston grunted and drove in harder. "Wild."

"Weston," I moaned as my orgasm blazed through me. So hot. So overwhelming, I trembled with it.

"Can't hold out, baby, not when your tight pussy clamps down."

Thankfully Weston's grip on my hips was iron-clad because my legs had given out, I was boneless. Floating on a cloud of bliss.

With one last thrust, Weston slammed home, stayed planted deep, and I waited for it. Waited for the feel of his cock swelling before I felt the throb.

"Love feeling you come, honey."

"Christ. Perfect. Beautiful. Sexy. Totally wild. No one better, baby."

God, I loved he thought that. Because there was no one better than Weston. Not anyone in the whole wide world and he was mine.

31

———

"Damn, brother, twice in one week?" Weston said to Alec as he entered the office.

Alec didn't reply, and it was then Weston took in his friend's frown.

"What's wrong?"

"Everyone here?" Alec asked instead of answering Weston's question.

"Yeah. Conference room."

"McKenna and Silver?"

Alec's inquiry immediately put Weston on high-alert.

"Out with Kennedy. There a problem?"

"Need a private conversation."

Before Weston could ask what the fuck that meant,

Nixon came into the reception area, Tank and Axel following.

Thankfully the two oversized puppies had learned some manners and no longer jumped on visitors like a pair of wild disobedient mutts.

"I'd say it's good to see you," Nix started. "But I'm thinking this isn't a social call."

Now that the shock of seeing Alec walk through the door had worn off, it was clear Alec was not giving off a happy vibe.

"Got a few minutes?" Alec asked.

Nix jerked his head toward the conference room and moved to the hall with Alec on his heels. Weston waited a moment, not liking the feel of Alec's visit. Unable to fight the urge, he pulled out his phone and sent a short text to Silver asking about her lunch, and only exhaled when she messaged back saying she was having a great time.

The impulse to call his woman, just to double-check she was okay was curbed when Nix barked Weston's name. *She's fine* he thought to himself as he made his way into the conference room.

"Hope that job offer was real," Alec started, but said no more.

"Say what?" Nix's eyes cut to Alec.

"Gave my resignation three hours ago. It was

accepted and even though I offered to remain on the job for four weeks, they cut me loose."

The room went utterly still. No fucking way would Alec Hall leave his job at the Department of Homeland Security unless some serious shit was going down.

"They cut you loose?" Nix clarified.

"Yep. Officially unemployed."

"So whatever you suspected was going on that made you give them that resignation was confirmed," Nix continued.

"Fuck yeah. No one wants me around a case, when I feel in my gut shit ain't right. I started asking more questions, got bullshit answers, asked some more, got pushback, gave notice, and my boss was all too happy to collect my security badge and send me on my way."

"What doesn't feel right?" Weston asked.

"Don't like the way shit went down with Silver. Don't like how Jason Scott got cut a deal, really don't like how everyone wanted to drag their feet with Howard Sposato, and to top all of that, the takedown was too fuckin' easy. It was like all the players knew we were coming, and they were prepared."

Weston's stomach lurched and desperation was taking over. He knew firsthand how easy it was for shit to go sideways. How vulnerable their women were. Micky had been snatched right out of her own goddamned house and Kennedy was taken from a public parking lot.

No fucking way in hell was his woman gonna be taken.

"Not unusual for powerful men to have their attorneys on speed dial and at the ready," Chasin reminded Alec.

"No. But it's pretty fuckin' unusual to have said attorney sitting at your table, the day DHS comes in with a taskforce to take you in. Funny, it was almost like he was waiting for us." The sarcasm in Alec's tone couldn't be missed, therefore no one in the room did. Though the new information sent more than a chill through Weston.

"That's something you failed to mention to us," Nix growled.

"Yeah, I know. I was trying to get some answers before I brought it to you. Never got those answers. So here I am, out of a job, hoping your offer was legit."

"You know the offer stands," Nix returned.

"Silver in danger?"

Alec's gaze swung Weston's way and he braced. "Wish I could say for certain the answer to that was no. But you know me, and I don't blow sunshine and I don't make promises I can't keep."

"Fuck!" Weston's hand went to his hair, and with a

vicious tug, he stepped away from the table and started to pace. "Her ass is swinging. Everyone in that office knows Silver brought us the intel."

"Yep," Alec clipped.

"So she's in danger," Weston concluded.

"Right now, Sposato, Chapman, and Scott are too worried about saving their asses and spinning this to worry about revenge," Alec informed him.

"And you know this how?"

"Considering all three men were out in under twenty-four hours, I've been following them, watching their meets. And when the opportunity arose, I bugged their homes. Nothing's been said except strategizing how to get their asses out of drug charges. Don't have access to their phones, and that's where I'm hoping Micky can work her magic."

Weston stopped wearing a hole in the carpet and looked at Nixon's stone-cold expression. Weston figured his face looked the same. Glancing around the room, he noted Chasin, Holden, and Jameson, all wore identical scowls.

"When the girls get back from lunch, we'll brief McKenna." That was all Nixon said and changed the subject. "You moving to Kent County or you commuting in?"

"Moving," Alec answered.

"Right. There's an extra room in the farmhouse," Nix offered.

"Bring earplugs," Chasin grumbled, and if Weston wasn't so pissed he would've had a response. But he was pissed, more than pissed, he was downright furious that once again Silver was in the line of fire after he'd told her it was over.

"'Preciate the offer. May need to take you up on that until I find a place to buy."

That was interesting, Alec Hall wasn't a man to set down roots—buying a home would tie him to Kent County. Weston had been to the place he rented in DC. Alec had the option to purchase the brownstone in Logan Circle. It was a kickass pad, not worth the near million-dollar price tag being a one-bedroom, one-bath, but there was no denying the brownstone had character. But Weston had been surprised when Alec told him he turned down the offer even though the mortgage would be less than what he was paying in rent.

"You know the place behind Kennedy and me?" Jameson started. "After all that shit that went down, the bank owns it now. Lots of land, but the house is kickass. Bigger than you need, five bedrooms, but the price is right."

"I'll take a look when I leave here." Alec nodded.

"Can't say it makes me all warm and fuzzy the reason you're here finally accepting the job offer, but I can say I'm pleased to have you on the team," Nix said.

Alec and Nix locked eyes, and as happy as Weston was his friend would now be a part of the team, he was more concerned about Silver, and how she'd react learning she may have to take another leave of absence from work. There was no way in hell she was out of his sight until this shit was over. Weston knew all too well how fast life could change. One minute everything seemed great, the next it went to hell in a handbasket. And that was not going to happen to his Silver.

"PLEASE TELL ME YOU'RE JOKING," Silver whispered.

"Wish I were, babe."

They were sitting upstairs in Weston's office, facing each other, their knees touching and Silver's hands were in his. They were also holding tight. He'd just finished filling Silver in on the latest situation. Needless to say, she wasn't happy.

And Silver being Silver was using anger to cover up her fear. He could see it—her pretty face transformed right before his eyes. Had gone from happy and relaxed from her lunch with the girls to scared, then straight to pissed.

Weston had wanted to wait and talk to her after they'd gone home. He'd wanted to take her to their room, put her in bed, and hold her while he laid it out. Unfortunately, she was too smart for that. As soon as she'd walked into the office with Micky and Kennedy she knew something was going on, then she'd pushed to find out what that was. And considering they needed Micky to tap Alec's boss, Ellis Hopper's phone immediately, Weston didn't have the luxury of taking his woman home in an effort to cushion the blow.

Explaining the situation to Micky but keeping Silver in the dark, felt like a lie. Something Weston wasn't willing to do, not ever, so he'd made the decision not to wait. A decision he fucking hated to make, not only because it would freak Silver out, but it also meant she wasn't free from danger.

"Am I still in danger?" she asked, still whispering, verbalizing what he was thinking.

"There's a possibility, yes, but I'm gonna keep you safe."

"Wes—"

"Seriously, sweetheart, I need you to trust me."

"Maybe Alec's wrong—"

"He's never wrong," Weston cut her off. "Something we've all learned a long time ago, Silver—you never ignore your gut. So when Alec says he's got a bad feeling, not only am I listening, I'm making moves to protect you. Trust me."

And just when Weston thought they were sliding toward a stubborn standoff, Silver shocked the hell out of him.

"Okay."

"Call your boss and feel him out. Tell him you need more time off."

"And say what? My spleen's ruptured?"

"If you need to, yes."

Her eyes narrowed and her scowl deepened. "This isn't a joke."

"You're goddamned right it's not. And this might make me a dick, but right now I don't give two fucks what your boss says. What I do know, and what I do give two fucks about, is that you're not going back on rotation until this is over. And by over I mean, Alec gets the answers he wants and Hopper is cleared or taken down."

"I'll lose my job if I take off more time."

"Yeah?"

"Yeah."

"Then isn't it a good thing you no longer have rent?"

Silver's expression turned murderous. "If I lose my job I'm screwed."

"But you'll be breathing."

"That's—"

"You been kidnapped and held captive?"

"Yes!" she screeched.

"Your apartment been broken into and vandalized? Your car?"

"Yes." Silver's shoulders hunched forward and Weston hated it, hated having to remind Silver about what she'd gone through, but he needed her to understand.

"Right. So with all of that, and your name out there, Ellis Hopper knowing who you are, I'm not taking any chances. And by any, I mean you are not out of my sight for two seconds. I've lived it twice now—twice I've watched two of the strongest men I know crumble. Total devastation when their women disappeared. The kind of devastation you don't come back from, and mark this, Silver, neither of them would've if the outcome had been different. I am far from stupid, I've learned. And what I've learned is to protect what's mine. *And* I don't think I need to remind you, you might be carrying our baby. So there's no chance in hell you're not more than two feet from my side at all times."

Weston could feel his pulse throbbing in his neck and he braced for battle. There was not one thing that was going to stop him from keeping Silver safe. She could throw a tantrum, get pissed, be as stubborn as she wanted to be, but Weston wasn't budging. He remembered with great clarity what Jameson and Nixon had gone through—what they all had. Weston also knew losing Silver would mean his world stopped. There'd be no coming back.

So, no, she wasn't leaving his side.

"I'll call my boss. If he fires me, we'll figure something out."

Thank fuck.

Weston's hands spasmed in hers and relief washed over him.

32

I was sitting in McKenna's office, Kennedy sitting beside me, both of us watching McKenna listen in on the most mind-numbing conversation known to man.

Ellis Hopper was talking to a friend of his, they were talking about fantasy football stats and my head was going to explode.

"This is boring," Kennedy announced. "At least when we were listening in on Reggie, it was interesting."

I'd heard all about Kennedy's problems with the supreme jerk of all jerks, Reggie Coleman. I'd also been told how he'd made her life misery and his mistress had tried to kill her. And in a heartbreaking twist, Jameson had listened to Kennedy while she thought she was dying. They all had, the whole team.

Something I knew still upset Weston. And three days ago when he'd told me I was in danger again, he'd made it blindingly clear he was not over it and he would not allow a repeat performance starring me as the kidnapped party.

Needless to say, my boss was livid I'd called out again and while I was fairly certain I was going to be fired—and with a possible baby on the way—that stressed me out. But Weston was right, at least I'd be alive to be stressed.

A lot had happened in the last three days. What had not happened was my period. I was officially late. Weston and I had also decided we would take a test tonight but not tell anyone until at least after the wedding if it was positive, which I was pretty sure it was going to be.

I'd also spent three days sitting in the office basically twiddling my thumbs because there wasn't anything I could help with and I wasn't allowed out of the office without one of the guys at my side. That was something Weston had agreed to yesterday when I was starving and Weston had been tied up on a call. While he'd been sitting on hold, he'd decreed Holden could walk with me to this awesome little coffee shop around the corner that also had amazing sandwiches so I could get lunch before I died.

That may've been a small exaggeration, but the way my stomach had been growling and twisting in hunger pain, it wasn't an exaggeration by much.

So that brought me to now, sitting in McKenna's office bored out of my skull, but I was breathing.

"I'd rather listen to fantasy football than nasty Reggie nailing Deloris," McKenna grumbled. "If there was ever a time that ear bleach needed to be a real thing, it was then."

"Okay, not that part," Kennedy conceded, and scrunched her face in disgust.

"Was it really that bad?" I laughed.

"Bad doesn't describe it," McKenna started. "Let's just say Nix wasn't all that happy with Reggie for a variety of reasons, most importantly what he was doing to Kennedy, but also because I was turned off from his favorite position for a good long while."

"Remember when Jameson called in the middle of us listening," Kennedy started on a giggle. "And told Holden not to let me listen?"

"Seriously?"

"Oh, yeah. Holden was bitchin' the whole time we were watching talking about how doggie-style sex was ruined for him."

"I think he's lifted the ban..." McKenna mumbled.

"Yeah, Jameson says he doesn't have a good feeling," Kennedy returned.

I was a little lost in the conversation, and out of all of the guys, I knew Holden the least. He lived in his Airstream. Which I had to admit was awesome. Weston had taken me on a tour of the farm and Holden had been home and showed me around his place. When we'd got back to the farmhouse, I told Weston I understood why Holden wanted to live in the Airstream—it was *that* cool. But he explained that while Holden liked his privacy that wasn't why he held himself slightly apart. It was because Holden was going through something and had been for a long time and refused to talk about it even though everyone knew.

I found this to be extremely sad. Holden was a nice guy—funny, smart, good-looking—and I didn't like thinking about him alone brooding. But I didn't know him well enough to talk to him about whatever was bothering him.

"About what?" I asked Kennedy.

McKenna's eyes snapped to mine before she whispered. "This is top secret. Well, not from our guys, just from Holden. He doesn't know we know." I nodded my understanding and McKenna continued. "He's hung up on a woman. Has been for a long time. Charleigh was his, but she wanted more, Holden didn't think he could give her what she needed so he stepped aside. Shortly after he let her go, she started dating one of Holden's teammates. They got married, had a daughter, then he died in combat."

"Oh, no. That's horrible."

"Yeah. But what's worse is, Holden never stopped loving her. And when Paul—that's her husband—died, his last words were to Holden asking him to take care of his family. Holden couldn't do it. Couldn't face Charleigh or her daughter. So now on top of being in love with her for years, he feels guilty for reneging on a promise he made to his dying friend."

"Poor Holden."

"You got that right," Kennedy agreed. "Jameson says Holden screwed up big time letting Charleigh go. No one could believe he walked away from her. But it's been years since Paul died. A few months ago, Charleigh was having some problems, no one knows what, but she called Holden and asked him to go down to Virginia and he went."

"He went? Oh, man. Bet that tore him up."

McKenna nodded and told me, "Remember a few weeks ago when Holden left again?"

"Yeah."

"He went back to Virginia to see Charleigh again,"

McKenna finished. "Nix says something happened, because since Holden's been back, he's off."

"Off?"

"Different. Nix is really worried."

"He wouldn't hurt himself, would he?"

I couldn't bear the thought of Holden sitting in that Airstream all alone suffering.

"No. Absolutely not. But he's changed. He normally jokes around and he is the funniest out of the guys. It's all an act of course because he's really torn up inside, but he doesn't even pretend to be happy anymore."

"That sucks," I said and sat back in my chair.

Ellis Hopper disconnected his call and silence fell.

I felt horrible for Holden. I knew what it was like to be all alone and I knew the loneliness that surrounded you. It was like a heavy blanket, but instead of keeping you warm, it was cold. It chilled you straight to the bone. And that aloneness didn't lessen when people were around, it made it worse. It reminded you that while you were trapped in your life —having nothing, no one—the world around you kept going.

As the seconds ticked by I remembered I no longer felt that loneliness. Even when I'd been on rotation and was alone in my bunk at night, I wasn't lonely. I'd missed Weston, but I wasn't *alone*. He was still with me, miles had separated us, but I could still feel him. My hand went to my still-flat stomach and I remembered something else Weston had given me, something beautiful, precious.

"You okay?" McKenna asked.

"Yeah. Just thinking about Holden. It wasn't too long ago I felt like him. Only I hadn't lost someone I loved so I imagine I actually don't know what he's feeling because that kind of loneliness, that bitter cold, has to be worse than anything I've known."

"You were torn up inside?" Kennedy asked.

"You could say that. I'm sure you've heard about the showdown with my dad." Kennedy nodded and her face gentled. That felt nice—before I met Weston I couldn't remember anyone showing me any sort of concern. "My dad's...my dad did the best he could raising me. I know he loves me. I know when I was a kid he thought he was giving me this grand life. Off on adventures to faraway places. And in some ways he did. But when I got older he ignored what I wanted, what I needed. Even after I begged him to let me go to a regular high school, have friends, do normal stuff. I told him I was lonely, I felt like I was some sort of freak being raised on a boat, homeschooled. He told me high school was boring and friends were overrated and always let you down. So, yeah, I was very lonely. And I was torn up inside over my mom. Everything she said to me, her leaving, her coming back to say more awful stuff, before she just left and never came back. My dad never addressed any of that either. He simply went on with his life, hiding his pain, so I thought that was what I was supposed to do, too. Hide it, lock it away, pretend it didn't hurt. Without knowing what I was doing, I turned into her. Not the mean parts, but the stubborn, self-centered, bitchy parts."

When I stopped speaking I realized two things. The first being I'd shared—and I'd shared a lot—more than I'd ever done with anyone, save Weston. The second was I'd never had friends, not real ones, close ones where I felt safe enough to admit what I had to Kennedy and McKenna. Weston gave me that. Then there was something else that Weston had given me. Strength.

"You know," Kennedy started. "I admit, I thought it was cool how you grew up. All the places you've been. But I never thought about the flip side of that."

"Sorry about your mom leaving," McKenna murmured and I knew she meant those words.

I also knew she'd lost her mom when she was young, and the stepmom who raised her not too long ago.

"Don't be. She wasn't a very good one. It was good when she left, but it would've been better if my dad had helped me deal with it. Instead, it festered and grew into fear."

"Is Weston helping you deal with it?" Kennedy asked.

"Yeah."

"Good." Kennedy smiled huge.

"So..." McKenna smiled. "Any thoughts about where you want to live?"

Yes, I had thoughts on *where* I wanted to move and *who* I wanted to move in with, but it hadn't been discussed further than me staying with Weston while I was looking. And now with the possibility I was pregnant, I wasn't sure where Weston's head was at.

"Well, I was gonna start looking for apartments, but then with Alec's news, that's on hold," I told McKenna, omitting the part about the baby and how that might change everything.

"Will you be looking in Kent County?"

"Yeah."

Both women smiled at me then looked at each other.

"You know..." McKenna's eyes came back to mine. "The house that's next to mine is coming up for sale. Mr. Webber, that's the man who owns it, came by last night to tell us. He actually offered it to me and Nix. We don't want it, but we were thinking it would be perfect for you and Weston."

"Um. I don't think I can afford that," I told her somewhat disappointedly.

"We'll see."

"We'll see what?"

"Nix is gonna talk to Weston about it."

"But—"

"I'm ordering lunch," Alec said, poking his head into McKenna's office, cutting off our conversation. "Anyone want anything?"

"Yes," I blurted out.

I was starving, even though before Weston and the guys had left to go meet with Jonny Spenser, he'd gone out and gotten me two blueberry muffins. Both of which I'd scarfed down in record time. I did this in front of Weston, and without shame. He said nothing as I stuffed my face, as a matter of fact, he'd lounged in his chair behind his desk smiling at me.

After Alec took our lunch orders he left to go back downstairs. He was using the conference room as a makeshift office until something more permanent could be arranged.

"What do you think about Alec quitting DHS?" I whispered.

"It's a good thing. Nix has been trying to get Alec to work for Gemini Group for months," McKenna explained.

Before I could ask anymore questions my cell vibrated in my pocket, my boss's name flashing, and I debated not answering. To say my boss was pissed was a gross understatement. As a matter of fact, his response to my made-up illness was over-the-top. He was normally a laidback guy.

"Sorry, it's my boss. I need to take this." I stood and quickly walked down the short hallway, ducking into Weston's office and answering before it went to voicemail.

"Hi, Travis." I tried my best to sound sick. I wasn't sure what a ruptured spleen entailed. I assumed it was painful, though I was then seeing the error of my ways not doing a thorough internet search of symptoms and treatment.

"Check your texts."

"Huh?"

I got no answer because after Travis's bizarre demand, the line went dead.

I was thinking Travis was now mostly a dick, and he was probably texting me my exit papers.

Shit. I was going to be so screwed.

My phone vibrated. I pulled up my texts and tapped on his name.

Then pain sliced through me. My world stopped and I wished with everything inside of me I could turn back time. Memories flashed in my mind, cold and heartless.

You embarrassed yourself, you sure as hell embarrassed me.

I stared at the image of my father beaten and bloody and didn't know what to do. Couldn't begin to comprehend what was going on. So many thoughts were racing through my head I jumped when my phone buzzed again.

"Hello?" I managed to choke out.

"Don't do it, Scout!" I heard my dad yelling and my body froze. "Whatever it is, don't do it."

"You got one hour to get to the boathouse and call in or your father's dead."

"What?"

Suffice it to say, I was in shock. Totally and completely paralyzed.

"One hour, Silver, or dear old dad kicks the bucket."

"I can't make it to the boathouse in an hour," I told him, looking around for Weston's Jeep keys. I'd seen him toss them on his desk that morning. "I'm too far away."

"Yeah. I know exactly where you are," Travis's voice rumbled in my ear and I snatched up the keys. "That reminds me. Ditch the boyfriend. I got someone sitting outside watching. You don't come alone, anyone follows you, Dale's dead. I'm not fucking around."

I could hear my dad screaming in the background and what I heard sent chills down my spine. My dad was crying out in pain.

My eyes screwed tight and tears started to form. All I could see was my dad's face—not bloody and beaten but with anguish as I yelled at him.

Dale Coyle thinks of no one but himself and the next great thrill. I'm done, Dad.

I'd said that, to my own dad. The man who'd raised me. Loved me the best he knew how.

Oh, God.

"Don't hurt him," I begged.

"Then you better drive fast, Silver. Your time starts now."

The line went dead and I stood rooted in place unsure what to do. Then I became unglued when the visions of my father being brutally assaulted invaded my mind.

He may've been a crap dad but he was my dad. I

had to go—had to. There was no other option. As quietly as I could, I walked down the hall, passing McKenna's office, down the back steps, and waited. Thankfully Jameson, Holden, Chasin, Nixon, and Weston had all gone to talk to Jonny Spenser, leaving Alec there to watch over us. The last I'd seen Alec he was going back to the conference room, which I'd have to pass in order to get out the door. I slowly made my way down the corridor, peeked into the conference room and it was empty.

Thank God.

I had no idea where Alec was and I wasn't looking a gift horse in the mouth. I made a mad dash to the front door, opened it barely enough for me to slip out, shut it as quietly as I could, and took off down another set of stairs, then across the street to where Weston's Jeep was parked. I did all of this without thinking. I was on autopilot. All I knew was I had to get to my dad before Travis killed him.

I started the Jeep, pulled away from the curb, and drove as fast as I could through town.

What was I doing?

Weston was going to be furious.

My phone rang and I pulled it out of my pocket, checked the caller ID, almost relieved it wasn't Weston.

"Travis," I answered.

"Good, you're on your way. And you followed instructions. New plan. Head to BWI."

"The airport?"

"Yes. You have two hours."

"Why?"

Not that it mattered why. Nothing mattered anymore. Travis was threatening to kill my dad. I'd offered myself up in exchange. Weston would be so furious with me he'd never forgive me—that was, if I lived through whatever Travis had planned.

"Why the airport?" It was hard to hear with the wind rushing all around me but I couldn't miss the impatience in his tone.

"No. Why are you doing this?"

"Because you fucked everything up. And if you'd just come back to work like you were supposed to I wouldn't've had to involve your dad."

"What?"

"Jesus Christ, for someone who's so smart, you really are a dumb fuck. You should've minded your own goddamned business. Homeland Security? Really?"

Stupidly. Belatedly. Naively it hit me. Gary wasn't the only one in on it, Travis was, too.

"You're an asshole," I told him. "And not just

because you kidnapped my dad. But because I liked you, thought you were a good guy when really you're a piece of shit allowing drugs to be transported down the canal."

"I'd be careful not to let that mouth of yours run away with you. I'm the *asshole* who's holding a gun to your father's head."

I fought the urge to close my eyes as tears once again began to fall.

...you're a maniac.

What kind of daughter said that?

Most of my life my dad had been selfish, but he was still my dad and he didn't deserve this. My throat clogged hearing about anyone holding a gun to his head.

"Two hours," Travis barked and the line went dead.

I couldn't let my dad die. I couldn't let the last thing I said to him be in anger. I couldn't do it.

What was I doing?

I was speeding down the highway in Weston's Jeep making the worst mistake of my life. I knew it. I knew what I was doing but I couldn't take my foot off the accelerator. I couldn't stop thinking about how I'd told my dad to leave, all of the horrible stuff I said to him. He loved me, I knew he did.

And Weston, he loved me, too. Thinking about him was like a dagger slicing through my heart.

"What the hell am I doing?" I screamed.

Then suddenly everything hit me. Weston. The baby. The conversation from three days ago playing in my mind.

Total devastation when their women disappeared. The kind of devastation you don't come back from, and mark this, Silver, neither of them would've if the outcome had been different.

I am far from stupid, I've learned. And what I've learned is to protect what's mine.

Then I remembered what he'd said to me last night after he made love to me sweetly, kissing my throat, my neck, telling me he loved me.

Hope our kid gets your pretty eyes, baby.

I realized I couldn't do it. My foot eased onto the brake and I slowed down and reached for my phone.

"On our way, Nix is driving—"

"Weston," I cut him off.

"Where are you?"

"I need help."

"Baby, where the fuck are you?"

"On my way to the airport."

"The fuck?"

"I need you, Weston." Tears clouded my vision and

I frantically tried to blink them away. "I'm so sorry. I can't do it. I can't."

"Can't do what?"

"I need you," I repeated. "Need you right now. I'm so sorry. Should've trusted you earlier."

How could I have been so stupid? So selfish? God, I was worse than both of my parents combined. But my thoughts went to my unborn child and I knew I was going to let my dad die. I knew it and guilt hit me so hard, so deep, I wasn't sure I would be able to live with myself. But I knew, I knew with every fiber of my being, I had to protect my baby.

33

Weston's whole body locked tight hearing Silver hysterically telling him she needed him. He could also hear wind rustling through the phone. Fear was edging in along with confusion. He'd left Silver at the office less than two hours ago. Alec had stayed behind to watch over the women while the team talked to Jonny.

"Silver, baby, I need you to calm down and explain to me what's going on. Are you driving?"

"I swear, I trust you," she sobbed. "I'm so sorry."

"Where am I going?" Nix asked from beside him.

He had no answer so he concentrated on Silver. "Baby, I need you to tell me where you are so I can come help you."

"I'll call Micky," Holden said from the back seat.

"I'm almost to Queen Anne's County."

"Queen Anne's County," Weston repeated.

Nixon slammed on the brakes, executed a U-turn, and headed back out of town away from the office.

"I got a text from Travis. They have my dad. It's bad, Weston. Someone's following me."

The tenuous hold he had on his fear was slipping.

"Tell me exactly where you are."

"I just passed that pizza place with the red roof on 213."

Weston knew exactly where she was but none of the dread dissipated. She was obviously in his Jeep. The top was off, there were no doors, she was completely exposed.

"Listen to me, Silver. We're fifteen minutes behind you. I need you to slow down so we can catch up. But do not pull over."

"They're gonna kill my dad. I can't do it. I can't."

"Can't do what?"

"Travis knew I was with you. He knew when I left the office. He said if I didn't come alone my dad was dead. He'll know I can't do it, and he's gonna kill him."

"We're gonna figure it out. Just let me get to you first."

"Someone's following her," I told Nix. "Travis Yagger has Dale. Wants Silver in exchange."

"Fuck," Nix clipped.

"Micky says there's been no calls to Ellis Hopper and she's tracking Silver," Holden added.

"I have to let him die," Silver sobbed again and Weston's vision clouded.

"Please calm down. I need you to drive slow and careful, Silver. We're gonna get your dad."

"I can't do it. I'm sorry."

Fucking hell, she was killing him.

"Almost there. Hold on, baby."

"All of this is my fault."

"There's your Jeep," Nix unnecessarily told Weston. He could see Silver's hair flying in the wind three car lengths in front of them.

"I have another call coming in," Silver told him.

"Don't answer it. We're right behind you."

There was silence for a few beats, then Silver spoke. "I'm sorry I left. I'm sorry I didn't call you."

"You did call, baby," he reminded her. "Hang tight, it's almost over. There's a convenience store coming up on the left. Get ready to pull in."

Weston watched as Silver turned on her blinker, the car right behind her doing the same.

"We need that plate," Weston announced.

"On it," Chasin said.

Silver made the left, the black pickup behind her doing the same. But when Silver pulled into the store's parking lot, the truck kept driving down the small side street.

Nixon made his turn, pulled in behind Weston's Jeep, and before the SUV had come to a complete stop, Weston was out rounding the back of his car to get to Silver.

Without a word, he unbuckled the seat belt and yanked her into his arms.

"Weston." Her face went into his neck and her body shook, and on a wail she screeched, "I killed him!"

"Fuck, baby, fuck."

He couldn't think about her dad, where he was, or what he was going through. Silver was safe in his arms and that was all that mattered to him. All he could think about was that she'd called. She hadn't given herself up to save her father.

The squealing of tires pulled Weston from his thoughts and the sound of automatic gunfire had him reacting. On instinct, he took them both down to the blacktop, rolled them so his body was covering hers, then rolled again, angling Silver under the Jeep.

There was another burst of bullets, glass shattering, his team shouting, but he lay motionless protecting Silver the best he could. When the second volley stopped, through the ringing in his ears, Weston heard Nixon call out for a SITREP.

Not until after Chasin, Jameson, and Holden yelled out they were not hit did Weston finally speak.

"Silver, baby?"

"I'm okay."

"Roll back to me, sweetheart."

She did as he asked and his breath caught when he saw the gash on her shoulder and scrapes down her bicep.

"Shit," he grunted. "Easy, Silver, keep coming."

When he finally had her out from under the Jeep he could see all of the abrasions from the pavement.

"Need to get Silver to the hospital!" Weston shouted.

"She hit?" Nixon asked, crouched behind him.

"I don't need a hospital. I'm fine."

"Silver, I took you down hard. Wasn't thinking. Need to take you in to get checked out."

"Weston—"

"The baby, Silver. We're going in," Weston growled, losing the last of his patience.

Silver's face went pale and he heard Nix grunt from behind him, but he didn't care Nix knew, he didn't care they'd agreed to wait to tell everyone. At that moment, Weston didn't give two fucks about anything or anyone except Silver and their baby.

"Okay," Silver whispered.

"Go. Take Jameson with you. The rest of us will wait for Jonny."

Jameson didn't wait for direction, he jumped into the driver's seat, started the Jeep, and waited for Weston to get Silver into the back. Once Weston was in and had Silver wrapped in his arms, Jameson took off.

"Oh my God," Silver muttered, and Weston followed her eyes to the demolished SUV.

Bullet holes riddled the side and the windows were blown—a total loss.

"It's just a car, babe."

"It's...no, it's not. Someone tried to kill you. All of you." Silver shoved her face into Weston's neck. Tears, God, so many tears drenched his tee.

"You're safe now, baby. Promise."

"My dad," she wailed. "I couldn't do it. I couldn't do that to you. I couldn't force you to lose us. Me and the baby. I'm so sorry, Wes—"

"Shh. Silver. Everything's gonna be all right."

Silver was silent the rest of the way to the hospital. Weston held her while she cried, his body strung tight, fear gripping his insides. Something pricked the back of his throat, making him swallow it back. Heat scorched his gut and burned his soul—Silver picked him.

She'd fought a mighty battle, and chose Weston and their child over saving her dad.

Weston knew Travis wouldn't give up Dale in exchange for Silver. He knew that once Silver had shown up he would've killed them both. And if Silver would've been in the right frame of mind she would've known that, too. But she wasn't and didn't and she still chose Weston.

Jameson pulled up in front of the emergency exit, Weston jumped out, and carefully lifted Silver out.

"Be right in." Jameson didn't wait for a response as he pulled away.

Weston ushered Silver into an empty waiting room and went directly to the reception desk.

"My fiancée's pregnant and had a fall. She needs to be checked out immediately."

An older woman with perfectly coiffed, white hair and hot-pink rimmed glasses that would've normally made Weston chuckle looked from him to Silver and she smiled sweetly.

"Come on back, lovely, let's get you checked out. Through that door over there."

The woman motioned to the left and two double doors opened.

Weston didn't delay shuffling them through the door. The woman met them in the hall, did a full-body scan of Silver, and Weston watched her flinch.

"Oh my. We'll get those fixed right up for you."

For a small hospital that the county had been fighting for years to keep open, the emergency department was top-notch. A curtain was pulled back and the older woman stepped aside and motioned for them to enter.

"The doctor will be right in to see you."

He helped Silver onto the bed and got her settled, noting she hadn't uttered a word.

"Babe?"

"What if I hurt the baby?" she mumbled.

Fresh pain washed over him seeing the torment in her beautiful hazel eyes. Eyes he hoped she gave their children. Eyes that couldn't hide the beauty she had within or the strength that she possessed. As fast as lightning, they could go from shooting fire to soft and sweet.

She was safe, he reminded himself. And their baby would be, too. It had to be—he didn't think she'd survive the guilt if it wasn't and he knew he'd never recover from the loss.

"Everything's okay. Just a precaution."

"But—"

A woman came into the room, cutting off Silver's rebuttal, and Weston turned, giving the doctor an assessing once-over. Shoulder-length brown hair, gentle features, kind eyes. He instantly liked her.

"Hi there. I'm Dr. Webb. Miss Reba said you're pregnant and had a fall?"

"Yes," Silver croaked out. "I haven't taken a test to confirm but I'm late."

Dr. Webb smiled and Weston really liked the way she was looking at Silver.

"We'll start with a pregnancy test and go from there."

Over the next ten minutes, Dr. Webb examined Silver and his admiration for the doctor grew. Gentle touches and firm reassurances. By the time the doctor was done, Silver looked somewhat relaxed under the circumstances.

When Dr. Webb left the room Silver turned to him and started to speak, "I need to—"

"No, baby. Later. All you need to do now is relax. We'll talk when we get home."

"But—"

"Do you trust me?"

"Yes." Silver's quick response took his breath.

No hesitation.

"Then sit back, and let me take care of you right now."

She nodded and laid her head back on the bed. It couldn't be said that Silver was relaxing—her hand was tight in his, her body stiff, her breaths coming out as pants. But Weston knew that was the best he was going to get under the circumstances.

Over the next thirty minutes, people came and went. Thirty minutes that felt like a lifetime, and just when Weston was going to get up and ask what the hell was taking so long, Dr. Webb returned to the bay, pushing a machine into the room.

With a gentle smile, she announced, "Congratulations. You were right."

"I'm pregnant?" Silver breathed.

Yes, his woman uttered the word on a hopeful, excited exhale, and when Silver's eyes slid to his and she finally smiled, his world stopped, his breath caught, and he knew nothing would ever come close to what he was feeling in that moment. Not even if Silver gave him ten more babies and gave him that look each time she told him she was pregnant.

Nothing in the world was better than this—hearing for the first time he was going to be a father. Seeing

Silver's beautiful smile and her eyes dancing with happiness.

Best day of his life.

"You're too early in your pregnancy to use a Doppler to hear the heartbeat. I'm going to do an internal ultrasound." Dr. Webb nodded toward the machine and explained how the noninvasive procedure worked.

"Okay."

Dr. Webb politely left the room, drawing the curtain closed after she reiterated Silver needed to be undressed from the waist down.

"You okay?" Silver asked as Weston helped her out of her jeans and panties.

He looked up from his crouched position and stood. Both of his hands cupping her cheeks, he leaned in close. "Oh, yeah. You?"

"Yeah. I'll feel better after Dr. Webb tells us I didn't hurt the baby."

Silver's smile died and Weston bent forward, finally doing what he'd been dying to do since he'd pulled her from his Jeep.

Their lips touched. The kiss was brief, gentle, tender, but he hoped Silver understood the depth of his gratitude. Weston poured everything he was feeling into that kiss, knowing he'd never find the words to tell her how happy he was, how much he loved her. He didn't need to make vows in front of friends in a church or any other place. He silently made an oath to God, to Silver, to himself, to always take care of and protect what he'd been given.

Treasure.

"Everything's fine, baby. And you didn't do anything," he muttered against her lips, then helped her back into bed.

Ten minutes later a whooshing sound filled the room and Weston knew he'd been wrong. Hearing his child's heartbeat for the first time, that was the best moment of his life.

"Everything looks perfect. Nice, healthy, strong heartbeat." Dr. Webb's gaze left the monitor, her eyes going between Weston and Silver before the doctor settled on Silver and asked, "Do you have any questions?"

"Yes. About a million, but I can't think of any right now."

The doctor's smile widened and her eyes became infinitely softer. "I bet you do. Make an appointment with your OB and in the meantime write your questions down so you don't forget them. You're fit and healthy, Silver. I don't think you have anything to worry about. Your abrasions are superficial. Keep them clean, and do not scratch the scabs as they heal. But other than that, you're fine. Baby's perfect. Try to relax and enjoy your pregnancy."

"Thank you."

"You're very welcome." Dr. Webb stood, took off her gloves, tossed them in the trash, and moved to the curtain. "My information will be in your discharge papers. Call me if you need anything."

"We will," Weston answered, but remained seated, not willing to let go of Silver's hand even if it would've been the polite thing to do.

"Congratulations."

And with that, they were alone.

"You're gonna be a dad," Silver whispered.

"Thank you."

"Why are you thanking me?" Silver smiled.

"Sweetheart, you just gave me the world."

THE DRIVE back to the farmhouse was much like the drive to the hospital, only Jameson drove a little slower.

Without having to tell him, Jameson knew what was in the Jeep.

Precious cargo.

WESTON CAUGHT sight of Silver sitting on the couch as he and the team went over the information McKenna had found on Keith Yagger, Travis's brother. The man whose license plate she run while he and Silver had been at the hospital. They didn't know if Keith had been driving the truck therefore been the shooter or if Travis had stolen or borrowed his brother's truck. Answers they wouldn't have until they found Travis and Dale.

Gone was the excitement and joy.

Anger bubbled to the surface, so much fury Weston was barely containing it.

A day that was supposed to be filled with bliss was marred with grief overshadowing their happiness.

"Ready to roll?" Nix asked.

"Give me a second."

Weston made his way to Silver and pulled her up from the couch.

"I'll be back as soon as I can."

"Okay."

"I got this, Silver."

"Okay."

Fuck, she was breaking his heart.

"Do you trust me?"

"Yes."

His hands came up to cradle her face. Silver's hands went to his waist and her fingertips dug in.

"Love you, baby."

"Love you."

Weston leaned down, kissed her forehead, then straightened and looked over her shoulder. Finding Jameson staring at them, Weston knew he didn't need to tell his friend to watch his woman. Jameson knew what Weston was entrusting him with.

His whole world.

FORTY MINUTES LATER, the team was at their destination. A small rundown house in the middle of Nowheresville, Delaware.

McKenna had traced Travis's phone to that location and had continued to monitor Travis's and Hopper's phones.

No calls had been made.

"Weston." Alec stopped him as they exited the SUV.

"Not now."

"Brother—"

"Not fucking now."

Alec's face got tight and he lifted his chin but remained quiet. Weston knew Alec felt like shit, he'd explained he was in the bathroom when Silver had slipped out. Further, he'd apologized repeatedly.

Five men surrounded the house and waited for Nixon to give the order to enter.

"I've got eyes on Coyle," Chasin's voice came over the radio.

"Alive?"

"Cannot confirm."

"Fuck."

"In three." Nixon wasted no time counting them down.

Alec jacked the door open, Weston readied his weapon and stepped over the threshold. Then pain seared through him.

"Fuck!" he roared, as the burn of the bullet had him stumbling.

34

"What's taking so long?" I asked no one in particular.

I felt a hand on my shoulder and I nearly jumped out of my skin. "Takes time, girl," Jameson's voice rumbled. "Why don't you go up and rest?"

"Rest? You think I can rest?" It had taken damn near everything inside of me not to shriek.

How the hell was I supposed to rest when Weston was off God knows where trying to find my dad?

As soon as we'd made it back to the farmhouse from the hospital, Weston had ushered me to the couch, McKenna, Kennedy, and Mandy had swarmed, and Weston had left me with them to go talk with the guys.

One hard look from Alec told me he was pissed beyond belief at me, punctuated by the way he'd stomped across the living room to join the man-huddle.

During that time, I couldn't hear what they were discussing, but even if the guys hadn't been speaking in hushed voices, I still wouldn't have been able to hear over the rapid-fire questions the women were throwing at me.

Neither Kennedy nor McKenna seemed pissed. They looked more concerned than anything, sprinkled with a liberal amount of relief I was safe.

Jonny had shown up a few minutes after Weston, Nixon, Holden, Chasin, and Alec had left. He came straight to me, pulled me into an awkward hug—awkward because I barely knew the man—but there was no denying his concern had felt good.

Now Jameson, Jonny, and Zack were playing sentry while I paced the house, unable to get the vision of my dad beaten and bloody out of my head. To make matters worse, I was replaying the last time I saw him. The horrible stuff I said. And guilt was threatening to consume me.

I knew when I made the decision to call Weston, there was a chance I was killing my dad. I knew it and I still did it. Then all hell had broken loose and I'd almost gotten the team killed.

Jesus, what had I done?

"Silver?" Jameson turned me to face him. "You need to sit down, try to get some food in your belly, and calm down. If you can't do that for yourself, then do it for the baby."

And that was when it hit me. Shame hit me and my eyes closed. I'd been blessed with his perfect gift and already I was screwing it up—not taking care of it. Contrition surged through me, tearing at my insides.

"Trust Weston to take care of your dad," Jameson continued. "I've been where you are. I've stood in your shoes when someone I loved was taken from me. You don't think I was replaying every moment I had with Kennedy? The stupid shit I'd said to her when we were starting out. I was. I remembered it all."

"How did you know that's what I was doing?" I whispered.

"Because it's written all over your face. Because I've been where you are. Because when you've been where you are right now, you never forget the fear. But, Silver, you need to take care of yourself and the baby. That's your only job right now. Weston's got the rest."

"I'm so scared," I admitted.

"Know that, too. But it's only been three hours. They'll be home soon."

"How do you know?"

"Because we're damn good at what we do. Because

I trust my team. Because I know Weston will stop at nothing to take care of you."

I nodded because I knew Jameson was right. About all of it. But the wait was killing me. Everything I could possibly think of that could go wrong was filtering through my mind, torturing me with what-ifs.

The door slammed open. Jameson moved quick, pushing me behind him, his big body shielding me before he relaxed and moved aside.

My breath caught in my throat, and my vision blurred as a bloodied Weston stalked across the room.

I couldn't take my eyes off the red staining his shirt. Blood.

He was bleeding.

Weston made it to me. His hands going to my face, he forced my eyes up to meet his.

"Your dad's been transported to the hospital. He's stable." I didn't let out a breath of relief. Mainly because there was no oxygen in my lungs. They'd seized, completely non-operational. "He's gonna be fine, baby."

"You're hurt," I wheezed.

"I'm fine—"

"You're hurt."

"It's just—"

"You're bleeding!" I screamed. "You're hurt and bleeding. Why aren't *you* at the hospital?"

"Baby—"

"You're hurt, Weston. Yourehurtyourehurty-ourehurt!"

All of my words jumbled together as I shouted at Weston.

His grip on my face tightened and he brought his forehead to mine.

"Listen to me, sweetheart. I'm fine. It's a graze. Jameson will stitch me later tonight."

"Jameson will stitch you up?"

"Not the first time," Jameson cut in. "Few months back, gave him thirteen."

"He did what?" I was back to shrieking.

"Stop worrying about my arm and let's get you to your dad. He's asking about you. But fair warning, he's pissed as shit you were gonna give yourself up in the exchange."

"He's pissed?" I tried to pull back but Weston kept me where he wanted.

"Learned a few things about your dad today. His intentions might be misguided but he loves you some-thin' fierce. Would've rather died today than you putting yourself in harm's way."

"He said that?"

"Straight out, Silver. Said he wanted to die before you were hurt. Travis knew where you were, he wanted your dad to come and get you. Dale refused. He took one hell of a beating, but held out."

"Wes—"

I didn't get anything else out before the sob I was holding in ripped through me and Weston pulled me into his arms. And for the second time that day, my tears soaked his shirt.

"Hey, Dad," I whispered.

"Hey there, Scout."

I glanced around the room and focused on the monitors in an effort to regain my composure. My dad looked horrible. Even with all the blood cleaned away, his face was a mess. I'd been told he had broken ribs, his wrist was fractured, and he had a concussion.

"Dad—"

"I was a jerk," he cut me off. "See that now."

"Dad—"

"Trying to live my dream through you or pushing my dream on you. Not sure which, but I know I did wrong. Know I shoulda listened to you when you were a teenager. Know I was selfish not wanting to give up my time with you, what I want for you, so blinded by it, I never stopped to think about what you wanted. I'm sorry about that, Scout. Hope one day you can forgive me."

Weston's hand in mine flexed and I glanced up at him.

He was the picture of strength. From his messy hair, his chiseled jaw, the beard he'd let grow making him look even more menacing. All the way down to his powerful thighs. He stood next to me, holding me together.

Treasure.

He'd thought that was what *he'd* found, but he was wrong. That was what he was giving me. He was the something special I never thought I would have. The very person I was meant to be with, stand next to, the man I was meant to spend my life with. I'd known it all along. But right then, I knew I'd never lose it. I'd never let it go to waste. I'd cherish him for the gift he was —always.

"I shouldn't have said those things to you, Dad. I'm sorry."

"Damn right, you should've. I needed to hear them. If you'll let me, I'd like to make it right. I know it's asking a lot, but I hope you'll forgive me."

That was twice my father had asked me to forgive him.

"Nothing to forgive, but if you insist, I'll make you a deal. You forgive me for being the worst daughter in the history of daughters and I'll forgive you. Though I will say again, I don't think there's anything to forgive."

My dad smiled at me, shook his head, and looked at Weston.

"Stubborn," my dad mumbled.

"Not telling me anything I don't already know, Dale." Weston chuckled.

"Right."

"That wasn't me being stubborn."

"Right," my dad repeated.

"It wasn't. I know when I'm being stubborn."

"Okay." My dad laughed.

"I wasn't—"

I didn't get to finish because Weston's lips were on mine, silencing me.

"Only you can be stubborn and argue about being stubborn, while *being* stubborn."

"But—"

"You gonna argue or visit with your dad?"

I glared at Weston a moment, contemplating whether or not I was ready to give up my snit or if I wanted to argue some more, when my dad's very loud laughter filled the room.

"Damn," he grouched. "Sucks it hurts so bad when I finally have something to be happy about."

I turned to my dad, snit over, and smiled.

Weston didn't have broken ribs so it didn't hurt when he laughed. So that's what he did. The sound of it filled the room and settled over me.

"We have some news for you, Dale," Weston started, and plastered me against his side.

"Good news, I hope."

"The best news," I told him.

And that was when it finally hit me, the joy and excitement. All of it came crashing over me, and for the first time in my life, I felt nothing but happiness.

35

Two days later, Weston stood in bright October sun, a slight fall chill in the air, with Silver tucked close, and watched as Nixon and McKenna took their vows.

It was then that Weston knew, that was the very spot, with the beauty of Nixon's land surrounding them, where he wanted to marry Silver.

"Mrs. Swagger." Silver giggled as she pulled Micky in for a hug.

"Congratulations," Weston added.

"Thank you." Micky looked around the small tent and smiled.

"Everything's perfect, just like you said it

would be."

"Yeah," she agreed. But Weston knew the moment they'd lost McKenna's attention.

Her eyes went lazy when she spotted her husband. A look he'd seen from Silver, a look he'd work his ass off to keep getting for the rest of his life.

———

"YOU'RE THERE," Weston growled, and lifted his head from the crook of Silver's neck. "Fuck baby, so good."

"So good, honey. Harder."

Weston gave his woman what she wanted and drove deep, her pussy clamped down and he knew she'd found it. Silver's nails dug into his back, her sexy legs wrapped around his waist and he pounded deep until he found it.

"Love you, Silver," Weston groaned and stayed rooted.

His cock throbbed as he spilled himself into Silver's hot, tight pussy. But he wasn't thinking about how good it felt. He wasn't thinking about the beauty she created every time they came together. Not how she went wild for him, how she mewed his name, begged him for more.

No, Weston was thinking about the day he'd make

her his wife. And how that day was going to be soon.

———————

THREE DAYS later Weston put a bid on the house next to Nixon and McKenna. Two hours later his offer was accepted.

———————

A WEEK LATER WESTON, Nixon, and Alec were sitting in a fancy restaurant in DC across from Ellis Hopper. They hadn't been invited, nor had Ellis offered them the seats they were now occupying when they'd found him eating lunch alone.

"You still don't get it," Hopper said. "That's your problem."

"Get what?" Alec snapped.

"How to play the game."

"What fuckin' game is that? You scratch my back, I scratch yours? Or more to the point, you give fuckwits a heads' up they're about to be arrested and they line your pockets."

"No money was exchanged," Hopper defended.

"And that makes it right?"

"What it makes is smart. That's the part you don't

get. In this city, it's good to be owed markers. Even better when those markers belong to powerful men."

"You're right, I don't get it. Never will. But I have learned a few things."

"Pray tell, Alec, what have you learned?" Hopper asked, irritation lacing his tone.

"How to play the game." Alec leaned in. "Travis is dead, the half-wit brother of his as well."

"You're wasting my time telling me something I know," Hopper complained.

"Right. I'll get to my point then. Silver Coyle is off-limits. You'll spread that far and wide. Anyone thinking about retribution should think again."

"That's not in my control."

"You better make it in your control, Ellis, you don't handle that situation you'll find yourself in a world of hurt. You may like to be owed markers by powerful men. But I like to hold the strings of weak men who conspire and betray the oaths they've taken to uphold the law."

"You don't—"

"I have everything I need to bury you. Anyone moves in on Silver or Gemini Group I'm holding you personally responsible."

"It's a good thing you've resigned," Hopper sneered.

"Yeah. Good thing."

With that, Alec stood and the rest of the men followed, then they followed Alec out of the restaurant and stopped on the sidewalk.

"Piece of shit," Alec grumbled.

Ellis Hopper had nothing to do with Silver's father being taken and beaten. He had nothing to do with the drugs being moved. The only thing Hopper was guilty of was tipping off Sposato. Travis had acted out of greed and anger, roping his brother into a kidnapping scheme that hadn't ended in the way they'd hoped. But it had ended with both of them no longer breathing. Something Weston didn't feel remorse about.

"Ready to go home?" Nixon asked.

"Fuck, yeah. I close on the house this afternoon," Alec announced.

"You and Jameson, neighbors." Nix chuckled and shook his head. "Glad you came to your senses and came to work for us."

"Yeah. My checkbook doesn't agree with the pay cut," Alec snickered.

"Right."

As much as Weston was enjoying his friends' banter, he wanted to get home to Silver. They had a lot to celebrate.

Or they would when she accepted his ring.

36

Alec Hall walked into his house and tossed his coat over the back of the couch and looked around. There was no doubt the house was too big. He didn't need five bedrooms. He didn't need the acreage that came with it. The formal dining room, formal living room, along with a study. But he also couldn't deny it was perfect.

The previous owners had taken great care over the years as they upgraded the kitchen, the three bathrooms, and the floors. Alec had also purchased the house for a song. The bank wanted out from under it, and Alec had gone in with a cash offer.

So now, Alec was the proud new owner of a too-big house and more land than he knew what to do with.

Something Nix had said he'd help him sort out come spring.

Alec wandered through the great room into the kitchen, opened the fridge, and pulled out a beer. Before he could pop the top, there was a knock at his door.

He wasn't expecting company. As a matter of fact, he'd just left everyone he knew at McKenna and Nixon's house. A surprise engagement party for Weston and Silver. It was still early, but there was only so much he could take of everyone's could-not-be-missed happiness. Even Jameson's grumpy ass was smiling and laughing. Something Alec never thought he'd see from the man who'd spent years with a perpetual scowl.

It wasn't that Alec wasn't happy for his friends, because he was, but that didn't mean that the celebration wasn't a stark reminder he was thirty-eight years old and alone, with nothing but a string of hookups and uninteresting women in his past.

The knock came again and Alec set down his unopened beer and made his way to the front door. Tapping his hip, he felt his sidearm, and opened the door without looking. Something in his line of work he shouldn't have done, but these days, Alec felt like living on the edge.

On the edge of what, he did not know. He just knew he needed something, anything, and nothing beat the adrenaline rush of a good tussle.

A man he'd never seen dressed in an ill-fitting suit opened the storm door, and the woman standing next to him moved slightly behind the pudgy man as if she were seeking protection. The sight almost made him smile. He got that a lot. He'd also been told more times than he could remember that the way he looked scared most people.

"Alec Hall?"

"And who are you?" Alex returned.

"Are you Alec Hall?"

"Yeah. And you are?" Alec repeated, not concealing his annoyance.

"Detective Johnson, DCPD. This is Miss Walters from the family liaison unit. May we come in and have a word?"

"What's this about?"

"May we come in?" Miss Walters asked. "I'm afraid what we have to tell you may take some time."

Alec stepped clear of the door and waited for the pair to walk into the entryway.

"Follow me."

He moved them into the great room and offered

them a seat. Detective Johnson declined but Miss Walters sat and opened her briefcase.

"Mr. Hall—"

"Alec."

"Alec," the detective began. "I'm very sorry to inform you of this, but Jamie Fields has passed away. A car—"

"Who?" Alec questioned, and the detective jerked in surprise before he looked at Miss Walters who was now shuffling through the papers she'd taken out.

"Jamie Lynn Fields," the woman semi-repeated as if that would somehow make Alec remember who this Jamie person was.

"Sorry. I don't know a Jamie Fields or any other Jamie for that matter. I think you have the wrong Alec Hall."

"But, sir, you're listed on the birth certificate."

"Come again?"

"Ms. Fields listed you on her daughter's birth certificate. Your last known address matches—"

"I'm sorry, did you say her daughter?"

"Yes."

Now Alec knew they had the wrong man. He certainly didn't have a daughter.

"You've—"

But before Alec could explain they'd made a trip to

Maryland for no reason, Miss Walters proceeded to rock his world. The very foundation of it crumbled as the woman explained that Jamie Fields had planned for her death, she left strict instructions on what was to be done with her daughter in the event of her demise, and Jamie had also left a sealed envelope with Alec's name scrolled across it in pretty handwriting.

Alec stared at the letter like it was a venomous serpent ready to infect him with a deadly toxin. The woman shook the envelope, urging Alec to take it.

He reluctantly took it and ripped it open.

Just like a Band-Aid, he thought to himself. Open it, read it, then tell these people he was not the man they were looking for.

But even as he told himself that, dread had started to take root.

Alec,

If you are reading this then something has happened to me and I now owe you an explanation. One I never wanted to give but knew in my heart you deserved. All we had together was one night. It was a great night. Well, for me it was. I had left my disaster of a marriage six months before I met you and that night was the first time I'd felt the stirrings of the old me returning. Then I saw you sitting at the bar and you stole my breath. So handsome, but like me, you looked lost. When I sat next to you and you turned your piercing blue eyes on me and smiled, I knew I was going to do something crazy. And I did. I hit on you. But instead of catching my play you laughed at me.

Jesus Christ. Jesus fucking Christ.

He remembered her. All of it. Only she didn't introduce herself as Jamie, she called herself Lynn.

Jamie Lynn Fields.

Shit, the woman was pretty. Not beautiful, but pretty. Girl next door that looked way out of her element sitting in a swank bar in DC, even if she'd been dressed to the nines. She was right in her assessment—she looked lost. What Alec hadn't known was that she recognized that same observation.

And Alec had laughed at her lame attempt to pick him up, but instead of it being a turn-off it had been cute as hell. So he'd decided he'd turn the tables. Not even two hours later, he'd taken her back to his place. After that, there hadn't been any talking. The next morning, she was gone. No goodbye. No note. Nothing. Lynn had vanished and all Alec had felt was relief he didn't need to have the uncomfortable talk about why there wouldn't be a second time.

Christ, he was a dick.

Alec shook off the memory and went back to the letter.

I'm sorry about the way I left. I'd never done that and I'm sure right about now you're rolling your eyes because I'm sure you've heard that a thousand times, but it's true. I married my high school sweetheart. He was my first. Then I spent the next fifteen years in a loveless marriage to an asshole who didn't like me much, but that was okay because I didn't like him. You were the second man, I'd ever slept with.

Now to the hard part, the part I struggled with the whole time while I was pregnant with Jocelyn.

Alec stopped reading and sucked in a breath.

Jocelyn.

Jesus Christ.

His eyes went back to the page.

That night at the bar, you made it clear—crystal clear—you were not the type of man who wanted to settle down. I knew Jocelyn's existence wouldn't be welcomed. But please understand for me, she was the best thing that had ever happened. I wanted her from the moment I found out she was growing in my belly. And I'm sorry, Alec, but nothing was going to stand in my way of having her.

I know I meant nothing to you. I'm simply a woman you met in a bar, spent the night with, and then I was forgotten. But to me, outside of my beautiful daughter, you are the best thing that ever happened to me. If I had not met you that night. If I hadn't found the courage to sit next to you. If you hadn't taken me home, I would've missed out. I wouldn't have had Jocelyn. And she is the single best thing I have in my life.

I hope you can accept my apology. I know it is a lot to ask, but I also know you're a good man, an honorable man. Please take care of our daughter. Please love her and care for her. I don't know what happened to you in your past to make you look so lost, but I hope you find a way to let it go. I hope you find everything you're looking for. Just so you know, I did. The second Jocelyn was placed in my arms I found everything. I love her, Alec. Please make sure she never forgets it.

Jamie Lynn

Alec looked up at Detective Johnson and growled, "Where's my daughter?"

Check out Alec's Dream

RILEY'S REBELS

If you are interested in joining Riley's Rebels
newsletter sign up here:
https://www.subscribepage.com/RRsignup

ALSO BY RILEY EDWARDS

Riley Edwards

www.RileyEdwardsRomance.com

Romantic Suspense

Gemini Group

Nixon's Promise

Jameson's Salvation

Weston's Treasure

Alec's Dream

Red Team

Nightstalker

Protecting Olivia - Susan Stoker Universe

Redeeming Violet - Susan Stoker Universe

Recovering Ivy - Susan Stoker Universe

Rescuing Erin - Susan Stoker Universe

Romancing Rayne - Susan Stoker Universe

The Gold Team

Brooks - Susan Stoker Universe

Thaddeus - Susan Stoker Universe

Kyle - Susan Stoker Universe

The 707 Freedom Series

Free

Freeing Jasper

Finally Free

Freedom

The Next Generation (707 spinoff)

Saving Meadow

Chasing Honor

Finding Mercy

Claiming Tuesday

Adoring Delaney

Keeping Quinn

The Collective

Unbroken

Trust

ABOUT THE AUTHOR

Riley Edwards is a bestselling multi-genre author, wife, and military mom. Riley was born and raised in Los Angeles but now resides on the east coast with her fantastic husband and children.

Riley writes heart-stopping romance with sexy alpha heroes and even stronger heroines. Riley's favorite genres to write are romantic suspense and military romance.

Don't forget to sign up for Riley's newsletter and never miss another release, sale, or exclusive bonus material. https://www.subscribepage.com/RRsignup

Facebook Fan Group

www.rileyedwardsromance.com

facebook.com/Novelist.Riley.Edwards

twitter.com/rileyedwardsrom

instagram.com/rileyedwardsromance

goodreads.com/15080716.Riley_Edwards

bookbub.com/authors/riley-edwards

amazon.com/author/rileyedwards

ACKNOWLEDGMENTS

To all of you – the readers: Thank you for picking up this book and giving me a few hours of your time. Whether this is the first book of mine you've read or you've been with me from the beginning, thank you for your support. It is because of you I have the coolest job in the world.

Made in the USA
Las Vegas, NV
01 October 2022

56352782R00252